The black bird lifted off the rooftop. And in my vision, I followed. Only when I got to the ridge, that Raven wasn't alone. My breath caught in my throat when I saw dozens of black birds perched in the trees that surrounded the clearing.

I held my breath, trying not to rile them. Taking one step at a time, inching my way back, I kept my eyes on them…until I backed into something that didn't move. Something warm.

"Hello."

I screamed.

I fell hard to the ground. The Ravens took off with their wings thrumming the air to a deafening roar. A black swarm filled the sky. I covered my head, afraid they'd attack me, but when that didn't happen, I looked at the guy standing over me.

I was staring up at Nate Holden.

Also by *USA TODAY* bestselling author
Jordan Dane and Harlequin TEEN

IN THE ARMS OF STONE ANGELS

ON A DARK WING

Jordan Dane

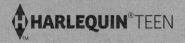

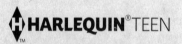

ISBN-13: 978-0-373-21041-1

ON A DARK WING

Copyright © 2012 by Cosas Finas

Recycling programs
for this product may
not exist in your area.

To the many friends I have made in Alaska, then and now.

Good friends are like stars.

You don't have to see them to know they'll always be there.

abbey chandler # prologue

Palmer, Alaska

I had countless excuses for missing the bus that afternoon, five years ago. In the grand scheme of the universe, what was five minutes? I could have carved out five minutes from talking to my friends after school or taken five minutes off my stop at the 7-Eleven. Three hundred lousy seconds to grab a Pepsi and a bag of Cheetos. No big deal, right? When I saw the school bus pull away from the curb from across the street, I didn't even run to catch it.

In the endless dreams I've had since then, I never run for that bus. *Not once.*

Even in my sleep, I couldn't change what I did. It felt like my feet were stuck in cement. It had been way too easy to reach into my backpack and make a call on my cell phone—a call that changed my life forever. The choices I made that day, all of them led to that one moment when the school bus drove off and fate took over. I would learn a lesson I wasn't prepared for.

Death would be my willing teacher.

All the strangest parts of my memory lingered to taunt me. Not the pieces I needed most. Guess that was my punishment. My memory had holes, a damaged and wounded thing. No amount of therapy or hypnosis or father-daughter talks has ever shed light into those dark corners.

Dad says he doesn't blame me, but I can't see how that's true. *I blame me.* I can't even look at him without feeling my own guilt and shame. I'm stuck where I am, unable to move on. I sure as hell can't go back and fix it. So I did the only thing I could.

I quit talking about it. *I had to.*

I should've been the one who died. It should have been me. I cheated Death and lived past my expiration date, but my lucky break would come at a price. I'd become obsessed with what happened the day I got my mother killed.

Guess you could say I was dying to know the truth.

Five years ago

"This is the third time this month that you missed the afternoon bus, Abbey."

"But, Mom, it wasn't my fault." I strapped the seat belt across my chest as my mother pulled our SUV from the curb and headed for the Parks Highway. "I was reading in the library and I lost track of time. I swear."

The sun had already gone down for the day. A steady chill settled into the night air. In Alaska, that's how the dark side of the year happened. The days were short, making everyone crave sleep. The long summers made up for it, but in the dead of winter, it felt like life had been put on hold. If you didn't get outside at lunch, you missed any hope of seeing daylight before darkness played the bully and took over.

"Oh, yeah? You were reading, huh?" Mom gave me that look—the one that said she wasn't buying it. "What were you reading, hotshot?"

When Mom turned onto the highway that headed home, I rattled off a book title that I knew she'd never read. I guess lying came naturally, like a rite of passage or something.

"How were the Cheetos?" she asked.

"What?"

"Your fingers are a dead giveaway, Abbey. You were at the 7-Eleven, weren't you? Is that why you didn't make the bus?"

I looked down at my hands. Even in the dim glow off the dash, I saw my fingertips were colored. Like, seriously neon orange. My mind raced with what I'd tell her, but I never got the chance. I looked up a split second before it happened.

I never even screamed.

On pure instinct, my body grew rigid. When I braced a hand against the dash, Mom looked at me. An eighteen-wheeler had crossed the center lane veering straight for us. I couldn't even warn her. If Mom hadn't turned her head in time, and yanked the steering wheel right, we would've hit that monster truck head-on.

On impact, the high-pitched grind of tearing metal punished my ears. Our SUV flipped and rolled. As our windshield caved and shattered, shards of glass cut my face and hands. All I saw were flashes spiraling in front of me like I'd been strapped into a roller coaster barreling straight down a dark track, twisting and turning in agonizing jerks. My seat belt pinned me. When the dashboard crushed into my chest, everything else caved in, too. The crash happened so fast, yet went on forever. When the SUV finally came to a dead stop, an eerie quiet settled in.

My ears were ringing and when my eyes blinked open again, I saw the blur of the dash, fogged by wafting smoke. The headlights off the eighteen-wheeler caught smoldering debris and suspended it in the rig's beams. I felt a sudden urge to move, but I couldn't. When the warm taste of blood filled my mouth, something felt seriously wrong.

Momma. Please…help me.

I searched for her, but couldn't move my head. I didn't even sense her next to me. I felt alone, cocooned in pain and deepening shadows. How long I lay there shivering, I didn't know, but eventually I sensed something that, to this day, I have never forgotten.

A strong presence filled the SUV.

Soothing heat replaced the numbing cold that had settled in my bones. It made me want to close my eyes and sleep, but a strange urgency wouldn't let that happen. I strained to stay awake and searched the shadows, waiting for a glimpse of something…*anything* to explain the eerie feeling.

After an intense light stabbed my eyes and sent a shock of pain down my spine, I saw movement. Something eclipsed the truck's headlights. It drifted toward me, inching closer until it hovered over my body. The brilliant glimmer swept over me and through me. Even though I could see through it, the light took shape and substance. The ghostly flicker turned into a body with arms and hands…and finally a face.

A boy's face.

I was only ten, but he looked older, like a high-school boy. He had the most intense eyes that I'd ever seen. Beautiful. They were deep blue and reminded me of the frigid depths of the ocean. His eyes were the only real color on his face, but that wasn't the most incredible thing about him. White tufts undulated and billowed within the boundaries of his filmy body, beautiful and peaceful. He conjured memories of a perfect summer day with me lying on my back on a grassy hilltop, picturing animal shapes in the drifting white clouds.

When I shifted my gaze back to his eyes, I saw a long tunnel with a glimmering light at the end of it, a light eclipsed by the vague shapes of bodies undulating on a watery surface. Those wavering images calmed me. At that moment, I felt a part of them, as if I belonged. He comforted me in a way no one ever had.

The boy fascinated me. I must have had the same impact on him. He stared at me with such concentration that it looked as if he was memorizing my face. *Who are you?* I wanted to ask, but I couldn't make my lips work.

When he reached out his hand, a strong impulse made me take it.

"A-Abbey?" My mother's choked whisper broke his spell over me.

I pulled from his grasp and shut my eyes as the haunting sound of her voice held me without even a touch. *Oh, Momma.* In the many nightmares that would follow, her voice would punch through the illusion of that strange boy and slap me with the harsh reality of what I'd done. That would be the last time I ever heard my mother's voice.

She died that day because of me and I had a hollow ache deep inside that left me grieving over something I could never change.

Five minutes.

Five minutes would have meant everything.

abbey   chapter 1

Palmer High School—Alaska
Present day

Although the last five minutes dragged on for an eternity, I watched the final few seconds tick toward the top of the hour and braced for my edge. If I got out first, I might stand a chance of beating the crowd. When the period ended, the bell rang and I made a mad run for the door, but my social-studies teacher, Mrs. Akkerman, raised her voice above the noise and royally jacked me up.

"Abbey Chandler, please stay after class."

Damn it! She nailed me, solid. With all eyes on me, I turned around. I couldn't even pretend that I hadn't heard her.

"Ha. Loser," Britney Hartman mumbled under her breath as she shoved me aside. She rolled her eyes and heaved a sigh, like I cared about the added drama.

I could've totally come up with something cool to say, but Britney had already turned her back—*the coward*—and she got swallowed up by the horde of mindless zombies that crowded the hall. Okay, I admit I may have instigated her resentment from elementary school.

In Girl Scouts, she had all the badges and her mother ran the show, making sure her precious suck-up daughter got more than her share of recognition. Me? I'd never been a joiner, but that didn't become apparent even to me until I hit Britney over the head with a confetti egg in front of the whole troop. Pieces of colored paper stuck in her hair and she bawled like a baby. What can I say? She egged me on.

Even her mother got into it and expelled me from the scouts, stripping me of the one badge I'd earned for Food Power. (I made a food pyramid of healthy food groups out of junk food. Oh, the irony, but what the hell. It tasted good after.) Britney hated me for my project, too. She begrudged me the one badge I had. I caught her grinning when her mom stripped it off my sash in front of the troop. Our feud had deep roots.

After my chance to let loose my inner smart-ass on Britney had come and gone, I slouched against a wall near the classroom door and waited for the room to clear as I chipped the navy glitter polish off my stubby fingernails. Pretending to be busy, I avoided catching the smirks I knew would be there if I looked up.

Being the second to last day of school, you'd think Mrs. Akkerman would lighten up and cut me some slack, but forget about it. Teachers never had a concept for how bad it felt to single a kid out, especially on Taco Thursday. I didn't care about much. Most days I felt invisible, totally forgettable with no special talent. But damn it, give me my tacos.

Now there'd be a long line in the cafeteria. I'd be late and my best friend, Tanner Lange, would be pissed for making him wait. Adding to the suck factor, the other kids stared at me as they left, like I had an epic defect or something.

In elementary school, kids knew about the way my mother died and they treated me different, but it didn't take them long to see I didn't need their pity. I didn't want it. When the classroom cleared, Mrs. Akkerman called me over with a wave of her hand.

"I just wanted to ask you…" When she stopped, I looked up. *Big mistake.*

She looked down at my clothes. My hoodie and jeans were more than a little wrinkled. They were clean, but I had to pull them from a cold dryer. I'd left them overnight and didn't have time to run them on hot that morning.

"How are you doing, Abbey? You getting enough sleep? Are things okay at home?"

I hated looking at her. She had a sickening expression on her face, like I had something majorly wrong with me. But I knew why she bombarded me with questions. Guess I'd brought it on myself.

Earlier in the year, she assigned a project to keep a daily journal of everything we learned in her class. I know, sounds lame, right? Well, it was crazy lame. I bought a notebook just for her class and started that journal, but on day one, I got drool on the first page from where I'd fallen asleep. After it dried, I wrote one line.

Fell asleep today. Will try again tomorrow.

By the time I turned in the assignment, every page had the same entry and enough dried spit to keep a CSI team busy for weeks. When she saw my journal, my teacher called my dad in for "a talk." She told him she worried about me being depressed and possibly suicidal. If you haven't guessed, Akk the Yak had been a former psych major.

After my dad blew past any concern he had over my mental state, he embraced his dark side and went parental on me. I had to put up with a lecture about my work ethic, but Mrs. Akkerman ended up giving me a B+ anyway—*for doing nothing.* I knew other kids had gotten worse grades, despite filling their journals with enough excrement to fertilize the Matanuska valley. That confused me until I figured it out. If she thought I intended to slit my wrists, she didn't want to put me over the edge with the stroke of her red pen. I milked the whole suicidal thing for the rest of the term.

"I'm doing...better. Really." I had to say "better" to stroke her ego. "And things are good with my dad." I lied again.

Of course, that wasn't the end of it. Once she opened her mouth, she spewed strange stuff that I only half heard. I stood there and took it, but the whole time, I screamed in my head, *"I'M NOT LISTENING, LA, LA, LA, LA, LA, LET ME FRICKIN' GO, ALREADY!"*

By the time she was done, I had to navigate the crowded halls like salmon swimming upstream to get my rocks off on some eggs. *Out of my way... No, left... Walkin' here.* I kept my head down, clutching my book bag to my chest to hide my wrinkles, but dead ahead a pod of jocks took up half the hall. Where there was one, more would follow and aggregate in mass quantities, like an unspoken rule or something. Everyone put up with their sense of entitlement to the halls before lunch. When these guys were ready to chow down, some pathetic dick weed would always let them cut in line.

I had to get in front of them…*pronto.*

Normally I walked around them and held my breath. Some of them stank, but since I was late, I shoved my way through the wrestlers. They were like a solar system of varsity letter jackets with the smaller guys hanging out on the edge in a circle around the bigger, no-neck dudes. Making eye contact in this planetary system had always been *verboten* in my rule book, but when I saw Nate Holden, I stopped dead.

At that moment, I had two really good reasons to forget how much my life sucked and Taco Thursday paled in comparison to the reason standing next to me. Nate Holden stood talking to his buddy Josh Poole. His deep voice tingled in my ear and made my belly twist into a major knot, the kind of thing that felt terrible and amazing at the same time.

Even with his back to me, every side of Nate Holden was excellent. I loved how his dark hair curled at his collar and he always smelled good, but with a full frontal, his hypnotic blue eyes made me forget to breathe. Whenever he talked, his lips could mesmerize me for hours, too. Being next to him felt like getting sucker punched—*and liking it.* He'd always be out of my league, an unreachable boy from an alternative universe who came to me in my sleep and tortured me. *Sweet torture.*

Nate Holden had been a constant reminder of how messed up I was. He was the complete opposite of me, someone I had no business even wanting. We had absolutely nothing in common. Brownie points for him. But that didn't stop me from practically stalking him. Deduct said brownie points. I played scenarios in my head, where he needed me as much as I wanted him. How sick was that?

That would never happen. My fantasies were the only way I'd ever get close to someone like him.

"Where the hell have you been?" A voice came from nowhere and intruded on my fantasy like cold water dumped on my head.

"What?"

I turned to see Tanner Lange roll up in his wheelchair. I considered him my best friend, poor guy. In truth, he was my only real friend, even if he got a little rude at grazing time.

"I had prime real estate staked out in the cafeteria. I had to give it up to come looking for you. What happened?"

Looking back over my shoulder, I stared at Nate as I mumbled something about Akk the Yak keeping me after class, but Tanner didn't buy my excuse.

"You've been stalking him again, haven't you?" He shook his head, but I saw him losing his battle with a smile. Tanner had cute dimples that gave him away every time. The whole bashful-boy routine came easy for him and he wore it well.

I took a deep breath and forced myself to turn my back on the one thing (besides Tanner) that made school even remotely tolerable, Nate Holden. After I slung my bag on Tanner's wheelchair, I climbed on back to scoot us down the hall.

"Coming through, people," I yelled, making engine and horn noises. "Make a hole."

It took us over thirty minutes to get through the line and get to a table, only we had to share our spot with the Scrapbook Club, the glue and stickers brigade. *Talk about useless!*

"You gonna eat your tomato?" Tanner didn't wait for my answer.

He reached across the table to score the tomato slices on my chopped lettuce. I thought about stabbing him with my fork, but that's not how you treat a guy in a wheelchair—at least not while anyone was looking.

"Chandler, you should consider dialing it back a notch with Holden." Tanner leaned in and whispered. "You're a little obvious, don't you think? I'm disturbed by your drooling. It's nearly put me off of my taco experience."

"You're disturbed, all right. Anyone can see that." I rolled my eyes.

Although I knew he had a point, I couldn't help it. I was a junkie and Nate fed my addiction. The boy was seriously worthy. He was smart, got good grades, and he risked his sweet neck doing volunteer work for a mountain rescue team. If he had any flaws, no one could expect me to point them out, because I was blind. Seriously blind.

"It's a good thing I'm secure in my manhood or else I'd be a little uncomfortable with your courtship ritual." Tanner stuffed a taco into his mouth.

"Yeah, good thing, Chuck Norris. I can see how messed up you are about it. How're the tacos?"

"Are you gonna eat…?"

"Don't even think about it." I glared at him. I wasn't so wrapped up with crushing on Nate that I'd let Tanner scarf a taco off my tray, not on my watch. "Damn, dude. You're like a human garbage disposal. Seriously. You've got a tapeworm or something."

"I'm blessed with a healthy metabolism. It runs in my family."

"Yeah, well…I wish you'd share it with me. The only

reason I hang with you is, I'm hoping lean and mean is contagious."

I had totally justified body image issues, but never cared enough to go cold-turkey off the junk food, and forget about breaking a sweat. Exercise was for mice in a cage with a wheel and nothing better to do.

"Now I know you're lying. I know the real reason you've lowered your standards to hang with me." Tanner leaned across the table again. Only this time, he didn't whisper. "'Cause when I start driving, I'll have all the choice parking spots."

"You've nailed it, Lange. I'm after your handi-crap parking. You've got me figured out. But, dude, I'm tellin' ya, some days that's not good enough." I looked at him sideways and smirked. "So why do you tolerate me?"

"Two reasons. You're my only friend with boobs."

I rolled my eyes and scrunched my face. "What's the second reason?"

"You do the math, Chandler. You've got two of 'em, duh."

When Tanner shrugged and kept eating, it gave me a chance to partake in the Nate Holden experience when he finally walked into the cafeteria and the Red Sea parted. If Palmer High had royalty, Nate would be crown prince and I'd be the cursed troll who lived under the bridge. Nate stood close enough to our table for me to overhear him talk to Josh about their trip up Denali. A climb like that would be epic, but it worried me. People did it. Some never come back. I had met one of the unlucky ones once. His body was still up there, frozen in ice.

I had plenty of motivation to talk Nate out of the climb of his life—a trip he'd been talking about forever—but he'd never listen to someone like me. I wasn't even on his radar. We occupied the same planet and breathed the same air, but that's where anything we had in common came to a dead stop.

"You comin' over tonight?" Tanner had turned his attention to his chocolate pudding cup. "I got a recording of a new Japanese reality TV show that's pretty sick. You could check out my new radio. Dad says it should pick up the frequency Nate will be using for us to track his climb."

Expedition teams on Denali carried portable radio transceivers used to get weather alerts and for emergencies. Our plan had been to eavesdrop on Nate's climb.

"Yeah, sure. That'd be great."

Tanner was an army brat whose father did the daily commute to Fort Rich so his mom could live in Palmer to be near her family. His dad doted on his only son, especially after Tanner was paralyzed from a four-wheeler accident at thirteen years old. Racing too fast with his buddies on a mountain trail, not far from Palmer, Tanner slid around a corner and his back wheel caught a boulder that sent him careening into a ravine. He got pinned under the vehicle. Once they freed him, he had to be evacuated by helicopter, but the damage to his spinal cord had been too severe. A lapse in judgment had cost Tanner his legs and since his father had bought him the four-wheeler, against his mother's wishes, the terrible incident nearly shattered his family.

Tanner had been strong and athletic once. He had friends, too. But after things got rough, his buddies went on with their lives, leaving Tanner to deal with his. I'd been one of the few people who stuck around. Birds of a feather, I guess.

My best friend had his own reasons for listening to

Nate's Denali expedition on his radio. It gave him a chance to imagine going with him. Tanner never had to tell me that. I figured it out on my own.

An hour later

This time of year I always felt an edge of impatience for summer to get here. Spring breakup in the Mat-Su Valley was the ugly butt end of an Alaskan winter. Breakup was nature's equivalent of being forced to eat brussels sprouts before you could dig into a hot-fudge sundae. With the sun nudging aside the night sky, each day gained five to ten minutes of light. Summer solstice would be right around the corner in June, when the days got seriously longer.

Despite the fact that slushy mud was the terra not-so-firma today, I could live with the sloppy mess because summertime in Alaska had always been worth waiting for. School would be over soon. One more day and I'd be done. *Adiós, M.F.* Since nothing much happened on the last day, except cleaning out our lockers so nothing fungal grew in them over the summer, I was totally ready for a vay-kay from school.

I hadn't come straight home. Tanner's mom let me stop at Taco Bell, in case I hated what Dad made for supper. I scored like a hundred things of free salsa to eat with the bag of Doritos I kept in my sock drawer. On the drive home, I sucked on an open packet of honey that I'd gotten from the drive-thru window. The honey was supposed to be drizzled on sopapillas, but I liked it straight up. When I got home, I waited until Tanner and his mom drove away before I crept around the back of my house. I climbed the stairs to the main floor, careful to avoid the creaky parts of the steps.

Dad hated when I sneaked in the back way, avoiding the entrance to his business. I mean, there was a time that the way we lived didn't bother me, but after the other kids dropped the pity routine and abused me for real, that's when I became painfully aware that where and how I lived was different. Sneaking in the back had become my way of keeping a low profile.

When I got inside, I tossed my coat and boots on the floor, saying, "I'm home," barely loud enough for me to hear. I hoped my dad wouldn't notice, but my luck wasn't *that* good. Dad's voice came from the basement.

"Can you come down here, honey? I could use some help."

I rolled my eyes, even when there was no one around to see it. In my opinion, eye rolls were never wasted. I trudged to the basement where Dad had his business, feeling the weight of my body with every step.

When I got downstairs, I plopped into a chair in Dad's workroom and said, "What?" While he worked on Mrs. Capshaw and fixed her gray hair with a brush, I stared out our frosty basement window. The glass glowed bright orange. The ice crystals were lit from behind by the sun going down. I grabbed my cell phone and took a picture of it, trying to ignore my dad.

"Work your magic with the curling iron, will ya, Abbey? You always do a great job."

Dad didn't see the irony. He thought I did a good job with hair when I barely touched mine.

"She looks pretty, doesn't she?" Not waiting for an answer, he pointed a finger and said, "Do something up here? She needs some lift."

Mrs. Capshaw had her eyes closed and a faint smile on her face. I knew Dad had something to do with that. When I got to work with my curling iron, Mrs. Capshaw's silver curls caught the faint orange glow coming from the basement window. The sunset made her hair look real pretty and under fluorescent lighting, the wrinkles on her face didn't cut into her skin as deep.

I had no concept of turning seventy-five years old. At fifteen, that seemed like an eternity to me. I wondered what I'd do as my face changed. Would I freak at the first wrinkle? When would I stop obsessing over my fat thighs and my nonexistent boobs? And at what point would I quit hoarding Kit Kat bars or lose interest in Nate Holden, the love of my pathetic life?

Did I have to wait until I died like Mrs. Capshaw?

"Is that good enough?" I asked.

Dad focused on the dead woman lying in the coffin. "Yeah, that works. She looks ten years younger, don't you think?"

I swear, I don't know why people say that. When someone is seventy-five, does ten years really make a difference?

"Yeah, she looks…better." I lied.

How could someone look better dead than alive?

Most kids my age have never seen a dead body, but not me. After Mom died, I knew death wasn't a joke, but every kid in town made me the poster child for sick humor. I'd been around corpses my whole life. When it came time to bury my mom, I knew what would be behind the curtain of Oz and hated everything about the funeral business. My dad, Graham Chandler, ran the only mortuary and crema-

torium in a small town of 4,000 people, a business that had
been in his family for generations.

I lived in a house with a mortuary in my basement where
the big-screen TV should have been. With the ground frozen for a big chunk of the year in Alaska, Dad stored bodies
in our house, waiting to plant them with the spring thaw.
Our first floor had a funeral parlor with visitation rooms
and enough Kleenex boxes to soak up the Matanuska River.

So being an outsider came with the territory—with good
reason. I made the weird kids in my school feel good about
themselves. I knew what it felt like to have no one show up
for a sleepover. I see dead people, *literally*. My father makes
his living off them. He likes to call it job security. According to Dad, it's a great way to meet people without really
trying. Eventually everyone comes to you.

But from my darkened corner of the world, my dad and
his *"business"* only reinforced my D.O.A. social life. Living
with Dad made "normal" impossible. It wasn't easy being a
teenager—*period*—but to do it when your father tells people
embalming fluid runs in his veins?

I used to think that was funny.

"I got good news." While Dad fussed with Mrs. Capshaw's dress collar, he smiled and avoided looking at me.
That wasn't a good sign. *Ever.* "I got that time off and I've
made all the arrangements."

"What are you talking about?"

"Our trip. Don't you remember me telling you about it
last week?"

Dad could have said something, but did he really expect
me to listen? Remembering stuff from a week ago was
like…a whole week ago.

"Like I told you before, after your last day of school

I made arrangements to go to our cabin. This is a good time for me to take off. We'll practically have the whole lake to ourselves. The fishing will be great. And we can... remember your mom, stay through her birthday this time."

"But Dad...I can't. You never said..." I had trouble breathing.

My father clinched his argument by bringing up Mom's birthday. His "ritual" of going to the cabin was about the two of us remembering her. He'd made a whole ceremony thing, whether we stayed for her birthday or not. Before we left the lake, we burned candles near the shore. The two of us. We talked about her—and to her—like she was still with us. Guess she was.

I'd gone with Dad to our cabin near Healy, Alaska, every year since Mom died, more out of guilt than really wanting to. I had done it for him, but being reminded how she died only made me feel worse. I made sure Dad never knew how I felt. It didn't take a crystal ball to know he'd send me to more shrinks. After I quit talking about what happened the day of the crash, I went along with our trips to the cabin, making it seem like I'd put it behind me. It was easier than telling him the truth—that I hated remembering how she died, especially with him.

To make things worse, I didn't want to leave town when Nate could use my positive vibes. I needed to know he'd be okay. With him heading for a dangerous climb, I had to be in town, to listen to the radio that Tanner had set up. Dad would ruin everything.

"Come on, honey. This is our tradition. We do it every year."

"Can't we skip it? I mean, for one year? I've got things to do. I can't..."

He never let me finish. "What things?"

I heard the anger in his voice and he got that funny look on his face, like he'd go ballistic. Dad came with a warning label. Whenever he was about to blow, two wrinkle lines showed between his eyebrows and his nostrils flared. He had that look now, the same one I probably had, thanks to him. These days, we really knew how to punch each other's buttons.

"What's so important in your life that you can't take time off for your old man? You used to like going to the cabin."

Operative words—*used to*—but I'd grown out of wanting to spend time with him. I wasn't a kid anymore. Our ritual at the lake only reminded me of what I had taken from him…from us. I didn't see the point, not now. With Dad glaring at me and expecting an answer, my heart pounded and my face got real hot. I thought he might see straight through me to the guilt I had over Mom's death that always threatened to choke me. I couldn't tell him how I felt about Nate. Telling him would spoil everything. It would be the worst.

"I'm not going, that's all." I turned before he saw the tears welling in my eyes. I didn't want him to know he could still make me cry.

"Abbey, come back here. We're not done." He yelled after me, but I wouldn't go back for round two.

I grabbed my coat and put my snow boots back on. I had to get out of that house—a mortuary filled with dead people. I was tired of sharing my life with the dead. They'd turned into a constant dark memory of my mother. I had two more years of high school. I should've been looking forward to them, but I couldn't see where things would ever get better.

After my mom was killed, I couldn't deal with the unwanted attention. I curled up in a ball, not wanting to feel anything or do anything normal. Not feeling was the only way I got through it. For some kids, that made it open season on me, especially after they found out what Dad did for a living. I became a target for every cruel joke in town. The abuse caught on like wildfire. Even if I wanted friends and a normal life, I knew that would never happen.

Kids called me the ghoul next door, Zombie Queen, a citizen of Cremation Nation, and Necro Girl—I'd heard it all. I *hated, hated, hated* being reminded of my never-ending link with death.

Why didn't Dad get that?

Twenty minutes later

Tanner didn't live far from me. I'd walked to his house plenty of times. After the sun went down, the heaping piles of melting snow reflected blue haze over everything. With my boots crunching into the slush, I heard the strange echo of my own footsteps. I'd heard that noise before and it always sounded like someone following me. I turned and looked back, peering into every shadow, looking for anything that moved.

I felt like the dumb babysitter in a slasher movie, a seriously stupid chick who opened the door to a guy who cut out her heart and watched it beat in his hand, even after everyone in the theatre had screamed, *"Don't open the door!"*

But I didn't see anything, not this time.

"Damn it," I whispered. I hated being scared.

I spun and looked around. I didn't see anything in particular, but I felt something or someone watching me. I felt cold and my feet were numb. Even my goose bumps had goose bumps, but that strange creepy feeling didn't go away, no matter how much I wanted to laugh it off. This time when I ran, I heard my footsteps and my mind played tricks on me. I didn't want anything to be there, but I swear to God, this time I saw something move.

"Who's out there?" I yelled and my voice cracked. *Babysitter chick, revisited.*

When I picked up my pace, I heard it—a loud caw in the trees over my head. It could have been a crow, but when it eclipsed the moon, I saw the size of its shadow on the snow. It was big. Real big. I looked up and got dizzy. Everything spun and sweat trickled down my spine. Without the sun, the night sky closed in and the trees stirred like bodies skulking around me.

That's when I heard the bird again and felt a cold sweep off its wings. It happened so fast that I could've sworn I felt it. Its wings fluttered and swiped against me, stinging my cold skin. I ran and covered my head with my arms. When it cackled, the shrill sound magnified. I ran and didn't look back.

Not until I got to Tanner's.

I crawled up the tree outside his window in record time. With adrenaline pumping through me, my heart felt like it would explode. I tapped on his window so hard that I almost cracked it. Tanner sat at his computer and he nearly jumped out of his skin. He fumbled for his mouse and shut down his system. His move to hide what he was doing would later strike me as odd, but at that moment I felt so blasted scared that his bizarre reaction didn't weird me out.

"Okay, okay, I'm coming. I thought you'd use the front door." He rolled his wheelchair to the window and let me in. If I hadn't been so wrapped up in myself, I would've totally said something about the way he avoided looking at me. "Are you okay? You look like you've seen a ghost."

"Yeah, maybe."

I locked the window behind me, something I usually didn't do. I pressed my face to the glass, cupping my hands around my eyes to block out the light from Tanner's room. When nothing moved in the dark, I finally felt safe enough with Tanner.

"I'm just being stupid," I told him. "As usual."

Tanner had "Not Meant To Be" by Theory of a Deadman playing loud. I loved the lyrics to that song. It was about a love like the one I felt for Nate. When I turned, I watched Tanner back up and make room for me in his bedroom. He couldn't afford to be a slob like me and leave his clothes on the floor. He needed to roll and his wheels took up space. I could've told him about the damned bird, but when I saw his face, that didn't seem important anymore.

He looked like I'd caught him doing something bad.

"What were you doin' online?"

Tanner always clocked time on his computer. He had mad skills, way better than I did. Guess when a guy had trouble getting around in the physical world, a virtual one was the great equalizer. Online he could be anyone he wanted to be. In his posts, he could say anything he wanted to about himself. I know. I'd read his stuff. I sometimes got the feeling that his online life had more importance than the one he really lived.

"Nothing. Just the usual stuff."

Tanner slouched into his wheelchair and didn't look up. He acted strange, even for Tanner.

"What's wrong?"

"I said, nothing. Give it a rest, Chandler." He snapped back, something he usually didn't do, either.

"Is that your new radio?" I pointed to the only thing in the room that looked like a damned radio. *Like, duh.*

"Yeah. I need to find out what frequency those guys will be using, but once I get that, we should hear what's going on."

Now I clammed up. If Dad got his way, I wouldn't be listening to Tanner's radio and hearing Nate on Denali. I'd miss out on the biggest adventure Nate Holden would have in his lifetime, all because Dad didn't trust me to stay home by myself.

"What's the matter with you? I thought that's what you wanted. It's all you've talked about," Tanner said as he crossed his arms and stared at his computer, working his jaw like it hurt. He grew tense about something and I couldn't let it go.

"Dad and I had an argument. He's picked this weekend to do a little father-daughter bonding. He wants me to go with him to our cabin. Why do *I* have to go? I mean, why can't I just stay home?"

"Seriously, would you leave you at home?"

I ignored him.

"I just don't see the point anymore. You'd think we could skip it this year. I mean, he didn't even consider my feelings at all."

"But isn't this the trip that he makes about your mom? What's wrong with that?"

Tanner was my best friend, but I'd never told him much about the day my mom died. Telling him everything would make it too real, would make me more of a freak. I didn't want anyone to know, especially not the only real friend I had.

"What's wrong with you? You're supposed to be my wingman and have my back," I said, using "wingman" the way Tanner and his military dad did. "Why are you on his side?"

"I'm not on anyone's side but yours."

"It doesn't feel like it." When the silence between us built to a combustible stage, I saw that Tanner wouldn't give in, so I did. "What's wrong? You look like your dog died. Pretty serious, considering you don't even have one."

It took him a while to answer. He stared at the floor and didn't move. When he finally did speak, he shocked the hell out of me.

"Maybe you should go with your dad. It might not be a bad idea to get out of town now."

"What? That's crazy talk, Tanner. You sound like you're channeling your mom. What gives?"

I wanted to yell at him—*at anybody*—but when I saw his face, I couldn't do it. I knelt by his chair and looked at him, saying, "Talk to me. Please." He didn't say anything for a long time, but after he took a deep breath, he rolled his wheelchair back to his computer and finally told me what bothered him.

"There's something you should see. You're not gonna like it, but don't kill the messenger."

Minutes later

"Abbey, don't go," Tanner called to me as I crawled through his bedroom window, not looking back. "Talk to me. Please!"

I don't even remember the trip back to my house. I ran until my legs and chest burned. My tears made the whole thing a blur. By the time I got home, I knew my face and eyes would be red, but I didn't care. I couldn't get those images on Tanner's computer out of my head. A part of me wished he'd never shown me, but a bigger part was glad he did. It would have been worse if I didn't know and had to face everyone at school, like a dumb ass.

This time, I burst through the front door of my house and headed straight for my room. I peeled off my coat and boots and dropped them on the floor as I ran through the hall and up the stairs.

"Honey? Are you all right?" My dad called after me. I really didn't want to see him, but I had to. I stopped and waited for him to find me in the hallway. I kept my back to him so he wouldn't see me crying.

"Yeah, I'm good." I cleared my throat and wiped tears off my face with the back of my hand. "I wanted to ask you, Daddy. Is it okay if we leave tomorrow…I mean, instead of waiting until Saturday?"

"But you have school tomorrow."

"I've already cleaned out my locker," I lied. "My stuff is in my room. Nothing is going on tomorrow anyway. You think we can get an early start?"

"Why the change of heart?"

I stood halfway up the stairs. When my dad came closer, I only glanced over my shoulder and forced a quick smile.

"I thought about what you said and I want to go. You were right. I really love the cabin."

"Yeah, I think we can make that happen," he said. "That's…great."

Whatever, Dad. I knew what he wanted me to say and I

said it, but that was the extent of my groveling. I bounded up the stairs, taking the steps two at a time. I had my own computer in my room. Once I got there, I shut the door and locked it. With shaking fingers, I booted my PC and grabbed my mouse to locate the same page Tanner had showed me. The closer I got to seeing it again, the more I felt sick.

With the number of hits the FarkYourself website got, I had no doubt that everyone at school would eventually see the photos of me or hear about them. Rumors would spread like wildfire. Someone had posted photos of me at the top of the thread. Anyone online with the ability and the right graphics software could use those photos to create any foul thing they wanted.

What made things worse, most of the jerks cut out my real body and replaced it with a gross fat one. Is that how I looked? They pasted my head onto anything obscene. The worst one had me doing sex stuff, things I'd never even seen before. Once my dad found out, I didn't know what he'd do. He didn't know much about computers. Would he believe anything I told him or would he think I had a bad rep at school? I wanted to believe he'd be on my side and protect me, but just knowing he'd see these pictures mortified me. How could I look him in the eye?

I was sick, *just sick*. And Tanner's words repeated over and over in my head. *"All of these people are anonymous and the site protects them. They can do anything they want and we won't be able to take it down."*

My real name had been posted, too. That was even worse than looking at those photos with Tanner in the room. I could tell he'd been embarrassed, too. I mean, sure, we joked about sex and stuff, but Tanner never made me feel weird about it and neither of us had ever crossed the line into gross—at least, for us. He'd *never ever* made me feel fat, either. Now after we'd both seen those awful pictures, I wasn't sure we'd ever see each other the same way again.

How could I face him? Face *anyone?*

"Even after you're older and are looking for a job, your future employer could find these." Tanner's words stayed with me and I remember his eyes filled with tears. I'd never seen him cry before.

We won't be able to take it down.

I'm totally screwed.

His words stuck and I suddenly knew what he meant. He was talking about both of us. Tanner had been "farked" on the site, too. I scrolled through the threads until I found what he'd been talking about. I'd been so wrapped up in me that I never asked what he meant.

"Oh. My. God." I gasped, covering my mouth with my hand. This time I had tears for Tanner.

On the thread they had on him, it started with an accusation and images that I knew in my gut weren't true. Tanner wasn't gay, but the photos were shocking. There were shower scenes in a gym and fake photos of him with other boys, each one more humiliating than the last.

"Oh, Tanner. I'm so sorry." There was nothing wrong with being gay—except if you weren't—and kids made fun of it like being gay was sick and perverted.

Whoever posted these doctored photos had hurt both of us, but Tanner didn't deserve the abuse. He'd done nothing wrong, except that hanging with me had made him fair game. These jerks had found a new way to hurt me through Tanner.

I shut down the page and cleared my search records, doing anything to destroy the evidence and remove it from my house, but I knew that wouldn't matter. Purging my system of what I'd seen didn't mean I could get it out of my head. I turned off my computer, not even waiting for my system to shut down. I hit the light switch and crawled into bed, covering my head with blankets until I only saw darkness. Yet no matter what I did, the images were still with me.

I wanted to puke. I wanted to scream. I definitely cried.

Some anonymous coward started it. It had to be someone from school. The photos they'd taken were from today, at the cafeteria. On some of the images, I recognized the clothes I had on and still had on—wrinkles and all. I didn't have the energy to change into my pajamas. I curled into a ball and gripped the blankets around me, sobbing into my pillow.

Tanner was right. I had to get out of town. I wasn't strong like him. Leaving would give me time to think. I didn't know if skulking away would be better than facing it head-on, like Tanner had chosen to do, but delaying the inevitable was something a coward did—*a coward like me.*

I don't know when I actually fell asleep, but I must have. I remembered tossing and turning and looking at the clock on my nightstand every hour. Only this time, when I opened my eyes, the clock read 2:35 in the morning. I'd slept for three hours straight, but that wasn't good enough.

I didn't want to be awake. Waking up meant I had to remember what happened and relive it. Being awake meant I still had to deal with what I'd do next, but a steady scratching at my window made me pull back the covers.

The full moon shined through the glass, nearly filling my entire window. With a tree limb eclipsing it, the moonlight cast an eerie shadow across my wall. The dark shape looked like a finger stretching into my bedroom.

"Damn it," I whispered.

I forgot to close my drapes. When I got out of bed, I saw I still had my clothes on, another bad reminder of what had happened. I stripped out of my jeans and peeled off my shirt, getting down to my undies and T-shirt before I headed for the window.

But a loud crash made me scream.

"Oh, shit!"

Something black hit my window and almost cracked the glass. I jumped back and hid in the dark. From the corner of my eye, I peeked over. When I saw movement, I pressed against the wall, too scared to move. An inky black shadow magnified across the wall of my room—the flapping wings of a bird.

I gasped and slid down, hiding in the corner. I don't know how long I stayed there. I lost track of time, but when it looked like the bird had flown away, I stood on shaky legs and crept toward the window. I shut the drapes real fast, but not before I took another peek. With trembling fingers, I reached for the curtains with the thud of my heart pulsing in my ears.

Dead bodies were in my basement, not exactly a comfort. Even though my dad slept in his bedroom down the hall, I had never felt so alone. I pulled back the curtain—barely enough to look out—and I nearly lost it.

"Oh, my God."

Below my bedroom window, a tree moved in the night breeze. At least, that's what I thought. It wasn't until I looked closer that I saw them. The tree was filled with ravens and crows. From here, it looked like hundreds of them.

When their iridescent black wings flapped, they caught the moonlight in their feathers and it made the whole tree look as if it would lift from the ground and drift into the night sky. The birds had gathered for a purpose that I didn't un-derstand, but for some strange reason, I knew one thing.

They had come because of me.

abbey   chapter 2

Next morning—too damn early

That thing with the birds last night left me spooked. I still heard them. Saw them. Their wings reflected the moonlight, shimmers of mesmerizing blue and purple that stayed with me in my restless, half-awake sleep. The rustling of their wings echoed in my ears, as if I'd perched on the branches with them.

Hiding under my blankets in the dark, I listened for them outside my window all night. Every creak in the house, every tree branch that moved in the wind and scratched at my window made my stomach lurch. I wanted to hear those devil birds fly away in one big rush, but that never happened. At some point, I must have closed my eyes and fallen asleep. I remember seeing the red digital numbers on my clock switch from 2:37 to 5:35 a.m. when my dad knocked on my door. By the time he woke me, I needed the distraction of our road trip to the cabin.

When I rushed to the window to see if the birds were

still there, the tree was empty. That made me feel like I'd imagined the whole thing, but not everything had returned to normal. After yesterday, I felt different. Don't ask me how. I just knew.

While I got dressed, every noise made me jump, even if I was the one who'd made it. Packing, I racked twice the steps between my closet and chest of drawers. I was forgetting everything. I even forgot how much I hated getting up before the sun beat me to it. My dad thought he missed something if he didn't get up early.

Yeah, right. Thank God I never inherited *that* gene.

As disturbing as it had been to stay up most of the night, because of the birds that gathered outside my window, I had more on my mind today. After I splashed water on my face, I reached for my cell and took it off the charger.

I wanted to text Tanner to tell him how sorry I was for not being a better friend after what we'd both seen online, but I stopped mid-thumb stroke. What kind of friend said something like that in a text message? I'd already been a real jerk for leaving town. Texting him would be a new low, even for me. I didn't use my phone much for actual talking, but I would've totally done it if I could be sure Tanner's dad and mom wouldn't hear his phone ring so early in the morning. Tanner would hate that.

"Shit." I tossed my cell onto my bed and raked a hand through my hair before I got back to work.

Rolling my clothes, I stuffed them into a knapsack and pretended Tanner sat with me, except for when I packed my underwear. I tried talking to him, but everything I said to fake Tanner sounded lame. Between the creepy birds stalking me and the anonymous online jerks who had posted porn on the internet about me and Tanner, I couldn't deal with any of it. It was too early and I was fried.

But as usual, I delayed the inevitable. Once we made it to the cabin, my cell phone would be hit or miss. In the mountains near Healy, the bars were virtually nonexistent. If I wanted to talk to Tanner before he left for the last day of school, I had to call him before we turned off the highway. I had a strong feeling that I wouldn't know any more about what to say to him than I did right now.

My life was a major suckfest, for real.

When I got downstairs with my junk, Dad loaded the car. I wasn't in the mood for talking. Maybe the birds were meant to tell me something, like I wasn't a good person and deserved the abuse. I felt responsible for what would happen to Tanner today, because I wouldn't be there. And for what embarrassment I'd cause my dad, after he got back to town and heard about those nasty shots online of his only daughter, I felt sick. All of it came rushing at me before the sun came up and I couldn't deal.

So I got in our SUV and left town with Dad—feeling pissed, ashamed, scared, loaded with guilt—and still not knowing what I'd say to Tanner. On top of everything, I'd be missing Nate's big adventure. With me being worried for Tanner and for Nate, I was in a pretty crappy mood.

"I thought we'd stop at that little café on the way up, get something to eat. You in?" Dad asked like I had a choice.

"Yeah…whatever," I mumbled.

With a lot on my mind, I stared out the passenger window with my arms crossed. I knew my dad hated me using the word *whatever,* but it was my only way to let him know I wasn't into his father-daughter bonding ritual anymore. *Whatever* sent a message that I didn't care about any of this and that he could make *all* the decisions. Dad usually ignored me when I got moody, but not this morning. For some reason, me not talking and my *"whatever"* had pushed him. Before we got out of our neighborhood, he pulled over the SUV, shifted it hard into Park, and turned toward me. When I heard the crunch of leather, the sound of him shifting in his seat, I couldn't make myself look at him.

"Is this how it's going to be the whole trip?" When I didn't answer, he kept talking. "You were the one who asked to go a day early. Now you act like I'm forcing you. What's up with you, Abbey? Talk to me."

Dad was being a shit and so was I. *That* gene, I'd inherited.

I crossed my arms tighter and only caught his reflection in the glass, his face silhouetted in the lights off his dash. I could have told him exactly how I felt about the timing of his trip and started our day with an argument, but I didn't want the hassle, not when I felt like such a loser.

"It's just early, Dad. Can we just…go?"

For a long moment, he didn't say anything and neither did I. I stared out my passenger window, waiting him out. Stubborn was my middle name and no one knew that better than my dad. When he finally heaved a sigh, I recognized his usual signal that he'd let it go. He shifted the car into gear and we were off again, but Dad was on edge now and I woke up that way.

Our father-daughter bonding trip had gotten off to a great start. *Typical.*

Almost two hours later

Breaking up our four-hour trip, Dad and I hit Trudy's Café almost every time we went to our cabin near Healy. It looked like a little Swiss chalet with souvenirs, T-shirts, refrigerator magnets (can't have too many of those little beauties) and key chains, shit like that. I could almost hear the yodeling. Off the Parks Highway, it was on our way, so stopping for a stackage of pancakes would have been very cool, except that I felt like a helium balloon, only without the helium. I carved a piece out of the center of my cakes and filled it with syrup to see if I could hold it in. A syrup dam. That pissed off Dad, but I guess that was the whole point. When he got up to pay the bill and sneak a visit to the head, I went outside to call Tanner. Avoiding the front parking lot, loaded with tourists in their mobile tin cans on wheels, I went for a quiet spot behind the restaurant.

I still didn't know what I'd say, but I hoped that when I heard Tanner's voice, something would come to me. After he answered on the second ring, I heard car noises in the background. His mother must have been driving him to school.

"Is something wrong?" he asked. "You never actually... call."

"Yeah, well. I had to catch you before I fall off the face of the planet. Getting bars at the cabin would be a major stroke of good luck and you know how that goes. Luck and me aren't exactly seeing eye to eye these days. I just wanted to say..."

"Look, you don't have to. I'll text you. Later, okay?"

"I know. You're not alone. Your mother's there, right?"

"Yep."

"Then just listen, 'cause my cell may not be working for much longer."

"Okay."

I took a deep breath and walked onto a small lookout point in back of Trudy's. Where I stood, I could see into a gorge that had a rushing river the color of jade. Looking at it made the morning chill dig into me and I crossed my arms, still holding my phone. When I pictured Tanner's face, it gave me the courage to say what I needed to.

"I wish I had guts like you, Tanner, but I don't. I'm defective. I haven't been a very good friend lately. I should have gone with you today...and faced the music."

"Yeah, well, I'm a trailblazer. Everyone knows the Silver Scorpion is a party on wheels."

The *Silver Scorpion* was a Liquid Comics graphic novel about a Muslim boy in a wheelchair who lost his legs in a land mine, but had the superpower to control metal with his mind. It was the creation of a group of disabled American and Syrian kids that Tanner had become fascinated with.

With his mother listening, Tanner tried to sound okay on his side of the conversation, talking about comics, but I knew better. I heard the worry in his voice...and the sadness. I knew he'd hate today. Hearing him on the phone made me wish I was there.

I didn't deserve him as a friend. I *seriously* didn't.

"Look, I'll be here when you get back," he said. "Thanks for calling. For real, I mean."

For my sake, Tanner made things easy on me. That's the kind of guy he was.

"Yeah, see you soon. First thing, I promise."

I wanted to tell him everything would be all right, but

I couldn't lie. Things were about to get a whole lot worse and I had no idea how to make it better for him.

Near Healy, Alaska

After we got to the cabin, Dad had me doing chores. On my suck-odometer, chores ranked in the red zone as something seriously wrong and unnatural, like anchovies on pizza, but I wasn't in the mood to talk anyway. I put away the groceries we'd bought from a small food store and put fresh linens on the beds and cleaned the kitchen while he chopped wood and cleared snow off the porch and back deck. The cabin was real basic. The front door had a mudroom for taking off our wet boots. The main room had a stone fireplace, a sitting area, and the kitchen. I had my own bedroom and so did my dad. We shared a bathroom that turned gross when he left the seat up—*which was like... always.*

By the time my dad got done with his ax, freaking me out like he was Jason on Friday the 13th (*so not funny*), he came in breathing a little heavy and got a fire going in our hearth. I smelled the wood burning and heard the crackling as I shut the door to my room. The place was always real quiet, which drove me crazier than usual. I had to have music in my ears and snag alone time behind closed doors, scarfing on a Kit Kat bar. Lying on my bed, I got completely wrapped in my tunes.

When one of my favorite Sara Bareilles's songs came on my iPod—"Gravity"—it reminded me of Nate. Listening to her sing about wanting to drown in love and being fragile always made me cry. I imagined Nate looking at me, really seeing me. In my dreams, I looked thin and smelled really good, too, like chocolate. Nate's blue eyes were the color of new denim and they always made it hard for me to breathe. Even in my daydreams, it was the same. I wanted to know what it would be like to touch a boy, for real.

The lyrics made me ache to kiss him…and hold him… and know what it felt like to really be in love. When my throat tightened, tears rolled down my cheeks and my room turned into a major blur, making it easy to cuddle up in Nateworld. I would never even come close to having someone like him and he sure didn't need me. He had a real life ahead of him. I could totally see him saving lives and doing real stuff, but that didn't stop me from fantasizing. I closed my eyes and blocked out the cabin to picture him with me now.

That would've worked, too—*except for Dad.*

He barged into my bedroom and ruined everything. I jumped off my pillows and wiped a hand over my face as I pulled the music from my ears.

"Come on, Dad. Knock." I couldn't look at him or else he'd know I'd been crying.

"I did. You had that music so loud, guess you didn't hear me."

I kept my back turned as I sat on the edge of my bed, hiding the raging blush that heated my cheeks. I wanted Nate to stay in my head, but Dad's intrusion messed that up.

"What's so important?" I asked.

"I can grill us hamburgers or hot dogs. What do you feel like?"

I knew he was hungry and he figured I would be, too, but everything Dad did bugged me more than usual. That

wasn't his fault. I felt tired and on edge for reasons he didn't
know. I took a deep breath and kept my voice calm.

"No, thanks. I'll get cereal later. I'm not hungry." I
stuffed the Kit Kat paper wrapper under my thigh.

"But you didn't eat much this morning. You always like
it when I grill. Are you sure?"

"I'm sure, Dad. Really." I still couldn't look at him. I
knew my eyes were red because they felt swollen and they
stung.

"Well, I'll make extra, in case you change your mind."

Before I could argue, he left my room.

"Nate, give me strength." I loved saying his name.

Picturing Nate made me forget about my dad not taking
no for an answer. After I listened to "Gravity" one more
time—without an interruption—I unpacked my stuff. I put
away my clothes and stashed the bags of chips and candy I'd
brought. My Kit Kat bars went on the windowsill where
they'd be nice and cold. I liked them that way. I opened
another one and had it half gone when I noticed that I'd
left something very important behind.

My damned cell-phone charger.

"Oh, no. No, no."

I dumped my knapsack on the bed and tore through everything, looking for it, but it wasn't there. I'd forgotten
it, damn it. Getting up that early, I knew I'd forget something major. Now I'd have to turn off my phone to conserve energy. Being on roam for a signal in such a remote
location, my battery would run down in a hurry if I didn't
try to salvage what I could. I'd have to save my call time for
emergencies or for text messages that I wasn't sure would
actually send. That meant no information about Nate. I'd
be cut off from anything that mattered to me.

Without a battery charger, my cell would be virtually useless. I knew exactly how that felt. Dad never had a phone installed at the cabin. That went against his weekend-warrior manifesto, he said. If I got desperate, I'd have to get him to drive me to the nearest phone, but that would only get him curious about what was so important. *Damn it!*

"I gotta get out of here." I sighed as I tossed my empty knapsack to the floor. "I can't breathe in this place."

If my cell had enough bars to work, getting to a high spot would be best. I had to call Tanner before my cell died. With the cabin walls closing in on me, I needed to get out. I swung open the door to my room and kept my eyes focused dead ahead. I never looked for my dad. I grabbed my coat and put on my boots outside in the mudroom. When I heard my father calling, asking where I was going, I pretended not to hear him. If he wanted peace and quiet, he'd get more of that without me.

Being around him only reminded me of how terrible I'd feel once he found out about the pictures of me posted on the internet. I never had "the talk" with Dad. That had always been Mom's job, like when she first told me about my period when I was ten. If Dad heard from virtual strangers about those nasty photos of me, that would be the first time we'd crossed the sex line. That wasn't something I even wanted to think about, much less live through.

With snow crunching under my boots, I headed for the lower ridge behind the cabin, to get those images out of my mind. It made me ill thinking about them, but I couldn't turn off the replay in my head. I climbed until I sweated under my layers of clothes and felt the heat rush to my cheeks.

Where I was going, I could think better. I hoped my cell phone might work long enough to talk to Tanner, but when I got to the first ridge, I soon found out that I didn't have the bars to make the call.

"Damn it." I tried holding my cell in the air and moved it around, but nothing helped. "Tanner, I'm sorry."

After I stuffed my phone in my jacket pocket, I slumped against a tree and took a deep breath to clear my head. The ridge overlooked part of the valley, one of my alone places. In the daytime, I could see across the lake and the rolling hills of evergreens. When smoke spiraled from the chimneys of the other cabins, it made the valley look like a postcard.

But on a clear night like tonight, the view was even more special.

The snow reflected the moonlight like I was walking on powder-blue marshmallows and the night sky took my breath away. Just for me, a gazillion stars twinkled across the universe and the northern lights shot ripples of green-and-red ribbons from one corner of the sky to the other.

"Holy…sh—shit," I panted, still out of breath. *"Gawh."*

The colors of the aurora borealis sent waves of light across the valley—and over me. Doused by shimmering magic, I stretched out my arms and spun with my head back until it made me dizzy. When I nearly lost my balance, I fell back on purpose, letting the fresh snow cushion my fall. Cocooned in a blanket of white, I watched the steam of my breath disappear into the darkness, the essence of my soul vaporizing into the night sky. I imagined what it might feel like to be completely alone. No Dad. No cabin. No worries. *Just me.* I heard the beating of my heart and, if I kept real still, the wind whispered through the trees and the snow crunched under me.

"Something good is coming...right? It's gotta be," I whispered and watched my breath drift over me like wisps of smoke. "Wish you were here, Nate Holden."

Even though I knew he couldn't hear me, I still pictured Nate lying beside me, making snow angels and holding my hand. After all the crap that had happened, being on the ridge with the dazzling light show blazing across the night sky made it all magic, like having him here could actually happen. I shut my eyes and made a wish.

But a sudden noise stopped me cold. I wasn't alone.

The loud caw of a raven made me jump. The haunting sound echoed over the valley. I sat up and looked around me, peering through the dark for that damned bird. When a chill settled into my bones, it made the hair shift on the back of my neck and my arms. I jumped to my feet and looked around. Even though I didn't see it, I knew the raven was there—watching me in the dark, laughing at me... and listening to my thoughts.

I ran down the trail, heading back for the cabin.

Whatever made all those birds come to my window last night, it was still with me. I felt it like the chill racing across my skin as I ran. Not even the magic of the northern lights and making wishes on Nate could make things better. My leaving town hadn't changed anything. I had a creepy feeling that whatever was coming, it wouldn't be good at all— *not even close.*

A few hours later
Palmer, Alaska

With the lights out in his room, Nate Holden was under his bedcovers in his boxers and T-shirt, staring at the framed poster of Denali hanging on his wall. His dad had gotten him the poster of the mountain and he'd dreamed about climbing it ever since he could remember—his rite of passage into his father's world. His alarm had been set for 4:00 a.m. but he knew he wouldn't need it. His body clock would get him up well before the buzzer went off.

Before he hit the sack, he'd texted Josh. His best friend seemed nervous, but as eager as he was to get the climb started. Since they were doing the climb for the first time tomorrow, they never talked about the bad stuff that could happen, unless his dad forced them. Nate didn't want to focus on that, but he had to admit that when he lay alone in the dark like this, he thought about it.

So when his door opened a crack, shining light from the hallway into his room, he appreciated the company. A tiny voice whispered to him.

"Can we come sleep with you?"

Hiding a smile, Nate rolled over and pulled back his covers to let his little sister, Zoey, scramble in next to him with her favorite stuffed moose. Her bare feet were ice-cold, but the rest of her was like a little heater. Zoey hadn't asked to sleep in his bed since she'd been five years old, but in the past two weeks, this had been her third time.

"I brought you a present," she said. "Wanna look at it?"

"Yeah, sure."

In her hand she held up a colorful beaded string. A small silver cross and a four-leaf clover glittered in the pale light shining in from the hallway.

"I made it. For you," she said. "It's a good-luck bracelet."

"Oh, wow. You did this, by yourself?"

"Yep." She rolled to her knees with a serious look on her face. "Let me put it on you."

With a smile on his face, he held out his wrist and watched her small fingers work.

"Don't take it off. Okay?"

In the shadows, when he saw she looked worried, his smile faded.

"Wearing your bracelet will be like you're there with me. I promise. I won't take it off. Ever." After he kissed her forehead, she sank under the blankets.

"G'night, Nate."

"Sweet dreams, monkey face. You, too, Mister Bullwinkle."

Zoey scrunched in closer and pressed the fuzzy moose against his chest. After her breathing got real steady and her arms loosened their grip on him, Nate knew Zoey had fallen asleep. She smelled like toothpaste and soap and something sweet.

When he kissed the top of her head, any worries he had vanished. He closed his eyes and dreamed of making his climb. With a blanket of white under his mountaineering boots and nothing but blue sky overhead, he stood on the summit of Denali. With his arms outstretched, he looked over the entire world from above the clouds and breathed in the thin air that few men had ever experienced.

Sweet…real sweet.

An hour later

Jackie Holden had a habit of making the rounds through the house before she went to bed—but her ritual had never been as important as it would be tonight. After she turned out the lights downstairs, she headed up the steps to Nate's and Zoey's bedrooms. Tomorrow morning would come too soon for her—the day her husband, Bob, would take their only son on his first climb up Denali.

Her first stop was Zoey's room. Although the room was dark, the light from the hallway shone on bright pink walls and the girly eyelet lace of her daughter's comforter. But when she poked her head into the room, Jackie saw that Zoey's bed was empty and her favorite stuffed toy was gone.

It didn't take Jackie long to figure out what happened and when she got to Nate's bedroom, her suspicions had been right. Amidst sports trophies, babe posters and one large framed print of Denali in Nate's room, she found both her children asleep. Zoey had crawled into bed with her big brother. Her son had his arm around his sister with his chin resting on blond curls.

Jackie couldn't help it. Her eyes filled with tears and her throat clamped tight.

Nate looked like his father, especially after he'd gained the extra muscle weight in preparation for his climb. His broader shoulders and muscular arms helped her visualize the man she always hoped he'd grow to be. If she ever stared at him when he was awake, Nate would be red-faced and would poke fun at her for being a mom, but when he slept, Jackie loved looking at her handsome son.

While she stood in the doorway, she realized she was praying. If she could stand there all night—every night—watching both her children sleep, she would have done it, freezing those memories in her mind forever.

But as she turned to leave, something made her stop.

A large bird looked to be perched on a branch outside Nate's window. Its silhouette eclipsed the moonlight shining through the drapes, making an ominous shadow. The bird flapped its wings and made a loud cry, shrieking into the night. The abrasive sound made Jackie jump. She rushed to the window to scare it away, so it wouldn't wake Nate and Zoey.

By the time she got there, the bird had gone, as if it had never been there at all.

What was that?

Although she didn't consider herself superstitious, when she replayed that moment over in her head, she couldn't shake the bad feeling. She knew what her husband would say, that she was an anxious mom worried for her son.

But as Jackie pressed her face to the window and looked for any sign of that bird, she could have sworn it felt like more than that.

chapter 3

Nate Holden stared out the window of the small aircraft, gazing over a vast field of ice and frozen peaks covered in snow that looked close enough to touch. If a guy were prone to intimidation, the sight could play real head games. Huge, gaping holes in the snowfield were visible, open crevasses waiting to swallow unwary climbers. His stomach lurched as they made their descent to the glacier near the base of Denali and a shiver of realization ran down his spine. He was about to embark on a feat few climbers had an opportunity to attempt.

Every man on his dad's team turned quiet now. They all peered out the windows of the noisy aircraft, together yet alone. The engine was too loud to have any real conversation, which was for the best. At a time like this, no words were necessary. Every man looked rapt in his own thoughts, mentally preparing for what would come. When his father thought he wasn't looking, Nate caught him watching over him. In charge of the expedition, his dad was all business. Even though his father was his rock, Nate wasn't as confident and strong. Doubt crept into his thoughts as the plane prepared to land.

His stomach churned with a strange mix of emotions. On the plus side, Nate had never felt so alive. On Denali, he'd cross a threshold into being a man, not some high-school kid. He'd leave his childhood behind forever. But on the negative side, he had to admit that the uncertainty he could no longer deny had been an epic buzz kill. What the hell was he doing here? In truth, he still felt like a kid. Until now, he had ignored the anxiety that was never far from the surface. He'd laughed it off with his buddies at school and had downplayed it with his mom so she wouldn't worry, but here on the plane, he couldn't go back even if he wanted to. Although he'd never admit it to Josh or his dad, Nate had more than the expected jitters about the climb—and it had a lot to do with what had happened last night.

Last night his usual dream of hitting the summit had turned dark, like a bad omen. Instead of walking the ridge toward the sunny peak, he dreamed of high winds that forced him to use fixed lines to cling to or else he would have been blown off the mountain. The nightmare had him battling huge black birds that pecked and clawed at his skin, making him bleed. At that altitude, he'd never given much thought to birds flying that high, but he'd read about it online after he got up that morning. He'd learned that ravens had been seen flying above the summit of Denali and that they'd been spotted at 20,000 feet on Everest, too.

But why would he have dreamt about something he didn't really know about until that morning?

For the first time, as if he'd been jinxed, he had dreamed that he never made the summit—and something far worse. Fighting off the birds, he'd lost hold of the tie line and fell off a steep cliff. His body plummeted to the ground, spinning end over end. As he fell, ice clamped over his mouth. When he called for help, no one heard him. The frozen rocks below careened toward his face. Before he hit, Nate braced his arms over his head.

He woke up before he struck the jagged boulders. Eyes wide, he'd leapt off his pillow with a gasp, panting. With his body covered in sweat, he shook all over. It seemed very real.

His sister, Zoey, never woke up. When she put her hand on his chest again, Nate felt like she'd brought him back from the nightmare of that dream, reminding him that he was at home and safe. Holding her tiny fingers in his hand, he closed his eyes, but never went back to sleep. Although the black birds felt like a bad omen, he chalked the whole thing up to nerves before the trip.

At least, he hoped that's what it was.

To get his mind off last night's nightmare, Nate nudged Josh without saying a word and pointed below, on his side of the plane. When his best friend leaned closer to check it out, he smiled and nodded. Other teams were making preparations for their first carry up the mountain to camp one. From the plane, they were mere specks on the ground, roped together in teams. The colorful gear on the white snow and all the activity on the glacier at base camp got him excited again. More than likely, these were international groups, from what his father had told him. Nate would have been intimidated if his father hadn't overseen his training.

Over the past four months, he and Josh had packed on twenty pounds of muscle weight, done cardio workouts, and taken on other winter climbs to ensure they were skilled enough to make this attempt. With his father's help, it had taken months of logistics planning to acquire the food, supplies, gear and make the other arrangements needed to support their team.

Denali was a seriously impressive and formidable mountain. In 1980, the State of Alaska had changed its name from Mount McKinley to Denali, but the federal government hadn't embraced that change. The name in Native Athabascan meant "the Great One." Nate didn't see how anyone could argue with that. At 20,320 feet above sea level, it was the tallest free-standing peak in the whole world. Although Everest was higher elevation wise, from base to summit Denali had it beat. Temps at the higher elevations had been recorded at 75 degrees below zero with wind chills documented at 118 below. The blistering winds could give them a fierce spanking if they weren't ready.

Nate squinted toward the ridge that led to the top until the mountain's jagged spine disappeared into the clouds that hovered like a crown around the summit. Tomorrow, they'd have to be up before dawn in order to cook and break camp by 6:00 a.m. Since the first leg of the trip after base camp would be the most dangerous—filled with many hidden crevasses covered over by ice bridges—it made sense to traverse the ice when it was the hardest in the early hours of the morning. That would give them the best shot at supporting the weight they'd carry in their backpacks and trailing sleds.

Because Denali was near the Arctic Circle, his dad had told him that the area would be plagued by a phenomenon called the Coriolis effect. That meant fierce storms, high winds, extremely heavy snowfalls and frigid temps were part of the equation. If a freak storm hit fast, climbers waited them out on the mountain. Teams had to be prepared. Their packs and sleds were heavier, filled with extra provisions.

Storms worried his dad the most.

Getting stuck on Denali in freezing storm conditions, without rescuers able to help, was beyond bad. That could mean a life-or-death struggle for survival. His father had tried to prepare him, but enduring the real thing would be the only way to gain experience. A tough lesson.

When the plane set down its skis onto the bumpy ice field of Kahiltna Glacier, Nate looked at Josh on the first jolt as a wake of snow and ice sprayed behind them and glistened in the dying sunlight. His friend smiled, but the gesture left in a flash. Turbulence in the small plane had made for a rough ride. He looked pale. Maybe nerves had gotten a grip on him, too.

Nate knew exactly how he felt.

Abbey

Near Healy, Alaska

After the first night at the cabin when I'd heard the call of a raven, I'd been on the lookout for any sign of the flock of birds that was stalking me. But just because I hadn't seen them, didn't mean they weren't there. I'd spent the day on the water, fishing with my dad. Actually, my father had done all the fishing. I only got my line wet, pretending to be interested. To go fishing, I must have been desperate for something to do. Staying at the cabin alone would be out of the question.

Since the ice had just broken off the surface of the lake, when Dad had paddled out in our aluminum canoe that morning, I heard the soft chink of ice colliding with the side of our boat. It sounded cool like we were in a mega bowl of punch with ice floating around us, but I guess the folks on the *Titanic* might have thought the same thing.

I didn't see anyone on the lake that morning. They didn't come out until later, at a more civilized hour. But I had to admit that Dad might have been right about the early morning. The lake looked fresh and new, as still as glass with a fine mist rising off it. The surface mirrored the morning sky—a pale bluish gray with wisps of clouds across it—and made the water look like an upside-down painting. The quiet of the morning made me glad I was there with Dad, even if he fished.

He'd told me that today would be a good time to go with the ice breaking apart, because the fish would be hungry coming off their winter hibernation. That might have been Dad's strategy, but I had no interest in actually catching a fish. Hooking one meant I'd have to clean it. *Gross.* Yeah, I knew how, but wanting to gut a fish was a totally different thing. So I slid down into the belly of the canoe and made myself comfortable in the bow as it rocked on the water. Listening to the soft splash of Dad's oar, I dozed off as he paddled the J-stroke across the lake to his lucky fishing hole.

"Did you sleep okay last night?" he asked. "I thought I heard you crying, but when I went to check, you had the door locked. Did you have a bad dream?"

I wasn't sure if he was making a point about me locking

the door or was really asking about me crying. As a kid, I felt comforted when he woke me from one of my nightmares and held me, but not anymore. I only felt weak. My dark dreams reminded Dad that I wasn't normal. So answering his question, without frills, was safer than assuming he had picked an argument about locked doors.

"I don't know." I trailed my hand along the water and stared dead ahead, not looking back at him. "I don't remember my dreams."

Another lie. The last thing I wanted to do was talk about my strange dreams with my father. Normally I loved sleeping. If I could make a career of it, I'd have my college degree by now. Sleeping meant I'd be in my room—by myself—with no one expecting me to do anything. I didn't have to answer to anyone. But over the past few nights, my dreams had been more like nightmares.

Even that morning, right before my dad came knocking on my bedroom door, I remembered that feeling of twilight sleep—the kind where I felt half awake and half asleep and didn't really care which had been more real. I had my eyes closed. The half-awake side had me dreaming about what I really wanted in my head—Nate—but it didn't take me long to screw that up.

My half-awake dream shifted into something dark.

While I lay in my bed that morning, I felt someone in the room with me, watching as I slept. My heart throttled my chest, and even though I fought it, my breathing got faster, too. I couldn't fake being asleep anymore, not if someone stood looking at me, but I couldn't make my eyes open, either. I lay there like a scared lump. My eyes were shut tight and I couldn't move. In that panic-stricken moment, I remembered feeling my mattress press down, like someone sat on the edge of my bed. If that wasn't creepy enough, a hand stroked my hair, but I still couldn't make my eyes open—not even to see if it was Nate.

The whole thing lasted only a few minutes, even though it felt like forever.

When my dad knocked on my door, I jumped and gasped for air like I'd been drowning. I sat up with a jolt and stared into every corner of my darkened bedroom, but I saw nothing out of the ordinary. The laundry fairies hadn't picked up my dirty clothes during the night to wash them. My room looked like a junk heap, exactly as I'd left it. Nothing had changed, but the weird feeling of being watched stuck with me.

Even now as I drifted across the lake in my dad's canoe, I felt eyes on me.

So the last thing I wanted was to talk about spooky stuff with a father who prepared the dead for their big send-off. He'd think I was crazy and needed more therapy. No way I'd tell him about the birds, or the invisible watcher, or Nate, or the incredibly cruel stuff happening to me and Tanner online with those cyber-bullies.

Maybe all of these things were somehow connected, but I didn't want to think about that, at least not until I went to bed tonight and got forced into dreaming again. I had a terrible feeling that my bad dreams were really a message—meant for just me—only I was too stupid to figure it out.

Anchorage, Alaska

After Tanner Lange rang the doorbell of a house off Seward Highway near the Chugach foothills, he sat in his wheelchair, waiting. He heard a guy's voice yell inside, "I got it, Mom."

Clenching his jaw, Tanner thought about all the reasons he'd forced himself to make contact with Jason Cheevers, a so-called friend who dropped off his radar after the accident that paralyzed him. He didn't think he'd ever have a reason to see Jason again, until now. Desperate times called for desperate measures. Jason was the one guy he knew who had the computer skills to pull off what Tanner wanted to do.

He'd been thankful Abbey left town and didn't have to deal with the jerks at school on her last day. She would've hated it. He tried not to dwell on what happened, but he couldn't help it. Some bastards vandalized his locker with the word *FAGGOT* painted in red. Anyone who hadn't known about the online photos got clued in after they saw his locker. And every time he turned his back, some asshole puckered his lips and made a loud kiss. Yeah, everyone thought that was funny.

The guys had been bad enough, but the sideways glances, whispers and pity-filled stares from the girls really put him over the top. Even though he could have let things die over the summer, hoping the online abusers lost interest, one thing made him mad enough to force his hand with Jason.

Abbey. She had been the reason why he'd lied to his mother.

He hated being the one to show Abbey that website. Seeing her cry had torn him up inside. When she ran from him, refusing to even come back and talk about it, he felt lower than dog shit. He didn't have a choice. She had to know before she got hit with it cold, but he still hated seeing her so hurt.

To make matters worse, she'd seen him cry. *What a complete tool!* With her beside him, looking at those damned photos, he had let everything out. The minute he did, he regretted it. Tanner wanted to fix things for her, not make her feel sorry for him. Now things were all screwed up.

That left him with few options. He could crawl in a hole and roll over like a wimpy asshole, or he could fight back—for both of them. It didn't take him long to decide what to do. For Abbey's sake, he had to try.

He told his mom that one of his buddies from his old elementary school needed his help in Anchorage. It had something to do with retrieving data off his crashed hard drive. With school over for the summer, his mother didn't make a fuss about accompanying him on a forty-five minute drive to Anchorage for his sudden weekend trip. She trusted him and even let him clock drive time behind the wheel, using his beginner's driving permit. His dad had modified hand controls and a ramp on the family van for him to use. Eventually he'd get the vehicle when he was old enough.

He hated deceiving his mother about his trip to Anchorage, but telling her what had happened and the real reason why he needed to see his old friend was too embarrassing. Even if it meant he'd miss Nate Holden's departure to Denali, Tanner felt sure that Abbey would understand. He'd been too distracted dealing with cyber-bullies that he hadn't even turned on the radio he had to track Nate's climb. He'd only be gone a few days.

With her engine idling, his mother had switched seats and was now behind the wheel and parked in the driveway, waiting to make sure someone was home. When the door opened, Jason stood there and looked down at Tanner. His red hair looked seriously messed up, like he'd slept on it wrong, and his blue eyes were bloodshot. He must have pulled an all-nighter.

After not seeing him in years, all the guy had to say was, "Hey."

"Hey." Tanner sighed. "Thanks...for doing this."

"No problem. Come on in. Let me take your stuff."

With Jason grabbing his overnight bag off the front step, Tanner turned to wave a hand to his mom as she pulled from the driveway. He hated lying, but he'd do it again, if he had to.

For Abbey.

Alaska Range—Denali

Until now, Nate had plenty to keep his mind occupied. Up since 4:00 a.m., he'd spent time hauling gear and supplies for his father's six-man team. They had all met in Talkeetna at the air-taxi service where his dad had chartered a plane to drop them at the Kahiltna Glacier of Denali. Between the morning drive and the flight time, the whole day had been packed with work.

Once they landed on the southeast fork of the glacier, his dad had the team review crevasse rescue procedures, organize their equipment, dig a cache for supplies they'd have to leave at base camp and pack their sleds for the long push to the first stop up the trail. All the logistics and prep had been a good distraction. But now that they'd made camp for the night and were waiting for the climb to start, Nate had too much time to think—and remember the nasty dream that had shaken him last night.

Sitting outside the tent he would share with Josh, he watched other teams take off, making their departure before his dad advised would be the best time to traverse the dangerous ice bridges. Watching them go made him antsy to fall in line. Apparently, Josh felt anxious, too.

Three times his friend went off to the latrines since they landed.

Nate wore four pairs of pants and layers of clothing underneath to stay warm, from his underwear layer to his insulated one on the outside. If Josh was dressed anything like him, that meant his buddy really had to go. A guy didn't peel that many layers just for something to do, not in this cold. Nate kept an eye on his friend, a guy he'd known since elementary school. After Josh came back to sit next to him, he had to ask.

"What's up with you? You look a little green."

"Nothing. Guess I'm nervous. I didn't sleep too good last night." Josh wiped his mouth with his bandana. "All this waiting around is getting to me. I'll be glad when we go."

"Yeah, me, too." Nate shifted his gaze toward his dad who stood talking to one of his clients. "Let me check to see how the weather is holding up for tomorrow. Dad should have an updated report by now."

Nate stood, but before he took a step, Josh tugged at his pant leg.

"Listen, Nate. Promise me. You and me, we'll stick close once we get going, okay? Guess I'm more tense than I thought."

Taking a knee next to Josh, Nate fixed his gaze steady on his friend.

"Yeah, sure. Until you get sick of me." He grinned. "You're not the only one with the jitters, but if you tell anyone, I'll deny it."

Josh punched his arm and chuckled for the first time that

day. "No worries. What happens on Denali, stays on Denali."

"You got that right."

If the weather held clear, Nate's father would soon give
the thumbs-up for their start up the mountain. Everything
would be a go for tomorrow. Before Nate went to talk to
his father, he gazed at the horizon. The sky had grown
darker and the temperature had definitely dropped since
they'd landed, but the weather looked good.

Covered in ice and snow, Denali stood before him, a dark
ominous shadow set against a sapphire-blue sky. With a sudden blast of cold air that made the breath catch in his throat,
the mountain sent him a message, a whisper of how dangerous she would be. Nate had a feeling this wouldn't be the
last time she'd remind him, but the twist in his gut wasn't
all bad. This climb was something he'd wanted to do his
whole life. At that moment, with a fresh dose of adrenaline
surging through him, he felt as wired as he'd ever been.

Abbey

Near Healy, Alaska

"You goin' to bed already, Abbs?" My father sat by the
stone fireplace, backlit by the crackling fire. "We could
play cards if you want."

Dad had taught me how to play poker. I'd gotten pretty
good at bluffing. My dad had no idea how much I used him
to practice lying with a straight face, even without cards in
my hand. But I wasn't in the mood to pretend to have fun,
not with everything on my mind. Not having a working
cell made it feel like I'd dropped off the planet. I had tried

texting Tanner, to see how the last day of school went for him and to find out when Nate would leave for his climb. With Tanner not responding, I had no idea if he even got my messages. Maybe they got sucked into a huge black wormhole. It could happen.

"No, thanks. I'm a little tired." I forced a smile. "Good night, Daddy."

"Good night, sweetheart."

Once I got behind closed doors, my smile totally vanished. I stripped out of my fish-smelly clothes, down to my boxers and T-shirt, and brushed my teeth before I crawled into bed. With the lights out, my room seemed darker. The moon cast only a pale glow through my thin drapes, fighting a cloudy night sky. With the winds stirring outside, noises in the cabin made me jumpy. Every scratch, creak and thump put me on edge.

It helped to have Dad up late. The lamp from the living room shined its light under my door until he went to bed. That's when my bedroom got nearly pitch-black. Whether I had my eyes open or closed, it didn't matter. It was so dark that I couldn't see a damned thing. It felt like I was trapped inside a coffin, unable to breathe.

"Get a grip, Abbs," I whispered.

Scared as I was, I knew only one thing could help me now. Time for some serious tunes. After I pulled the iPod from my nightstand drawer, I put my earbuds in and shut my eyes to focus on the music. Every song I'd downloaded had been recorded because it reminded me of Nate. In no time, I was in Nateworld and he was with me, at least in my imagination. Nate had been the one I went fishing with that day. Unlike Dad, he'd cleaned all the fish and cooked them, too. I even shared my Kit Kat bars with him for dessert. When it came time to play cards, Nate let me win. Now I imagined him with me in my room, kissing my neck and whispering to me in the dark.

"Everything'll be all right, Abbey. You'll see." He nuzzled my ear with his incredible lips and I felt his whisper on my skin. "I'm here now."

When I felt the weight of his body on mine, my face flushed with heat. I closed my eyes and imagined my fingers in his hair. The feel of his hands on me sent tingles across my arms and down my legs.

I fell asleep, dreaming of Nate and wanting to believe he'd make things better. Maybe he would.

Nate stared at the line strung out in front of him. He leaned into the blistering winds with ice crunching under his boots. Every step he took, more ice clung to him, making him move slower. It had gotten so dark that Josh was the only one he could see. The men in front of them were only vague silhouettes and his father was nowhere in sight.

"Dad?" When he yelled, no one turned. Not even Josh.

Every step had been a struggle to keep up with the rest of them. If he slowed down now, he'd be lost. Last in line, no one would see him. He had to keep going but the strong winds made every step feel like he waded through quicksand.

"Josh, I gotta stop. Please."

His friend trudged ahead. He didn't even look over his shoulder.

They were traveling over ice bridges. If the ice wasn't there, they'd fall into deep dark fissures, careening down into the belly of the earth. With every step he took, Nate heard cracks under his boots. The treacherous sound echoed through his head and followed him wherever he went. No place felt safe.

Dead ahead, a dark cloud welled up from the base of the mountain. It rolled across the frozen snow, heading straight for them. As it swallowed his father and the rest of the team, Nate felt the line tug him forward, pulling him into the darkness. He clutched at the rope and tried to hold it steady, but it cut into his hand through his gloves. The taut line burned down to his skin and drops of his blood fell onto the white snow at his feet.

"No…no. Can't…let go." Nate's eyes grew wide as he looked ahead.

Hidden in the storm clouds arose a swarm of black birds. They flew on the edge of the mounting gloom. Like an ominous dark blizzard, ravens spiraled from the sky and attacked him and Josh. Talons clawed his face and vicious beaks ripped his skin open, but he couldn't let go of the rope—until the mountain finally made him.

An ice bridge gave way and cracked open like a gaping wound in the earth. It swallowed him and Josh, pulling them into a dark hole. The bloody rope in his hands had been severed. They were free-falling deeper and deeper.

And Abbey fell in after him—*screaming*.

"NO!" I heard the sound of my own voice, crying in the dark. When I bolted upright in bed—covered in sweat—it took me a long time to realize that I'd been having another nightmare. I was in my dad's cabin, but something else was very wrong.

"Nate's in trouble." The words came from my mouth, like they were true, but how could they be? "Oh, man. That felt so…real."

I had no idea why I had that nightmare. The only thing I knew about climbing Denali, I'd picked up from YouTube videos after I'd heard about Nate's trek. Except for those birds, all of it seemed real as if I'd actually been there with him. Did I have a connection to Nate or was my nightmare part of my insane imagination, a jumbled mess of my own making? I had to know if something bad was about to happen to Nate, but maybe I was worried sick for him out of guilt for leaving town. I felt like a major screwup. If anything bad happened, I prayed that the dark cloud would be on me, not him.

I fell back onto my pillow and stared at the ceiling, listening to my panting in the dark as scary images of Nate assaulted my brain. No matter what caused the nightmare, I couldn't help it. I still had a strong feeling Nate was in trouble—because of me. Dreaming about those damned birds again had not been a coincidence.

Something bad was coming. Whatever it was, I'd be part of it.

chapter 4

On Denali—9,700 feet
Two days later—morning

For Nate and the rest of his climbing team, the first two days were spent establishing the next camp at a higher elevation and hauling gear and supplies between sites. With the intense sun, the snow had softened, making it hard to trudge through, but with the bright sunlight came the euphoric high that climbers get.

Nate had become addicted to it.

"Josh, check it out." He pointed toward the peak. "There she is. Isn't she beautiful, man?"

His buddy packed his sled for another carry. When he looked up, he smiled. "Yeah. I still can't believe we're here."

Nate already had his sled loaded. As he stood near Josh, he looked out over the trail they had put behind them. They were about to turn the corner, heading for the steeper ground of the 11,000-foot camp. At this altitude, the bright sunlight would have hurt his eyes except for the sunglasses he wore. He gazed down at the camps below. Gear of all colors was strewn over the pristine white snow. Vivid blues, yellows and reds made it look like a party. Sweaty clothes were hung on lines like flags waving in the breeze. Many of the climbers were cooking on their stoves. The smell of early morning coffee and pastas boiling were common, but Nate had a craving for something few climbers brought with them. He imagined the aroma of bacon frying and his stomach growled.

"Ah, man. No fair." Nate filled his lungs with mountain air. "Someone's frying bacon down there."

"Really?" Josh grimaced. "You can smell that from here?"

"Didn't I tell you? I've got one superpower. I can detect bacon from anywhere. Guess I'm still hungry."

"You're killin' me, Holden. Only you would pick bacon as a superpower."

Josh shook his head and got back to work. He had slowed down at the higher elevation. Nate noticed, but he didn't say anything. He felt too good to give Josh a hard time. The surrounding snow-covered peaks cut across a clear blue sky with low wisps of clouds hanging over their heads. On the summit, not even the clouds could reach the top of the world. That made him grin.

Temperature swings on Denali ranged from 100 degrees inside the tent on a sunny day to bone-chilling cold that came with harsh winds. The swings could happen within hours. Higher up the trail, his father had already warned the team. The weather would get worse. Count on it. But for now, Nate was as happy as he'd ever been. Days like this would stick in his memory, but confronting the treacherous challenges ahead and beating them was the real reason he climbed.

Anchorage

"Dude, seriously. Are you gay?" Jason Cheevers turned from his computer screen, his face scrunched in shock as he faced Tanner. His question hung in the air like the foul smell of feet in Jason's bedroom.

Tanner didn't blink. He said the first thing that sprang into his skull.

"I'll admit I'm gay if you can definitively refute that you're not a direct descendant of Sasquatch. You've got three minutes." Tanner looked at his watch. "Starting... now."

When Cheevers looked even more confused, Tanner rolled his eyes and slouched deeper into his wheelchair.

"Dude, you're giving me a headache." He heaved a sigh. "No, I'm not gay. That's the whole point."

"Wow, that's seriously messed up. No wonder you're pissed. Bet that makes it hard to get laid, huh?"

Stunned, Tanner stared at him. After spending two days with Jason Cheevers, he knew the guy's whole universe revolved around his dick. He assumed every other guy was just like him, even guys in wheelchairs.

"Tell me about it. Being on wheels, it's hard enough to get...a date." *Like try never*, Tanner thought.

He'd never been on a real date, but admitting that to this jerk would have been nothing short of pathetic. Tanner had enough regrets. Telling Cheevers about the

FarkYourself website was one more. But after grilling him for information, working off hypothetical scenarios and developing code, he finally had to concede he couldn't go any further without telling Jason the real reason he needed his computer expertise.

Tanner had run out of time.

Staying in Anchorage longer than two days would be a push for his mom to believe he was only retrieving stuff off a crashed hard drive, something he could do in his sleep. Two days with his old fair-weather friend, Jason, was about all he could stomach. All the guy talked about was his future in the NHL after his full-ride scholarship for hockey at the college of his choice. And he went on forever about how his family planned to vacation in Hawaii where he'd learn to surf. Not once did he ask about Tanner's life, like a guy in a wheelchair was an open book that everyone had read and knew the ending.

Spending time with Jason reinforced why Tanner had severed ties with him after he was paralyzed, besides the fact that the guy was a self-absorbed, egotistical tool. There had been an incident that had happened one winter night that really forced Tanner to think about who his real friends were. When Jason's father went out of town, Cheevers went joyriding in his old man's car and picked up some buddies. At that time, Tanner had been on his short list, but with no place for a wheelchair in the SUV, his wheels got tossed in the back.

After hitting a convenience store for munchies, Jason ran into a guy who told him about a wild party they could crash. Within minutes, they were parked outside an apartment building. The party was on the third floor with no elevator or wheelchair ramps. Jason could have changed his mind and found another place to go, but he barely looked over his shoulder in the rearview mirror at Tanner and said, "Sorry, man. We'll only be a little while." He turned off the engine, tossed him the keys, and left Tanner sitting in the backseat in a freezing car for what turned out to be hours. That hurt. Message received. It had been a harsh slap in the face.

But Tanner had gotten even.

He dragged his body out of the SUV through deep snow, started the engine with the key Cheevers had left him, and used a long ice scraper to operate the gas pedal. Tanner moved Jason's vehicle down a few blocks and waited for the jerk to come out looking for his ride. The guy freaked and sobered up real quick in the cold. Tanner wanted to find humor in what had happened, but at the time, the hurt felt too fresh. Jason thought that moving the SUV had been a lame joke. He never got the point and Tanner didn't bother explaining it to him.

Cheevers wasn't worth it then, and not much had changed. The only thing that had gotten him through two whole days of writing malware script and SQL injection code with the guy had been Abbey. He wanted to make things better, for her sake, even if that meant two whole days with an ass-hat like Cheevers. But now that it was time to tweak and upload the code, he'd need Jason to do it.

"Okay, cards on the table." Taking a deep breath, Tanner ignored his growing frustration and stroked Jason's ego. "You're the best cyber-bandito I know. I need you to help me, but you can't tell anyone what we're about to do."

"Cyber-banditos." Jason nodded with a lazy grin. "Cool, dude. I'm in."

A day later
On Denali—11,200 feet
-45 degrees

Only yesterday, the sun beat down on the mountain, teasing Nate with a false sense of security, but that's how things went on Denali. Euphoric bliss one minute, followed hard by a sudden fierce storm that could humble even the best mountaineering crew.

Now with the sun only a memory, winds had picked up to a body-numbing beating and the temperature had plummeted. Nate hunched his shoulders against the cold as he chopped his shovel through the hard-packed snow underneath. A newfound sense of urgency gripped him.

A storm was coming.

His team made camp, set up tents, but that wouldn't be enough. With hurricane-force winds and plunging temperatures expected, his dad ordered them to build fortified snow walls as fast as they could, to shelter each tent from the bitter cold windstorm.

With the sun down, Nate only had a headlamp to shed light on his work. When a large block of snow broke free, he grabbed it with gloved hands, lifted it to his chest and staggered to a spot he dug out around the tent he'd share with Josh.

His feet were numb with cold, but he still sweated under his gear. He was tired, but he felt good. His training had paid off. Through the blowing snow, he peered over the wall he'd finished, looking for his father who'd check on their progress soon. When he didn't see him, he turned back toward Josh. His friend was on his knees, shoving a block into place on his side.

"How're you doing?" he yelled. "You about done?"

With Josh not answering, that forced Nate to fight the blistering winds to get closer. He dropped to his knees next to his buddy.

"You okay?"

Breathing hard, Josh tossed his shovel on the snow. It took him a long moment to look up. "W-what?"

"I said, are you okay?" Nate yelled again.

"G-got a headache...th—that's all." Josh's shoulders slumped as he rubbed the back of his neck. He looked beat, but after Nate saw what Josh had done with his side of the barrier, he had to say something.

"Dad said to make the wall three blocks high, not two."

"He did?" Josh looked confused. "Guess I...forgot. Sorry, man."

"You sure you're okay?"

When Josh didn't answer fast enough, Nate reached for his arm and his friend waved him off.

"I'm fine. I can do this."

Nate knew better. At his pace, Josh would never finish his side of the snow wall before the storm got worse. The clock was ticking. If his father noticed Josh not carrying his weight, he'd play it safe and cut him from the team as soon as he could leave him behind, in good hands. Nate knew that meant he'd stay back, too. Even if that made his dad's expedition another man short, he wouldn't leave Josh.

"I know you can handle this, but I need somethin' hot to drink." Nate leaned closer. "I'll finish this. You get the stove goin' inside. Make us something."

After Josh nodded, he got to his feet and stumbled toward the tent. High winds made it hard to move, but Josh looked unsteady on his feet. At this altitude, his exhaustion showed, especially after they'd backtracked a steeper climb and double carried supplies from their last camp. But what lay ahead would be even more demanding.

The team would soon face a critical 90-degree turn. During whiteout conditions, Nate knew it would be too dangerous to attempt. With "Windy Corner" beyond that, it would be one of the most treacherous parts of the West Buttress trail. Both he and Josh had to bring their A game if they wanted to get past the steep icy slopes and make it through the threat of avalanches, rock falls and constant high winds.

But for now, they were stuck in their tents until the fierce storm blew over. No telling how long that could be. From what his dad told them earlier, other teams were trapped above them at the next camp. No one was going anywhere. With winds whipping over the top of their ice-crusted tent, they'd sleep with ice axes and boots ready, in case their tent imploded. The constant howling would make it hard to sleep.

Things were about to get brutal.

While Nate prepared to deal with what would come, he worried about Josh. Something felt off with him. Was he more scared than he let on or had something else happened?

Nate had to find out…*and soon.*

Forty minutes later

By the time he'd finished the snow wall, Nate crawled into the tent exhausted. His fingers were numb and he needed to hydrate. When he got inside and zipped the tent closed, he turned to find Josh asleep. His friend had left a lamp burning and had burrowed into his sleeping bag for the night.

"Oh, man." Nate shook his head and got to work on something to eat. Like Josh, he felt too tired to make the effort, but ignoring fuel for his body wasn't the answer. He had to stay strong and it would be important to take off his sweaty gear and dry it before morning. Sleeping in it, like Josh had done, would only make him miserable.

"You two okay in there?" his father yelled over the blowing winds and unzipped the tent opening to poke his head inside.

"Yeah, we're good." Nate forced a smile. "How's everyone else?"

"Our Chicago stockbroker is a little antsy with this weather, but everyone is holding up fine." After he nudged his head toward Josh, his father asked, "Sleeping beauty do okay today?"

"Yeah." It surprised Nate how fast he answered. "Thought the wind would keep him up, but I guess not."

"Some guys are like that. They can sleep through an avalanche." His dad grinned. "You guys did a good job on your snow wall."

"Thanks."

"According to the latest weather report, winds are at 60 miles an hour, but expected to get worse. Stay put. Don't go past the snow wall without roping up, except to use the latrine. In a whiteout, a guy could get real lost."

"Yeah, got it. Thanks, Dad."

His father turned to leave, but stopped. When Nate looked up, his dad crawled toward him and kissed him on the forehead, a move that surprised him.

"Wow." Nate smiled. "You tuckin' everyone in like that?"

"Only the ones I raised." His father winked. "I'm proud

of you, son. Hang in there. The storm will blow over soon. Promise."

"G'night, Dad."

After his father left the tent, Nate took off his gloves and stuffed them against his chest, under his long underwear, so they'd dry out overnight and not freeze solid. He cranked up the stove to boil water, but while he rummaged through his pasta stash for something to eat, he noticed a small glimmer that made him smile. Zoey's lucky bracelet dangled from his wrist, the one she'd made especially for him. Nate held the small clover charm in his fingers. He didn't consider himself superstitious, but maybe Zoey would bring him luck.

With a quick glance at his friend, he noticed that Josh was fast asleep. His buddy hadn't eaten and looked as if he'd be down for the count until morning. Whatever bugged him would have to wait until they could talk. Maybe after a good night's sleep, Josh would be better. Nate prayed that's all it would take.

Abbey

The next morning
Near Healy, Alaska

"Your mom's birthday is this weekend," Dad said as we finished cleaning up the kitchen. "Is there anything special you'd like to do?"

He always asked. The first two years after the accident, I racked my brain trying to make our memorial for Mom good for him, but somewhere I stopped making an effort. I thought he hadn't noticed, until I shook my head this time without saying a word.

"I'm not doing this for me, you know. I thought you would appreciate…"

"Appreciate what, Dad? Why am I the one who needs to remember?" My question came out harsher than I expected, but once I blurted it out, I couldn't stop.

"Mom's dead…" *Because of me,* I wanted to say. I stopped and clenched my jaw, fighting back the flood of emotions that always came when I thought of her. "She's gone, okay? At some point, we're both gonna have to…let her go. Don't tell me this is all for me."

Dad stared at me in shock. When he didn't say anything, it felt worse than if he'd yelled at me.

"I'm…s-sorry." My voice cracked. "I just can't do this anymore."

I threw down the dish towel I had in my hand and grabbed my jacket off a chair. Without saying another word, I ran for the door and slammed it behind me. Not even the cold mountain air stopped the hot sting of tears. I rushed from the cabin, leaving him behind. He didn't come after me. I didn't know which would've been worse. Sometimes I needed him to be the parent, to hold me and tell me everything would be okay, but Dad never knew how to do that, not like Mom had.

The problem was that I didn't just remember Mom on her birthday. I had her with me every day. I missed her so much. When she died, the love I felt for her didn't just stop. I couldn't shove it into a box like the clothes she would never wear again. She was the constant ache in my heart that never went away. My life had become nothing but a hole where my mother had been. I knew Dad needed us to be a family, even without Mom, but I felt lost without her. Dad and I were flying solo. Without her, we never learned how to really connect. Now I kept my distance from him because I had to.

I'd done this to us. We were both hurting because of me.

Shrugging into my jacket, I trekked up the trail behind the cabin and headed for the ridge that overlooked the valley. I wiped tears away with my sleeve, but when fresh ones came back, I quit denying that I felt like shit—and deserved to. I mean, why did I get a second chance and Mom didn't? It wasn't fair.

I needed time alone and I had a special place to go, somewhere I hadn't been in a long time. As I cut through the trees, the sun dappled me with its light, but as I climbed, the trees grew denser and the path became filled with deepening shadows. Ancient root systems dug deep into the soil. After centuries of dropped foliage, the forest floor had become spongy and pliable underfoot. It was quiet and peaceful. Ever since I'd found this path up the mountain, I sensed the presence of the souls who had climbed the trail before me. I don't know when the thought first struck me, but the trek to the upper ridge felt like a church. My kind of church.

I headed for a clearing that someone made long ago. It had an old stone fire pit and a view of the whole valley. The last time I remembered a fire burning in that pit, I was with Mom. I had shared my special spot with her. One night we'd made the climb, just the two of us, and roasted marshmallows on sticks.

I hadn't been back since. It was too painful.

But before I got my head wrapped around why I had come today, something weird happened. In the long shadows of the trees, a glimmer caught my eye. It flickered through the tree trunks and its glow warmed my face, but I couldn't tell where the light came from. Yet even though I had to shield my eyes from the brightness, I couldn't turn away. I stepped closer. When I saw movement rushing through the trees, I gasped as I looked up and saw it.

A raven.

It had drifted through the trees and perched on a limb near me. It hadn't made a sound except for the quiet flutter of its wings when it landed. The bird didn't appear to be afraid of me. Its shaggy-throated head cocked to one side and dead black eyes fixed on me. Seeing the bird up close, something primitive skittered across my skin. I couldn't take my eyes off it. I couldn't move.

I kept my feet planted, waiting.

For some reason, as I stared into that raven's eyes, I felt like the bird had come to me for a reason. On pure instinct, I shut my eyes tight and listened. The cool breeze rustling through the leaves and the chirping of small birds in the distance eventually faded to nothing but white noise before something amazing happened.

Everything went deathly still, like I'd been sucked into a cocoon, insulated from the rest of the world. With my eyes still closed, memories of my mother swept over me, warm and welcoming like hot cocoa on a chilly day. Her smile, her touch, the way she smelled, all of it rushed back like an old forgotten friend. For the first time in a long while, I actually felt happy.

It felt as if she was truly with me, even though I couldn't see her. I heard her humming in the kitchen like she used to and when I raised my chin, her perfume hit me from out of nowhere. Suddenly she was everywhere around me, as if time had rewound and the accident never happened.

Too bad that feeling didn't last long.

Just as a smile tugged at my lips, the bad stuff came in a powerful rush, too, things I had never wanted to feel, or smell, or hear again. In a cruel hoax, the stench of smoke and gasoline filled my nostrils until I could barely breathe. Grinding metal ran chills down my arms, like hearing nails on a chalkboard. When I finally heard the choked whisper of my name, I knew it was Mom—the last time I heard her voice.

"A-Abbey?"

I kept my eyes shut, waiting for her to touch me...to hold me. She was really with me. I just knew it, but I was afraid that if I opened my eyes, she'd disappear. That would feel too much like losing her all over again. So I did the only thing I could.

I prayed for the bad stuff to stop, even though a desperate sliver of me clung to the piece of my mother that I wanted to hold close to my heart. I felt torn. I didn't want to ever forget her, but if remembering her meant that I'd have to relive the accident, I knew I wasn't strong enough to go through that again.

"Please...stop this. I can't..."

I thought I had pleaded to the part of me that couldn't let her go until...

With an ear-piercing shriek, the purple iridescent raven lifted off the tree branch with ease, becoming a creature of the wind. Massive velvet wings beat in a flurry, caught the air, and defied gravity. Its powerful and explosive exit made me open my eyes with a start. But in doing that, the raven killed the intense connection I had with my dead mother.

I watched the bird fly above the valley until it vanished in the blinding light of the sun.

Something felt very wrong, but now I wasn't sure I wanted it to stop.

Next morning before dawn
On Denali
-55 degrees

Nate cracked his eyes open to an undulating blur of orange. It took him a moment to figure out what he saw. The ceiling to his tent billowed with the escalating winds, a reminder of the storm that still held them hostage on Denali. He felt the cold in the air, but as he listened to the wind, he only wanted to stay put.

The storm hadn't let up. If anything, it had gotten worse.

With the frigid air turning his breaths into vapor, Nate blinked twice and resisted the urge to yawn cold air into his lungs. Covered to his neck by his sleeping bag, he realized he hadn't moved once he finally shut his eyes. He'd collapsed into an exhausted sleep, but he didn't feel rested.

A little more sleep. That's all he wanted, but his mind wouldn't quit.

His brain had flipped to rewind for a reason. Something had awakened him. On Denali, fatigue dulled the senses. Yet he knew how important it was to stay alert, so he listened real hard and let his mind replay what had happened. Since he didn't hear anyone moving outside, he eventually took a deep breath and shut his eyes again.

But a steady persistent noise finally got his attention—something felt out of place.

He turned his head to see the tent flap unzipped and

whipping in the wind. That noise alone would have gotten him up, but what he saw next got his blood pumping. He grappled with his sleeping bag, yanking at the zipper until he shoved free of it to crawl on all fours across the tent.

Josh's sleeping bag was empty.

The only good thing was that the inside still felt warm. Josh couldn't have been gone long. Normally he wouldn't have been concerned. After all, a guy had to hit the camp latrine when nature called. But the way Josh had been acting, Nate got a bad feeling. After he put on his boots and shrugged into his parka, he grabbed a flashlight and gloves and crawled from the tent into the blizzard. Squinting in the direction of the camp latrine, he stood and faced the heavy winds, searching for signs of Josh. When Nate came up empty, he peered beyond the wall of ice they'd built.

In the distance, a slow moving shadow grabbed his attention. Someone was out there. Nate directed his flashlight into the murky gloom, but the beam only caught the heavy swirling drifts of white.

"Josh! Stop!" He cupped a hand near his mouth and yelled, "Stay where you are. Don't move!"

He had no idea if Josh heard him, but the shadow shrouded in blowing snow still moved and drifted farther from camp. In no time, the gale-force winds would cover his tracks. In these conditions, if Josh wandered too far, he might not find his way back. He'd be lost in the blizzard without a tie line, alone in a minefield of virtual death traps. Countless crevasses were hidden under the snow. If Josh broke through the ice, fresh snow would cover where he'd fallen.

Nate had no choice. If he didn't move fast—or if he took

time to get help from his dad—Josh could die. He looked over his shoulder toward the other tents and yelled.

"Josh is missing. I've got to help him. Tell my dad."

Nate didn't have time to wait for an answer. He strapped on a digital tracking beacon after he'd set it to transmit a standard signal and grabbed his climbing harness and ice ax before he vaulted over the snow wall, heading after Josh.

His best friend was in trouble.

Serious trouble.

chapter 5

On Denali at dawn
-55 degrees

Bob Holden woke with a jolt to the sounds of yelling outside. In seconds, one of his expedition team members, Mike Childers, had crawled into his tent.

"It's your son. He's gone. So's his friend, Josh."

Hearing about Nate, Bob fought to stay calm. But when he saw an edge of panic distorting the weathered face of his second-in-command, he grew more worried. Childers was an experienced climber and not prone to overreacting.

"Gone?" He grimaced as he unzipped his sleeping bag. "What are you talking about?"

"I swear, we thought we heard Nate shout something, but in the storm, we might have imagined that. By the time Joe and I went to check on the boys, they were gone. We can't be sure when that happened."

"Did you check the latrine?" Bob tried to keep his voice

steady while his mind grappled with worse scenarios. "Maybe they only…"

"We checked. They're not there. I tell ya, Bob. They're both gone. And with the snow like it is, we can't see tracks. We have no idea which direction they went…or when they took off."

Without hesitation, Bob shoved his boots on and shrugged into his jacket. He bolted out of his tent, shoving Childers aside. In the metal gray of morning, he peered through the blowing snow to search in every direction.

"Nate! Where are you?" He yelled with cupped hands at his mouth. "Josh!"

With Mike Childers and Joe Givens on his heels, he raced for Nate's tent and searched it. Their sleeping bags were cold, but given the temps at this altitude, the warmth would have been gone in a hurry. When he noticed Nate's ice ax, harness rigging, tracking beacon and flashlight were missing, he knew something was wrong. His son knew better than to wander off in whiteout conditions, especially after he'd warned him to stay put.

Backing out of the tent, he searched for tracks outside, but didn't see any. The snow had covered everything. Bob stared into the blizzard, feeling a deep chill to his bones. Nate and Josh were gone and without tracks to follow—or even a time frame—he had no idea where to begin looking.

"He took his ice ax and some gear, including a tracker," he told the men waiting outside the tent. Stan Edwards, the Chicago stockbroker, had joined Mike and Joe. All eyes were on Bob as the men waited for his orders.

"What do you want us to do? Call the ranger station?"

Mike said. "When the storm clears, they can deploy a high-altitude helicopter."

"I can't wait that long," he mumbled.

As he stared into the bleak horizon, filled with endless drifts of white, Bob Holden knew he had no right to ask these men to risk their lives to search for Nate and Josh. But he couldn't wait for a search-and-rescue helicopter, either.

He had to move now, even if he went alone.

Abbey

Dawn—near Healy, Alaska

Uncomfortable silence. That's what Dad and I had after our argument yesterday. We went through the motions of existing together. Mainly because both of us found excuses to be alone, outside the four walls that had closed in on us. I went for walks to think and skip stones on the water, always keeping my eye in the sky for that strange raven. Dad did his man stuff, chopping wood that we didn't need. I watched him from a distance through the trees. It felt like I saw a stranger, not the man who had raised me.

At dinnertime, I went to my room and told him I wasn't hungry. It was a relief that he didn't press for round two. Silence worked for both of us. By dawn, I'd tossed and turned enough. When sleep wasn't an option anymore, I slipped out of the cabin as the sun rose and worked my way up the ridge. Maybe the crisp morning air and the scent of pine would give me an idea what to do, besides saying, "I'm sorry."

I'd been a jerk, but I wasn't sure that I actually felt sorry. After Dad finally blurted out the truth, that he pushed

Mom's memorial every year at our cabin for my sake, guess we both had a lot to think about. What I'd said about us needing to let her go—and finding our own way to do that—had a ring of cold truth to it. So, yeah, I should've broken the ice and apologized for my blowup, but the way I saw it, Dad had a solid reason to apologize, too. Stubborn was a trait we both knew something about.

But as I neared the clearing on the ridge—the special spot I had shared with my mother—I saw the shadow of a man. If he hadn't moved, I never would've seen him standing in the trees.

"Oh, my God," I gasped.

The shock of seeing someone that early in the morning, it made me want to run, but something stopped me. When the man turned, I got a look at his face.

"You scared me, Dad. What are you doing up here? I thought you were asleep. I never heard you get up."

He wiped a hand over his cheeks, but not before I saw the glistening streaks on his face.

"Couldn't sleep." He avoided my eyes and cleared his throat. "What you said the other day, it got me thinking."

He had a low-key way of making me hurt all over, but maybe that was my conscience jabbing me in the gut.

"Dad, look...I'm sorry." Sorry was the one thing I didn't want to say, but it came out first. "I didn't mean to..."

"No, you were right. Guess I didn't realize how much I pushed you." Dad shrugged. "Maybe I was doin' it more for me. I don't know. I just...miss her."

I could tell he'd been crying, even though he acted like a tough guy now. I hadn't seen him lose it since the funeral. I stepped closer, unsure of what to do. That's when he surprised me again.

"Did you know that I proposed to your mother here?"

The shock on my face gave Dad my answer. The cabin had been in his family for a long time, long before he met my mother. I'd heard that he got down on one knee while they were here, but I'd never known exactly where…until now. It took me a moment to realize why Mom had never told me, even after I'd brought her to the private hideaway that I thought had been all mine to share.

"I don't think you ever knew, but I invited her up here once. This was *my* secret spot. We roasted marshmallows at that fire pit." After he shook his head, I realized that Mom never shared our secret with him. Finding that out about her made me smile. "Guess she didn't want to spoil the fun for me. She let me think I'd discovered this place."

I looked across the valley, fighting a chunk of regret jammed in my throat for not inviting him here, too. A part of me wondered if my mother's laughter—and the hopes she had for the love she shared with my father—still echoed in the trees that were rooted on this solitary ridge. It made me happy to think that was possible.

But from the corner of my eye, I saw Dad shift his gaze toward me. When I turned, he crooked his lip into a smile, like it took effort.

"Yeah, that sounds like her. She had a real subtle way of making us both feel special." He heaved a sigh. "God I miss her."

Long silences with my dad were familiar. He wasn't *that* guy, the one who filled the void with noise, but his grief felt like an even bigger wall between us. His connection to her made me feel left out and alone. He talked, but what he said sounded like words meant for her, not me.

"I still feel married. I go through the motions of living,

but it hurts, you know?" He stared across the valley, not expecting an answer. "She was the only person who knew the real me. And God bless her, she still married me."

Dad was in his own world—one that he had shared with her—and because they had a history longer than I'd been alive, I felt like an outsider.

"Man, I loved her...still love her." He shook his head and glanced at me over his shoulder. "And boy, did she love you. I just wish that I could be more like her, especially with you. I know it hasn't been easy, growing up without a mom. I wanna fix it, but to tell you the truth, I don't know how."

Dad was right. Mom had a way of making us both feel loved in a very special way, but I guess we never picked up on how she did that. I felt clueless on what to say to him, but it was my turn to make an effort.

"Being here at the cabin means different things for you and me. I see that now. I'm not saying we should stop coming, but I don't need a ceremony to remember her, Dad. Not a day goes by that I don't..." When I felt my eyes water, I let gravity do its thing. "Maybe I'll never get over losing her, but that's my choice. You don't have to fix it for me. You can't."

After a long awkward moment of Dad staring at me, like he saw me in a different way, and me not wiping tears off my face, he finally said, "You look like your mom, you know. You even sound like her."

I couldn't help it. I laughed.

"You're delusional."

What Dad said shocked me. I'd never be as pretty as Mom, or as smart, but he made me feel like I could be in some alternative universe.

"Maybe so, but not about that." He smiled for real this time and opened his arms.

For the first time in a long while, I collapsed into my father's arms. He pulled me to his chest and hugged me like he needed it, too. I'd come to the ridge to see if the weird raven would be there, to hook me up with its magic and connect me to bittersweet memories of my mother.

But at that moment, that raven had nothing on my dad.

On Denali at dawn
-55 degrees

Blowing snow distorted everything and played tricks on Nate's eyes. When he thought he'd made progress, getting closer to Josh, the winds made him slow to a crawl as if he stood still. Fighting the blizzard felt like he had slugged through bone-chilling quicksand.

"Josh! Stop!" he yelled at the shadow stumbling in front of him and flashed a light in his direction.

He stood close enough to recognize his friend's jacket, but something felt terribly wrong. Josh had to hear him, yet he wouldn't turn around. He staggered as if he were drunk. Although Nate hadn't seen a case of mountain sickness or cerebral edema before, he suspected Josh suffered from something much more than fatigue or jitters over the climb.

Brain swells happened suddenly. If Josh had one, it would explain his awkward walk and disoriented attention span, his memory loss and why he'd wandered off alone in a whiteout, against his father's repeated warnings. What had started out looking like a bad case of nerves had masked a worsening condition after Josh got to a higher altitude. He needed medical attention and a lower elevation, fast.

Nate struggled to pick up his pace, but when he got within a short distance from Josh, he noticed something. His friend had stopped. Even in the wind, Nate heard a sound that forced him to slow, too. The noise twisted his belly into a knot, even before he recognized it. A foreboding rumble from above them erupted into a deafening roar. When the ground shook under Nate's boots, he heard a loud crack echo from where Josh stood and he knew what would happen.

He couldn't warn his friend.

The ear-shattering noise made that impossible. With his feet pulled out from under him, Josh got sucked into a rush of collapsing snow. Ice cracked under his boots and opened a gaping wound deep into the mountain. A wall of snow had broken loose and engulfed him, heading straight for Nate.

Avalanche. Josh had been there one minute—and gone the next.

All Nate could do was brace for a punishing fall. A crevasse swallowed them both, dragging Nate into a deep chasm. On pure reflex, he braced his arms over his head as he fell and he gripped his ice ax and flashlight tight. Tumbling in with the fresh snow, he struggled for every gasp of air. Walls of ice pounded him as he twisted and careened on a free fall. The ice cut and scraped his hands as he dug in with his ice ax to break his plunge.

When he finally came to a stop, his head pounded. He had no idea if he was upright or head down and with the crushing weight of snow against his chest, he couldn't breathe. He needed a pocket of air or he'd suffocate in seconds. Even though it hurt to move, Nate forced his arms to work. With his ice ax still in his grip, he pushed through the snow before it hardened and shoved it away from his face.

But when his legs heaved against the packed snow that pinned his lower body, he felt the ice give way. He'd broken through the only barrier that held him. In an agonizing nosedive, he plummeted another ten or fifteen feet and hit hard.

"Ahh."

Slammed against icy boulders, he felt his last breath rush from his lungs. Heavy wet snow caved in after him and pummeled his back. He'd been thrust into murky darkness at the bottom of a cavern.

When everything stopped moving, a deathlike stillness closed in.

Nate lay sprawled on his belly, wedged between rocks and ice. He blinked and stared into the inky black until his eyes adjusted to the dark and faint glimmers of light came into focus. He could breathe, but his whole body ached. The only light came from the one he'd brought with him. Even though his flashlight had been partly covered in snow, it was within reach if he could move.

"Josh…" he whispered with a wince.

Nate wasn't sure he'd spoken at all. When he lifted his head, a jarring pain stabbed the back of his eyes and raced down his spine. Everything drifted in and out of focus. He felt dizzy as hell and wanted to puke.

"Josh," he called out again.

Not far from where he was, Nate saw a boot move under a mound of snow and he thought he heard a faint moan. Bad luck had sucked him into a crevasse with Josh, but at least they were together. Nate shoved the snow off and made sure he could move before he dug out his flashlight and crawled to Josh.

"I'm…h-here." He braced himself on an elbow to brush snow off his friend's face. "Can you hear me, Josh?"

To be able to work with both hands, Nate laid the flashlight on Josh's chest, shining the beam toward his head. The glow at that angle cast shadows on his face, making him look dead. That thought gripped Nate hard, but at least his friend was breathing. He did his best to clear the rest of the snow off and check him for injuries. Unconscious, Josh had broken an arm, but when Nate found blood on the snow near his leg, he knew the guy had worse problems.

"Oh, man."

His friend had a compound fracture below the knee. A jagged bone had broken through the skin. Although he had to stop the bleeding and get Josh stable, he had nothing with him for mountain sickness. And they had to deal with a bigger adversary—hypothermia. It could kill them both.

After Nate got his first murky glimpse of their predicament, he realized that falling into a crevasse had saved their lives. If they'd been caught in the avalanche, they'd already be dead. The crushing weight of snow would have suffocated them. Trapped in a cavern of ice with air to breathe had prolonged their lives—or delayed the inevitable.

It was too soon to tell if their stroke of good fortune would turn out to be a bad thing.

"H-hang in there, b-buddy." Nate's teeth chattered, making it hard to talk. "I gotta g-get h-help."

Nate rolled onto his back to shine his flashlight into the cavern. The avalanche had plugged the crevasse and caved in after them. The fresh wet snow was everywhere, leaving him no source for fresh air or sign of daylight. Without a clue where the surface was, he'd have no way to signal his dad, except for his tracking beacon if they got within range.

If he tried digging out, he could bring more snow down on them, robbing them of the only pocket of air they had, but not doing anything could be a death sentence. Being encased in ice below ground, the cold would get worse. All he had was his ice ax, his rope, and the flashlight in his hand, nothing that would keep them warm except the layered gear on their backs.

"Gotta…f-find a way." His voice sounded far off. It muffled in the emptiness of the snow and ice that entombed them.

With his forehead throbbing, Nate struggled to keep his eyes open. He thought of his dad and wondered if he even knew they were missing yet. His eyes watered when he imagined the worried faces of his mom and little sister. Thinking of Zoey, he tugged at his glove and looked down at his wrist, the one that had the good-luck bracelet she'd tied on him.

It was missing. Gone. And a pervasive sadness hit him hard. It felt like his connection to his family had been severed—taken from him. The hopelessness of his situation closed in.

"N-no. Stay f-focused."

Nate tried to sit up, but when he moved, he got dizzy. Blinding pinpricks of light spun in front of his eyes. He dropped the flashlight and collapsed back, staring into the frigid abyss with Josh unconscious beside him. Nate fought hard to stay awake, but eventually the cold won.

And everything went black.

chapter 6

On Denali

With howling winds gusting to 65 miles per hour, Bob Holden stared into the worsening blizzard surrounded by his team. His second-in-charge, Mike Childers, had already contacted the ranger station. As expected, the storm would hamper rescue attempts. The weather had to clear before any help arrived.

His team assembled in front of him with each man wearing full expedition gear under their climbing harnesses, ready to rope up. Even though they were prepared to search for Nate and Josh, Bob wanted them to know what they were up against and give them one last chance to back out—something he prayed they wouldn't do.

"I can't ask you men to help. Going out in this weather will be risky. If you decide to stick at camp, I understand. Nate and Josh are my responsibility. I have to do this, but you don't." Bob had to stop. To stem the emotion that threatened every time he thought about his son, he cleared his throat before he went on.

"We'll have a radio transceiver with us, but in case we get separated, there'll be another one here at camp, for emergencies."

Bob didn't have to say it. Everyone knew what he meant about getting separated. If he got into trouble, the rest of the team would have a way off the mountain.

"I'm going with you, Bob," Mike said. "I've packed the first-aid kit. And I think it's a good idea to take two sleds. The boys may need 'em."

"I'm coming, too," Joe Givens chimed in.

"And you're not doin' this without me." Stan Edwards made it unanimous.

Bob knew how important each man's contribution would be. The more eyes they'd have on the ground, the better the odds of finding the boys.

"Thanks. I can't tell you what this means to…my family. And Josh's." Bob made a point to look each man in the eye. "Since we have no idea what direction the boys took, we'll be searching in a pattern, using the camp as center point. We'll use wands to mark our way back, but once we're out of flags—" he took a ragged breath "—that's as far as we go."

Bob hoped it wouldn't come to that. He didn't want to think about not finding Nate and Josh, but Mike Childers helped distract him from his mounting fear.

"How does this search pattern work?" Childers asked.

Bob told them more about how they would search using the tracking beacon. He explained a method that he'd learned from an old Special Forces buddy who tracked hostiles in the jungles of Malaysia, a circular method Bob had adapted during hunting season to pick up animal tracks.

"We'll harness up, for safety, just like we did coming up. If you guys see anything, sing out loud enough for the next guy to hear you. We'll pass it down the line."

After each man nodded, Bob had one more thing to say before they headed out.

"If these boys are in serious trouble, they don't have much time. We gotta make this count."

Bob tried to stay focused, to clear his head of anything that would cloud his judgment. Nate and Josh's lives—and now the lives of these men—were in his hands. But no amount of objectivity could outweigh the rush of emotions bombarding him, especially since he hadn't told his wife what had happened yet. She'd be devastated. That's why he'd made the tough decision to stall until he knew more. Waiting at home for word would be pure agony for her, Zoey and Josh's family. But no matter how much he'd tried to remain detached and do his job, images of Nate and Josh flooded his mind.

Mike Childers had been the first man to pull him from his worsening misery. He put out his gloved hand. Without saying a word, he held it out in front of him, as if he were in a huddle. In a show of solidarity, each man did the same with Bob placing his hand last.

"We're gonna find 'em," Childers said. "You won't be alone when we do."

Bob swallowed, hard, and only nodded. Words would have been too tough.

Nate felt the comforting warmth before he opened his eyes. He had almost forgotten where he was until he blinked and everything came into focus. At first glance, nothing much had changed. He was still surrounded by ice, but when a brilliant pinpoint of light spiraled into something more, it made him squint.

The growing brightness hurt his eyes.

"What the hell…"

Gone were the scary shadows and the deathlike stillness of being trapped in ice. The light filled the entire cavern, blurring everything into an intense white, until a vague shadow emerged. Arms, legs and hands morphed from the light and took shape. The ghostly entity split from the bulbous masse and drifted over them. A guy his age, with blue eyes and a body Nate could see through, like a spirit or vision.

When the guy made of light settled over Josh, Nate got really scared.

"Josh. *Wake up!*"

He reached for his friend, but Josh didn't open his eyes. Nate wasn't even sure he was still breathing.

"Don't come any closer." He warned the spirit and put an arm over Josh. "Stay away from him."

But that didn't stop the thing. The entity swept its light over Josh until Nate couldn't see him anymore.

"What are you doing? Leave him alone," he pleaded. *"Please!"*

Nate tried shoving the strange vision aside, but his hands swept through the air, unable to feel anything.

Was Josh dead? *Is that how death came?* Helpless, Nate watched as the light washed over Josh inch by inch. In a slow realization, he grasped something he never wanted to consider.

Maybe they were *both* dead.

After the light finished with Josh, it turned toward him.

"No, stay back."

Nate shook his head and shoved away. When he moved, he hit a dead end with nowhere else to go, his back against a wall of ice.

"No. Don't."

The blue-eyed spirit with the ethereal body had come for him, but this time he didn't sweep over Nate, like he'd done with Josh. This time, the thing touched Nate's chest and his filmy hand went straight through. That seemed to surprise the creature, but it didn't stop the thing from getting closer.

"No! I'm not dead," Nate yelled. "I can't be!"

He didn't want to watch, but he couldn't look away. When the ghostly light came nearer, he stared into the spirit's translucent face as its fierce light speared his body. He expected pain, but instead came intense warmth.

"Please...don't do this," Nate begged, even though he knew it would do no good.

He had expected to fight the thing off, but he was shocked at his own reaction. The minute that being touched him, all the fight went out of him. He shut his eyes and let it happen.

Nate didn't even cry out.

Abbey

Near Healy, Alaska

Hugging Dad had brought a truce to the tension between us. Although I wasn't sure how long it would last, I felt happy that part of my life had gotten simpler. I even caught Dad smiling at me, for real. After we finished breakfast, he asked if I wanted to go with him to town, to stock up on red meat. When I asked him if his testosterone was running a quart low, he told me that he'd really gotten tired of fish. Cleaning them, gutting them, the smell, I wasn't sure what had gotten to him the worst, but he told me that he was seriously done with fishing for his supper.

"Yeah, I'll go with you. I can call Tanner in town, if you float me some coin."

After playing twenty questions with Dad on why I needed money for a public phone when I had my cell, I had to admit to him that I'd been lame and forgotten my charger. Dad had his own version of the eye roll. He raised an eyebrow, but at least he'd dropped the third degree.

"Then get ready. The train is pulling from the station in five minutes," he said. "But cover up that T-shirt. You're not going to town in that thing."

Dad acted like he hated my T-shirt, but since it used to be Mom's, he let me wear it when it was just the two of us. It was practically falling apart, but I couldn't get rid of it. When I had found it hidden in a drawer, after she died, I asked to keep it. He said yes with a sad smile and told me that he'd bought it for her when they were dating. That's all he'd said. Guess he wanted to hold on to that memory of Mom. Maybe he'd share it when I got older. I was okay with that.

Her T-shirt carried the name and logo of Skinny Dick's Halfway Inn, the one with two polar bears humping on the front. *Yeah, real subtle.* A local tourist hot spot near Healy, the inn was located on the Parks Highway, halfway between Anchorage and Fairbanks, hence the name. Since Dad would never let me be seen in public with Mom's old T-shirt, he always forced me to cover it up. Getting ready in my bedroom, I pulled my head through my tie-dyed Fly-by-Night sweatshirt, the one with a can of psychedelic Spam on the front. (Spam was practically the state food, or something.) When I slipped into Mom's old hiking boots with laces undone, head to toe I looked layered in Mom.

After I brushed my teeth, I grabbed my fanny pack and shoved all my personal stuff in it, the things most girls would carry in a purse. Dad was already outside and had the SUV running, but when I opened the passenger door, I heard a sound that stopped me cold.

The caw of a raven.

I looked over my shoulder and saw the bird perched near the stone chimney of our cabin. The damned thing looked as if it had been waiting for me.

"Ah, sorry, Dad. I changed my mind. I'm staying here."

"But I thought you wanted to use the phone in town."

"No, it's okay. There's something I need to do. I'll see you when you get back."

Dad stared at me with his face pinched. I thought he'd make me go with him, but after his expression softened, he said, "Okay. See you soon."

"Don't forget the snackage." I forced a grin, acting casual. "The really good kind. None of that healthy stuff."

"You got it."

I slammed his car door and watched him drive away. When I turned around, the raven was still there. It ruffled and preened its feathers, like it had all friggin' day. That made me impatient and I lost my cool.

"Primp on your own time, Poe. What's up?"

At the sound of my voice, the black bird lifted off the rooftop. In a seriously cool maneuver, it flew a circle around the cabin before it headed up the mountain. I didn't race to keep it in sight. I knew where it would go.

I followed it, only this time when I got to the ridge, the raven wasn't alone. My breath caught in my throat when I

saw them. Dozens of black birds perched in the trees surrounded the clearing, just like the ones that had stalked me
back home. Only this time, I was in the open without the
protection of hiding in my house.

"Holy cow," I whispered.

With all of them together, they scared me bad. Every rustling wing, every flap, every raspy caw made me tense. That
one raven suckered me into thinking he'd be alone, like last
time. But as I stood near the fire pit, I held my breath, trying not to rile them. I had visions of my eyes pecked out
and bloody. Even if I ran, I wouldn't stand a chance if they
ganged up on me. I was seriously outnumbered.

And with Dad gone, I was alone and without a working
phone. I didn't know what to do. I stared into the branches
that were filling up. More ravens darkened the sky and were
circling. Taking one step at a time, inching my way back
toward the trail, I kept my eyes on them...until I backed
into something that didn't move. Something warm.

"Hello."

I screamed.

The sound of a guy's voice came from behind me. My
whole body jumped. When I fell hard to the ground, the
ravens took off with their wings thrumming the air to
a deafening roar. A black swarm filled the sky, circling
through the evergreens and over the treetops. I covered my
head, afraid they'd attack me, but when that didn't happen,
I looked at the guy standing over me.

My eyes first stared at his boots before they traveled up
his jeans and eventually settled on his sweatshirt. It was the
exact one I had on, but what really spooked me and totally
had me confused was...

I stared up at Nate Holden.

abbey   chapter 7

"Are you for real?" I asked him.

Yeah, right. Like a faux Nate Holden would actually tell me I was dreaming. Of all the things I could've said, asking that question sounded stupid, even to me. It's just that I'd been fantasizing about him for so long that I thought this was the best one yet—or maybe I'd finally lost my mind.

With his dark hair in finger-tempting waves around his incredible face, Nate cocked his head and stared down at me. I must have looked silly, sprawled on the ground. But what he did next really surprised me. Instead of attempting to answer my lame question or make fun of me, he plopped on the ground across from where I'd fallen, with his long legs around mine.

I snorted a nervous laugh and said, "I mean, I thought you'd be on Denali by now. What are you doing here?"

Nate looked as if he was studying me and I did the same right back. His blue eyes were more beautiful than I ever remembered them. They were a deep winding road that I wanted to take. With him so close, I nearly forgot to take my next breath and time slowed to a soft pulse.

"Weather got…bad," he said.

His low voice sent a wave of goose bumps across my skin. He was really here—with me—and with my boots touching the inside of his thighs, being so close to him made my face heat up.

"So your father postponed your climb? Is that what happened?" I asked, trying to act calm. Nate was an outdoors guy. If he couldn't be on Denali, finding him near Healy wasn't exactly a stretch, but I was more than a little curious about how he found his way to my mountain.

He shrugged without saying a word. When he topped off his vague response with a lazy smile, he made my heart turn melty like chocolate-chip cookies hot from the oven. I wanted to stare at him forever—and touch him—but with me totally rattled, my mouth motored on like the Energizer Bunny.

"Aren't you…disappointed? I'm sorry. I didn't mean to say that. I guess postponing isn't canceling, right?"

I sounded like a moron, but he only smiled like I entertained him or something.

"Climbing Denali has been your dream." I leaned closer and softened my voice. "I'd be bummed if I had to wait… for something I really…really wanted."

I wasn't talking about climbing a mountain anymore. When his cheeks blushed pink, the combo of his smile and that shy-boy routine got to me. I wondered if he knew how girl killer crazy he was.

"But why here?" I asked. My gaze took a detour, trailed down to his lips and stayed there. "I didn't know you'd be in Healy."

"I came for…you."

Oh. My. God. I swallowed, hard. No way was this happening to me. I blinked like I had a piece of lint in my lashes and all my insecurities bubbled to the surface on a fast boil. My reaction grew more intense when he played with the laces of my boots, fingering them slow and easy.

"But I didn't think you knew—" *I existed,* that's what I wanted to say "—who I was."

"You're Abbey Chandler." He grinned and pulled his legs in, teasing me with the warmth of his body against my calves. "I've never forgotten you."

Never forgotten me? From what?

I narrowed my eyes, thinking about what he'd said. Nate acted strange. Coming from me, that said something, but before I asked about it, he did something I would never, ever forget. Without saying anything more, he got to his knees and crawled closer, not taking his eyes off mine. Better than any dream I could have ever imagined, he ran his fingers through my hair and down my cheek before he did exactly what I wanted him to. Slow and gentle, he held my face in both hands and kissed me, like I was precious and mattered. When I closed my eyes and felt his lips on mine, my whole body reacted. A tingling jolt raced through every strand of my hair and spiraled around in my stomach until it hit my toes.

The perfect kiss. *My first kiss.*

And it had come from the real Nate Holden, like I'd always dreamed it would.

Even after Nate stopped kissing me, I kept my eyes shut, not wanting it to be over. I felt him on my lips. I smelled his skin on the wind and the heady scent of pine and the rich earth would forever remind me of that perfect moment. When I finally opened my eyes, he didn't disappear like I had made him up. He really sat next to me.

"Why did you kiss me?"

"I thought you wanted me to. Was I wrong?"

Those big blue eyes waited for an answer. I swallowed with a loud gulp, one that I felt sure he'd heard. Nate sat close enough for me to feel the heat off his body. Even in the woods, he smelled damned good. I touched a trembling finger to his lips and he smiled. Guess he had his answer. I could have stared at him forever, but a bad case of jangling nerves kept my mouth talking.

"You never asked me about the ravens," I said. "I mean, it's weird, right?"

"Not really. Not for me."

"Oh, so they came because of you. Is that what you're telling me?" I grinned, but when he didn't crack a smile, I stopped. "How does that work? You snap your fingers and *poof,* they do what you tell them?"

Although I didn't know much about boys, Nate looked like he'd lost interest in birds. As if he'd read my mind and saw into my most intimate fantasies, he leaned in and teased me, brushing his lips against mine. As he kissed my neck, I shut my eyes, feeling absolutely everything.

But when his lips nuzzled my ear, he whispered, *"Poof."*

The ravens took off in one big whoosh. The sudden move scared me. When I leaned closer to Nate, he put his arms around me, to protect me. Black wings were everywhere. They flew through the trees and into the sky, heading for the valley below us. Like a wickedly good magic spell, he'd made them go. Was it a coincidence or had he really done it? I still felt as if I had imagined everything.

"Oh, wow. How did you do that?"

"You believe I had something to do with that?" He teased.

Now I felt like a moron. He'd been joking and I'd fallen for it. Even the damned ravens had been in on it. I wracked my brain to figure out a way to save face.

"I was kidding, too." I lied and changed the subject. "Nice sweatshirt, by the way. You have a thing for Spam or do you have a fake ID to get you into the Fly-By-Night Club?"

"Spam?"

"Yeah, I like it, too." After I looked down at my sweatshirt, I had a hard time meeting his gaze. "This was my mom's."

"Your mother crossed over."

He said it so matter-of-factly that I wasn't sure I'd heard him right—and he didn't actually ask a question. Crossed over? Even with my dad being in the funeral business, I'd never heard anyone real say it, not in a normal conversation that didn't involve weird psychics on TV.

"Is that some strange way of saying she died?" Although I heard the edge in my voice, I couldn't stop. "I didn't think you even knew me. Did someone at school tell you about my mom? I mean, we didn't even know each other five years ago."

Nate had me feeling anxious, something I never thought could happen. Even though he'd haunted my dreams plenty, I had to remind myself that I really didn't know him. When he only shrugged, like that was an answer, I pushed him for more.

"Did you read about it in the newspaper?"

"No, it's just that you always look sad." He cocked his head. "Is it because of her?"

He acted as if it was strange for someone to grieve over their dead mother, like he didn't comprehend the concept. And how did he know how I *"always"* looked?

"Well, yeah. She's dead and I miss her. Is that so hard for you to understand?"

"Actually I have an appreciation for death that comes from a…rather unique perspective, but I would like to hear how it's been for you since your mother's death."

"Oh, really." I narrowed my eyes. "Give me your email and I'll write you an essay."

He stared at me, like he was processing what I'd said.

"You seem angry."

"Very perceptive, Sherlock." I narrowed my eyes at him. "How I feel about my mother is personal, but you act like I'm a freak for missing her."

"No, quite the contrary. What you feel for your mother touches me. It has from the moment I first…heard about what happened."

The compassion in his eyes took me by surprise. In an instant, he completely defused me.

"Look, everyone thinks that I have some inside track on the dead because of what my father does for a living." I sighed. "If that's all you're after, you'll be disappointed, because I'm not playing that game, not with you."

"This isn't a game, Abbey. Your feelings are important to me." When he reached for my hand, the warmth of his skin calmed me. "I'm not curious about the dead. It's the living I want to know more about. I want to know about you. The depth of human emotion is complicated and extraordinary. It fascinates me."

"What? Are you writing a book?" I pulled my hand away.

"No, it's just that I find a mother's love such a powerful force. How did it feel to lose that remarkable bond at such a young age?"

"Okay, that's it. If you want the 411 on death, you can Google it." I got to my feet and stood over him, brushing off the back of my pants. "And please stop talking about my mother, like you knew her."

I went to the edge of the clearing and looked over the valley. When the sound of boots came up behind me, I felt Nate's hand touch my hair. It surprised me that I let him do it.

"If you want me to stop talking about her, I will. The last thing I want is to hurt you, Abbey." He kissed the top of my head and squeezed my arm. "But I hope we can talk more. I like…being with you."

His soft voice and the affectionate kiss brought on my tears. I didn't want to cry, but he'd peeled back all my defenses until I had nothing left but my soft underbelly. Talking about my mom always did that.

I wasn't sure I'd ever willingly open up about losing my mom. Even talking about her with Dad had been tough, but Nate made me almost want to. He'd kept me off balance— like he pulled the rug out from under me and caught me when I fell all at the same time. Maybe the dreams I had about him had made me feel like I'd known him for a long time, but something about him definitely felt familiar and safe—and strangely comforting.

"Look, I gotta go." I took a deep breath and wiped away my tears before I turned to face him. "My dad's gonna be home soon."

"Whenever you come, I'll be here. I promise."

I wanted to see him again and I had every intention of arranging that, if I could, but he jumped ahead of me with his promise.

"How did you know what I——? Never mind." I shook my head. "So anytime I come here—even at night—you'll be hanging out, is that it?"

"Yes, unless you're afraid to come after dark."

"I'm not afraid. I come here all the time at night."

"Then, yes. I'll be here."

"Okay." I shrugged. "Guess I'll see you...*whenever.*"

I headed down the trail, looking back over my shoulder. Every time I did, Nate stared down at me, smiling. What was behind that knowing smile? That perfect boy. Why had he promised me he'd be on the ridge, whenever I wanted him to be? Eventually I lost sight of him, but I kept going, back to the cabin and my pathetic life. Being with Nate had been like watching a train wreck. It had been agonizing yet I couldn't turn away. He'd tortured and charmed me, enough to get me totally hooked.

But Dad would be home soon and I didn't want him to find me gone. He'd only go looking for me and I wanted to keep Nate Holden a secret—*my secret*—even though I hated leaving him on that ridge. I had a bad feeling that I'd never see him again, except in the fantasies that would really be sweet torture after today.

Trust didn't come easy. A part of me felt like Nate had set me up. That I'd come back to the clearing and wait for him while he'd be someplace warm, laughing at my expense because that's what most people did. They made fun of me. I was a joke, but when I thought about it, that didn't seem like something Nate would do. At least the Nate I thought

I knew from school. From everything I knew about him, he was a really good guy. He wouldn't do that, to me or anyone.

Yet I couldn't help it. Good things didn't happen to me. Why would Mr. Perfect kiss me? And why, of all things, would he talk about my mom? All of it weirded me out.

I wanted to feel like a normal girl who had been kissed by the boy of her dreams. Why couldn't that feeling last? But I guess I knew why. My defenses had grown a thick skin. They'd become my survival mechanism. Believing Nate had come for me felt too much like being stupid. People could be jerks, but it would kill me if Nate turned out like that. I didn't know what to think. I just knew something didn't feel right about him.

After Nate had pushed me to open up about personal stuff—and the death of my mother, a taboo subject—I had doubts about how well I knew him at all. I had to know if he had been on the level, but nagging uncertainty forced me into testing his promise—and there'd be only one way to do that.

After I left Nate, he was all I thought about the rest of the afternoon. I'd relived our kiss over and over. I felt different, like I'd crossed over a line from being a kid. I honestly had no regrets. In fact I felt great about it, but a question lingered after I'd come off the high of kissing him.

Why did I let Nate do it?

I didn't even flinch or play hard to get. He was practically a stranger. Only the lofty pedestal that I'd put him on had earned him that kiss. At school, we'd never even talked, but being alone with him in the woods—on my turf—must have burned all my inhibitions. I let him kiss me because of the fantasies I'd had about him for so long, but why had he kissed me? At school, he always seemed to look through me.

Maybe it had been more about being alone with that one special boy. I wanted him to kiss me and he did. That moment had been about me wanting to feel like a regular girl, without all the baggage that usually came with being me. So the big debate raged inside my head the rest of the day. While I pretended everything was cool with my dad, in my mind I juggled my feelings over what had happened with Nate.

Despite him making me feel uncomfortable about my mom, I was more than ready to see him again, even though I knew Dad wouldn't like it. I guess that's why I decided to spend time with my father after he got back from town. He probably would have questioned my judgment over seeing a strange boy in the woods, but seeing Nate wasn't his decision. It was mine.

After Dad got home from town, he dumped all the good stuff on our kitchen table. He really scored on the snacks. Chips, candy, dips and pistachios—all the best food groups of snackage. He did his parental duty and warned me that tapping into that mother lode would ruin my supper, but of course I ignored him. I had to force myself to eat every last bite of the steak and salad he'd made, just to prove him wrong. I was really stuffed, but I'd never give him the satisfaction of knowing he'd been right. It was like an unwritten rule or something.

After we ate, Dad started a fire using all the wood he'd chopped when we weren't speaking to each other. My eyes kept track of the clock. I had plans for later, plans I couldn't share with him. But sitting with Dad in front of the crackling fire, I looked up to see all the photos of Mom on the wall. Wherever I turned, her eyes followed me. Each trip to the cabin, Dad would bring a new photo he'd framed. He'd surrounded us with her. Finally, I had to break the silence.

"Can we talk…about Mom, I mean?"

Dad did a double take. When his gaze met mine, I couldn't read his expression, but I hadn't missed his hesitation.

"Yeah, sure," he said.

"The days after the accident are still a blur. I thought things would come to me over time, but that's never happened."

"You were in the hospital, Abbey. We waited for you to get better, before we had her funeral. Sometimes it feels like it happened a lifetime ago, then other times it feels like it was yesterday." He gazed at the family photo we had over the fireplace on the mantel, the last Christmas we spent with Mom at the cabin. "The doctors said there'd be parts of your memory that may never come back. You blamed yourself for what happened, but it wasn't your fault. I hoped that over time you'd…"

"I'd what, Dad? Get over it?" Despite what I'd said, I wasn't angry. I felt empty. "Guess that didn't happen." *For either of us,* I wanted to tell him, but didn't.

Sometimes I wished I had a better filter for what came out of my mouth. Every time I opened it, I spewed things about me. But lately, I'd been asking myself questions about the details I couldn't remember. I'd finally come to the realization that I needed Dad to help me. My memory had been a puzzle with missing pieces and until I found those pieces, I couldn't move on.

I asked the one question that only a daughter to a mortician could ask. It surprised me that I hadn't asked it before, but truthfully it took all my courage to ask him now. I wasn't sure I'd be ready to hear his answer or that he'd be willing to talk about it, but for some reason, I had to know.

"Did you do the work on Mom? I know I've never asked before, and if you can't talk about it, I understand."

He stared at me as if I'd crossed a line. I wasn't sure he'd answer me.

Even though he was my dad, my question felt out-of-bounds. Until now, I had always thought about mom's death as *my* tragedy, but that wasn't the whole story. Dad had gone through pure hell, too. I had been at the hospital, injured with psych doctors telling him all sorts of stuff about me. And his rock and best friend—the woman he had wanted to spend the rest of his life with—had died. He had to deal with all of that alone.

I felt the rush of blame that normally came whenever I thought about how Mom died, but this time I wanted to see our gut-wrenching ordeal through Dad's eyes. We'd never talked about the details of Mom's funeral, but for some reason, it was important to me now. I had to know what it had been like for him.

"I wasn't sure I could." His voice was low and quiet. "It took me a while before I made my decision, but in the end I did it, yeah."

I tried imagining how awful that had to have been for him, but nothing I'd experienced in my life would have helped me understand. Nothing.

"Why did you?" I asked. "That had to be really hard."

"It was the last thing I could do for her." He looked dazed and lost in his memories. Dad got that way sometimes. So did I. "And the honest to God truth was, I didn't want anyone else…touching her."

We sat in silence for a long time with only the noise of the fire to fill our emptiness. I felt like an intruder on his pain.

"That couldn't have been easy for you. I mean, after the accident, she must have looked…" I couldn't finish.

"Your mom, she had cuts and bruises, but I'd seen worse. She looked like she was sleeping. Every time I looked at her, I expected her eyes to open, so yeah it was hard. The hardest thing I've ever had to do. Doctors pronounced her at the scene, said she died of head injuries. They said she probably never knew what happened."

They were wrong, Dad. She called my name. I heard her, I wanted to tell him, but that would have been cruel. If it helped him to believe she died without feeling it, that was okay with me. I wish I believed that, too. She'd called my name. That meant she'd been alive and knew everything that had happened.

"Well, I don't know how you do it—" I shook my head and gazed into the fire "—working on dead people, I mean."

It took him a long time to say something.

"It's about respect for life and the human body," he said. "A funeral or a memorial is important. It's not about a life ended. It's about remembering a life lived. My family taught me that. That's how and why I do it. I didn't realize how important that was to me until I touched your mother for the last time."

I stared at my father for a long time after that, sneaking peeks when he thought I wasn't looking. He had the quiet strength to take care of my mother after she died, doing what had to be done even though he was hurting. Hearing him talk like this, I should have found comfort in it, but I didn't. I hated myself even more for screwing it up—for all of us. When Mom died, I lost my connection to Dad, too. It was like I'd lost them both. I mean, I'd always known how much he loved her.

But now that it was only the two of us, I wasn't sure how much he loved me.

Palmer, Alaska

The sun had already gone down by the time Tanner got home from Anchorage. For the last hour, he'd been sitting in his wheelchair, looking out his bedroom window with only one lamp burning. As he listened to the song "Not Meant to Be," one of Abbey's favorite songs, he thought about her. The lyrics put him into an epic tailspin, but they seemed to make her happy, so he played the song because it reminded him of her.

He imagined her skulking through the woods on her way to see him. Sometimes she'd come to his front door, but the times he liked best was when she climbed the tree and came through his bedroom window. He knew that wasn't going to happen tonight, but that didn't stop him from wanting to see her. Tanner gazed at the moon, wondering where she was and what she was doing, especially when he had so much weird stuff to tell her.

Jason's mom had insisted on making a home-cooked meal before Tanner left Anchorage, something different than the endless pizzas he and her son had eaten while they worked behind a closed bedroom door. Unlike Jason who never really seemed interested in Tanner's life, his mother was just the opposite. She focused completely on him and had been overly nice, the fake kind of nice that people with two healthy legs sometimes heaped on those who didn't. Tanner kept his mouth full of meat loaf and potatoes, and did plenty of nodding. It was the longest dinner he'd ever had. By the time his mother pulled into the drive to pick him up, Tanner had never been so happy to see her. Jason and his mom were probably relieved he was leaving, too. They'd done their bit for the handicapped, enough to feel good about themselves.

Abbey would've had plenty to say about Jason and his mom. With her usual slant on things, she probably would've had him laughing about spending two whole days in TV Land on a *Left It to Cheevers* rerun. She always noticed how people treated him and she said exactly what he thought before he'd even told her. She just...*knew.* He tried texting her again, but since she hadn't replied to his other messages, he had to assume she didn't get them.

But everything was in place and ready to go. Jason had helped him upload the code and now it had turned into a waiting game. He'd have plenty to do tomorrow, watching what they'd created unfold. He knew Abbey would have loved to be here when things started to roll.

Guess he missed his best friend—and not just a little bit.

Abbey

Near Healy, Alaska

I hadn't bothered to change clothes when I went to bed. I even kept my boots on. After I kissed Dad good-night, I pretended to be tired, but in reality I was more juiced than

I'd ever been. Doing something that I wasn't supposed to had fueled my buzz. I went to my room and sat in the dark, waiting. As I listened for Dad to go to bed, I watched the seconds and minutes tick down on my nightstand clock. When the cabin got real quiet and the red digital numbers on my clock flipped to 1:15 a.m., I grabbed my jacket and my dad's new flashlight that I had stashed in my room. I crept toward the front door, careful not to make any noise, and slipped out into the cold night air.

The first part of the climb up the mountain had been slow. I didn't want Dad to see the flashlight go on, so I went by feel in the dark with only the moonlight to guide me. I didn't turn on the flashlight until I got to the lower ridge. The chilly night air fed my adrenaline. As my blood got pumping from the trek up the mountain, I wasn't sure if my excitement had been about the exertion of the climb or imagining Nate as my reward for making the effort.

In all my dreams, I'd never pictured him in the dark, under the powder-blue dust of the moon. It was something I really wanted to imprint on my brain.

But as soon as I let myself believe he'd be there, I dashed my own hopes. The odds weren't good that he'd be there at all, especially at this hour. I had to prepare for the worst. Expecting good things to happen for me was a waste of time, but try telling that to my feet. No matter how hard I tried to slow down, my heart wouldn't let me. When I made the last turn, heading for the upper ridge, I searched the tree line above me, praying to spot him looking down like he'd done before.

I knew Dad wouldn't approve. The influence Nate Holden had over me was unnerving and exhilarating at the same time. As I got close to the clearing, I saw something that made me turn off the flashlight. I crept nearer to the break in the trees and peered through the shadows. A dim glow flickered through the evergreens. When I saw a fire burning in the pit, I held my breath and looked for him.

Nate Holden stepped from the shadows near me and eclipsed the flames, with his face shrouded in darkness.

"Gawd. You scared me," I gasped.

"But I told you I'd be here."

I couldn't see his eyes and I felt the warmth of the fire shift to cold when he stepped between me and the fire pit, but it wasn't just the sudden chill that made me uncomfortable. Our strange conversation from earlier had been unexpected. I had to admit, being alone in the dark with Nate had me on edge—especially when another frightening thought suddenly occurred to me.

What if Nate had only one reason for finding me in Healy—and it had nothing to do with liking me or wanting to get to know me.

Maybe he'd seen those doctored photos on the internet. Anyone seeing those gross pictures would get the wrong idea about me. They'd think I was a sure thing with a reputation. I didn't want to believe that Nate would be the kind of guy who'd hit on some strange girl to get laid, but maybe my fantasies about him had been all wrong.

The truth was that I really didn't know.

"I'm glad you came, Abbey." His low voice sent shivers over my skin. Only this time, I wasn't sure they were the good kind. With the flames behind him, his body had an edge of blazing orange that made it look as if he were on fire.

"You're here." I forced a smile. "Just like you promised."

"I never want to lie to you."

For the first time I noticed how carefully Nate worded everything. Never wanting to lie wasn't the same as saying he never would lie. I took a deep breath and walked by him toward the fire, hoping he wouldn't see my uncertainty.

I prayed I hadn't made a mistake in coming here.

abbey   chapter 8

Smoke off the fire wafted into the night air and faded into
the dark like the sound of our voices. I kept my distance and
sat across from Nate by the fire pit. When he hadn't tried
to kiss me again, I never thought I'd feel relief over that,
but I did, at least for a while. Even as we talked, I struggled
with my doubts—about him and me.

   What if I'd been right about him being a good guy and
now he'd think I acted weird? Had I sabotaged any hope of
a relationship with him? But if I let him kiss me and things
got heated, could I stop him if I had to? I hated thinking
he was a pervert. That went against everything I believed
about him. I knew about a couple of girls at school that he
dated. They weren't cheerleader types. He seemed to like
"normal" girls with smarts, but maybe that's why his interest in me seemed wacked. I was in a "lose-lose" situation
with no options. I couldn't explain my behavior without
saying embarrassing stuff. Yet if I was wrong about Nate

and he turned out to be a perv, I didn't want to think about how much that would crush me.

Nate must have sensed something in the way I'd been acting from the moment I got there. I'd been guarded, but as we talked I loosened up. He actually seemed interested in what I said, about anything. He listened mostly, which surprised me. Most guys loved to hear the sound of their own voices, but not Nate. He sat across from me, staring with those addictive blue eyes and giving me a glimpse of the occasional shy smile that I couldn't get enough of.

I'd never noticed before, but he seemed older. The way he talked, the words he used, they were different than I had expected. He had a calmness that made me want to be with him, but other things about Nate were the same as I remembered from school. Whenever he ran a hand through his dark hair—a gesture I'd grown fond of—I pictured helping him. The feel of his curls in my fingers was something I didn't want to only imagine. I wanted to know how it actually felt.

Being there with him felt like time had stopped. We talked for hours and the crackling fire warmed the bottoms of my boots as I rested my feet on the stones surrounding the pit. When the flames popped embers into the drifting smoke, the orange flickers spiraled up and disappeared into the darkness like the seconds ticking away from our time together.

"Do you kiss every girl you meet in the woods? Or did you try it with me because…"

I stopped from telling him everything. I couldn't bring myself to say it. If he hadn't seen the cyber-bully pictures of me on that FarkYourself website, I'd be outing myself. I didn't know what to do.

"Because why?" he asked.

"Nothing." I shook my head and forced a smile. "What were you going to say?"

"No, I don't kiss every girl I meet in the woods. You're the first, actually." Nate stared into the flames, with the fire reflected in the cool blue of his eyes. Like fire and ice, he was a contradiction and definitely not easy to read.

"No way," I said. "A guy like you has plenty of girls who…"

"But they're not you, Abbey."

What he said surprised me. Nate could shock me one minute and charm me the next. He had me off balance and I had no idea what to say.

"What makes me so special?" I asked him straight up, without playing it cute. I didn't need my ego fed. I really wanted to know.

"I see strength in you." He fixed his gaze on me. "You're not afraid to be different. Your mother must have loved you a great deal."

When he brought up my mother again, I glared at him, but he shrugged and said, "You asked me why you're so special and I told you."

"But why do you keep coming back to my mother? I don't get it."

"Because she's a big part of who you are…and who you'll become."

The things Nate said and how he said them really got to me. He pushed me to think and he caused me to question. I didn't know whether I should be mad or glad he was here. How did he know what I would become and why did he think I was some big deal? I didn't feel special.

Nate had a knack for messing with my head. Every time

I got comfortable with him, he brought up my mom on purpose, like he had an agenda he hadn't clued me in on yet. With him keeping me off balance, it made me want to return the favor by asking him something that might rattle him.

"So what scares you?" I asked. "Are you afraid of dying?"

Nate looked as if he struggled with what to say, but eventually he answered me.

"I'm afraid of feeling nothing. An eternity of nothing."

"Is that what you think death is?"

"No, but I know what... I mean, I can only imagine what an eternity of nothing feels like. It's my firm belief that death is...or might be a welcomed alternative. Death means a soul had lived in the first place. I appreciate what a blessing that could be."

"I don't understand. Are you talking about suicide?" I crossed my arms, unsure I wanted to hear his answer.

"No, of course not. Suicide is something I've never understood. To squander life, it's such a...profound waste."

"Then what are you talking about? You're scaring me."

"I'm sorry. That wasn't my intention. I'm talking about living, not dying." He looked up from the fire and fixed his gaze on me. "Life is about feeling absolutely everything. It's a miracle and a glorious blessing that I've come to cherish...recently. Even being able to communicate and speak is—"

I opened my mouth to say something, but he held up a finger and stopped me with one look.

"You asked what scares me and I'm trying to explain. Finding the right words is more difficult for me than you might imagine." He took a deep breath and moved closer to me as if he intended to confide something special.

The closer he got, the harder it was for me to breathe. He smelled like pine trees and rich soil, a mix of my favorite smells in these woods. With the heat of the fire, I felt dizzy. My eyes fixed on his lips until his hypnotic eyes drew me in.

That's when he had me.

With his voice low and sweet, he fed my addiction for him.

"Now that I've had a taste of life with its unrestrained joy and even its potential for boundless sorrows, I'm afraid of losing all that." He touched my cheek with a finger and adrenaline sent shock waves over my skin. "Feeling real passion and experiencing love for the first time, it would be simply cruel to have it taken away. Now that I know what life feels like—the good and the bad of what it can be—an eternity of nothing is what scares me most."

When he talked about dying being an eternity of nothing, that broke his spell over me like nothing else could have. What he said made me really sad and I couldn't ignore the guilt that had shaped my life.

"Is that what you think happened to my mother?" This time when he looked across at me, my eyes were filled with tears. "She died and everything good in her got sucked into some black void? Her life meant nothing?"

Even as I said those words, I felt an ache deep in my soul. I had wondered what death would have been like for my mother. I had a hard time believing in any God or heaven that would have taken her from me, but I'd been even more afraid that death was a vast wasteland of nothing with no "do overs."

"No, that's not what I meant. I was talking about me." He shook his head. "Maybe it was my mistake, to envy what I've never had. It was too big of a temptation perhaps. But now that I'm here, I can't go back. I'm not sure I can endure an existence of…nothing. Not anymore."

I felt so wrapped in my own pain that I had a hard time grasping what he'd said. I knew that had been my fault, but I had to understand.

"Wait a minute. What are you saying?" My voice cracked. "You make it sound like life is nothing but a crap-shoot. Whoever is lucky enough to get a chance, they get one shot and one lousy car accident can take that precious gift away."

"I'm sorry. That's not what—" He stopped and reached for my hand, but I pulled away. "I was only speaking for me. That's not what happens when a human soul moves on. When humans die, it's different."

"Oh, so now you're saying you're not human. Terrific." I threw up my hands. "Let me guess. You're Pinocchio, a splinter hazard who dreams of being a real boy."

"No, I'm human."

He forced a strained smile, but in the flickering light of the fire, he looked sad as he got to his feet. At first, I thought he would leave, but that didn't happen. Nate pulled a small knife from his pocket and sliced the palm of his hand before I had a chance to stop him.

"What are you doing? You're crazy," I yelled and jumped to my feet, watching blood drip down his wrist.

"I'm human, Abbey. Cut me and I bleed." He winced. "And if you stop kissing me that would cut me deeper than the knife. You're the reason I came here." He lowered his voice until I barely heard him. "Finding the right words hasn't been easy for me. I hoped you would give me a chance, but I'm afraid that I've said or done something so wrong that I'm beyond your forgiveness. For that, I'm deeply sorry."

Nate turned the tables on me again. I wanted to stay mad, at least enough to get satisfaction from it. But somehow he'd made me feel bad for pushing him. I wanted to get out of there. I could've ignored his apology and left without saying another word. That would've been the smart thing to do, but playing it smart wasn't usually my first choice.

Something made me stay and a strong urge took over. Until now, Nate had dictated how our conversations would go. I wanted my turn.

"You wanna talk about my mother. Let's talk." When I crossed my arms and turned to face him, Nate had trouble looking at me.

"Perhaps now isn't the best time," he said. "You're upset."

"Yeah, I'm upset, but I think we should talk about her. I mean, you were the one pushing me to do it, why back off now?"

"You're not ready to talk about her death. I can see that." He clenched his jaw. "I think you should go. The sun will be up soon and your father will be worried if he finds you gone."

"What makes you such an authority on me or my mother, huh?" I stepped closer. "You don't like me pushing back, do you?"

"It's not that."

"You're nothing like I expected, Nate. And I think you're right. It's time for me to go. Don't bother hanging around here, if that's what you do. 'Cause it'll be a waste of your precious time in Nothingville. I'm not comin' back."

I turned to leave, but he grabbed my arm, hard.

"No, p-please don't leave m-me. Something's h-happening… I c-can't…" The desperation and pain bleeding through his voice surprised me. It sounded like someone else said it. Even though the words came from his mouth, he looked surprised that he'd said them—surprised enough to lash out.

"What are you doing?" he asked. His voice turned harsh and he wasn't looking at me. *Who was he talking to?*

"I'm not doing anything. You grabbed me," I argued. I pulled away, but he wouldn't let go. "You're hurting me."

Nate gripped my arm tighter, until it hurt real bad. He wouldn't let go. The fire. The darkness. The blood where he'd cut his own hand. All of it scared me.

"I'm sorry, Abbey. I can't…" Nate looked down at his hand as if he were willing it to let go. "This isn't my do-ing. I swear to you."

"Let me go, Nate. Please."

"I'm trying."

At that moment, I saw something in his eyes that I never expected to see. *Fear.* Nate's beautiful eyes were wild, filled with a sudden panic.

"What's happening to you?" I touched his cheek. "There's something wrong with your arm…and your voice is differ-ent. Talk to me, Nate, please. You're scaring me."

"Not…my fault."

With great effort, he struggled to release his grip. His whole body shook as if he were having a seizure. But be-fore he let go, he leaned in with a pained expression on his face and whispered in my ear.

"Help m-me, Abbey," his voice cracked. "You're the only one who c-can."

Nate's voice sounded far away like a faint echo in my ear. He looked confused. Something was happening—*inside him*.

"What's wrong?" When I reached for his face again, he jerked his head away.

"I'm sorry, Abbey. I truly am, but please...come tomorrow."

After he let me go, Nate regained his composure, but not enough to look me in the eye. He headed toward the fire, barely looking over his shoulder.

"Tomorrow I'll be fine. We can talk then, but for now, just go."

I did as he told me and left. This time, I didn't look to see if he watched me. I knew he wouldn't be.

On Denali

Nate jolted awake and his gasp echoed in the icy cavern where he'd passed out next to Josh. His skin was beaded with sweat, despite the cold. And his heart hammered his ribs as his whole body shook, but his shivers weren't only from the cold. The nightmare that tortured him had been so vivid and strange—especially the knife.

He yanked off a glove and looked down at his hand, stunned. His palm throbbed in pain from a fresh cut with blood draining down his wrist. Although the wound hurt, it wasn't deep enough to worry about. But the instant the knife cut his skin, Nate felt something push through his body like a jolt of electricity. That adrenaline rush triggered an undeniable reaction in him, but how...and why? He felt split in two.

"This is insane." He shoved his glove back on.

Everything started with his vague memory of an entity

that had highjacked him. He'd dreamed that a malicious spirit had taken over, like a shape-shifter or a body snatcher in a horror flick. His thoughts, his movements, even the things out of his mouth weren't coming from him. He saw everything happening, but couldn't stop it. His body felt like a runaway train without brakes. No matter what he did to derail what happened, nothing worked until he felt that knife cut his hand. That instant of pain had awakened something. It gave him the courage to fight back harder and grab the girl's arm.

For a few precious seconds, he'd been in control.

And that girl, the entity had said her name—*Abbey Chandler*. For some reason, she felt special to him. The spirit's thoughts were jumbled inside, mixed with his own fears. Nate felt trapped and powerless, a prisoner in a crevasse of ice and held hostage in his own body.

What did it mean? *Was he dead?*

He grabbed his flashlight and turned toward Josh. While he'd been passed out, Nate was deathly afraid that he'd lost him. He shined the light onto his friend's slack face. When he saw him still breathing, he heaved a sigh of relief.

"Josh, you've gotta wake up. If you can see me, maybe I'm not dead." Nate reached his gloved hand for Josh's face. When his friend only groaned and didn't open his eyes, he said, "Or maybe we're both dead."

Their situation had been bad enough, but wondering if they were alive or dead made their ordeal more terrifying.

"Something's happening," he pleaded. "We need to talk. Please. I can't do this alone."

Nate heard the fear in his voice and hated it. He needed to stay strong and he had to think. He wanted Josh awake, but even if his buddy was coherent, what would he tell him? In his condition, Josh couldn't help. Anything Nate said to him would only sound out-of-bounds insane. Maybe that spirit was only a delusion, brought on by delirium. He could be sick, too.

Had he dreamed the whole thing? The idea of something slipping into his body and taking over, it sounded crazy if it hadn't felt so damned real. And Abbey seemed genuine enough. Something about her seemed familiar, yet he couldn't quite place her in his mind, not with everything he had to deal with. Although he hated scaring her, he needed to get her attention. He had no idea how far to go to break free. He was sure she'd heard him, yet Nate didn't know what to believe.

If a spirit had really possessed him, where was it now? How did he get control back?

"N-Nate? What h-happened?" Josh's eyes fluttered open. When he moved, he cried out in pain. "Ahh…shit!"

"Oh, man. Stay still. You've got a busted arm and leg, but you're gonna be okay."

"Where are we?"

Nate didn't have the heart to tell him the whole truth. "A freak storm hit us hard. You wandered off and got lost, but I found you."

"Why would I—? I mean, I don't remember…" He winced. "And my leg hurts real bad."

Pain. If they were both in pain, didn't that mean they were still alive?

"Yeah, I'm sorry. Wish I could do more, but there's something else." Nate put a hand on his friend's chest. "I think you've got mountain sickness. It makes you do crazy stuff, but none of this is your fault. You just need rest."

Rest wasn't the answer to Josh's problem. He wouldn't

get better without medical attention, but Nate didn't see the point in telling him things were about to get worse.

"We're stuck until the storm clears, but my dad is gonna get us off this mountain." He forced a smile. "You'll be fine. I promise."

Josh took a labored breath and his eyes watered. Nate knew him well enough to suspect his best friend wasn't buying everything he told him, but to his credit, he didn't push him for more. He let it go. After Josh shut his eyes again, Nate didn't have to put up a front anymore.

Josh wasn't the only one getting worse.

In the biting cold, Nate had a hard time staying awake. After his fall through the ice, he had all the symptoms of a concussion, with hypothermia compounding his deteriorating condition. Fighting nausea and a pounding headache, he worked through his dizziness and aching belly to use his tie line to immobilize Josh's broken bones and keep him from making his injuries worse. Moving to care for Josh had done nothing for Nate's head. The activity kept his body warmer, but he felt weaker. With every move, he got more sluggish and slow and all he wanted to do was sleep.

After he tended to his friend's wounds, he felt exhausted, but there was only one thing left for Nate to do. He had to deal with the hypothermia. He moved closer to Josh and wedged his body next to his, careful not to hurt him. The last thing he did was turn off the flashlight to conserve the battery.

He hated the dark. Darkness made it too easy to imagine being dead.

Like an anchor holding him steady, Josh's breaths grounded Nate and gave him what little comfort was left, but nothing made him feel safe—not when that thing lurked in the shadows. Shivering in the cold, Nate searched the inky black for any sign of the creature that terrorized him. Every time he nodded off, sharp pops of the ice or the hiss of settling snow jerked him awake and the shadows played tricks on his eyes. But before he collapsed into a fitful sleep, Nate found that his thoughts turned as dark as his prison of ice.

Despite what he'd told Josh to make him feel better, Nate had to face facts. His father had no way to know where they were and without pinpointing their location, no one was likely to rescue them. Nate's hope ran thin. Josh was sick and getting worse. It would only be a matter of time before hypothermia and his concussion would drag him down, too.

For the first time in his life, he was afraid of dying.

All he had left—for any sliver of hope—was his strange lifeline to Abbey Chandler. And the only way to reach her was to give up his freedom and his body to a dark spirit that scared the hell out of him.

Nate felt cold and sick—and he had no idea what to do.

chapter 9

On Denali

After gut-wrenching hours of wrestling driving snows and gale-force winds—and suffering through the dwindling hope of finding Nate and Josh alive after hours of enduring an unresponsive tracking beacon—Bob Holden clung to the only comfort he could. With the fierce storm receding, the sun had broken through the clouds. That gave him hope the ranger station could launch a more thorough rescue attempt, using their helicopter and more advanced equipment to track a digital beacon from the air.

"We're nearly out of marker wands," Mike Childers yelled over the sound of the wind. "But when this storm blows over, we won't need them. How are you holding up?"

Bob felt the subtle difference in the higher altitude. The air felt thinner and his lungs were working harder, but he only shrugged and shook his head. Childers didn't push it.

"I got an update from the ranger station," the man told him. "They're expecting a break in the storm in an hour or two. When it's clear enough to deploy a helicopter, they've got a high-altitude aircraft standing by."

"Good. We'll take a short break," Bob said. "But tell Joe and Stan to keep an eye out." After Childers left, he whispered, "God, please. Help these boys. Don't let it be too late."

With his cheeks chafed from windburn and his throat raspy from thirst, Bob ignored his discomfort. He didn't want a break, but the others needed one to keep their eyes fresh. He couldn't stop searching until he found Nate and Josh. Behind his polarized sunglasses, he peered over the tint-colored snow. From the red flagged wands they'd left to mark the way back to camp, to the narrow passage ahead that led to the summit, he saw nothing but a bleak stretch of white that tortured his eyes.

As his team rested and hydrated along the trail, Bob kept looking with his digital tracker, searching for a signal from Nate's beacon. He couldn't stop, even with the tracker dead silent. The blizzard that had hampered visibility was no longer a factor and the rays of sunlight piercing through the thick shroud of gray would help, too. While he searched, Bob remained tethered to his team. If anything happened to him, he trusted Childers and the others would know what to do. He ventured off the trail and poked the wand he had in his hand through the snow. Clamped to his boots, Bob's crampons dug into the ice underneath as he poked and prodded, looking for any sign of the boys.

Higher up the mountain, he searched for breaks or unusual formations that his trained eye would notice. With the visibility better, it didn't take him long to find something. A thick layer of snowpack had broken loose from a steep pitch and an avalanche had slid down in one massive chunk. The slab covered over the base layer of snow near him, but exposed a fractured ridge of ice pack higher up where the avalanche had broken free. The slide could have occurred naturally after such a bad storm, but his gut instincts warned him not to ignore it.

In his heart he wanted to believe that he'd caught a lucky break. The love he had for his son wouldn't let him see otherwise. If the blizzard had remained strong, he would have missed the avalanche. And if he and his team had remained at camp, waiting for rescuers, they would have lost precious time searching for the boys. They were fast running out of options. At least now they had a likely place to search until help arrived.

"Mike!" he called over his shoulder and waved at Childers.

Even though avalanches and rock falls were common in this steep section of the climb, he knew to pay close attention to anything out of the ordinary. Nate or Josh could have triggered the slide, especially under storm conditions with heavy snowfall. When Childers got within earshot, he pointed a gloved hand toward the slope.

"You see that sharp break in the snow?" After Childers nodded, he said, "That's a slab avalanche. The boys might have triggered it or gotten caught in it. It's a long shot, but we've got nothing else until help arrives."

"Yeah, I'm with you. What do you want us to do?"

"Use your trackers to search the perimeter of that slide, especially along the debris line. And use a wand to poke through the snow as you go. Look for any breaks in the ice underneath or debris like clothes and tools. Nate had his ice ax, tie line and a flashlight with him. We might get lucky.

If we can narrow down the search grid for the rescue heli-copter, it could make all the difference."

"Do you know if both boys have their beacons?"

"Unfortunately, Josh left his behind. I saw it in his gear before we left camp."

Two signals might have made it easier to track them, but Bob was thankful that Nate had thought to take his. That showed he was thinking, but as Bob shared his thoughts with Childers, he fought the doubts mounting in his head. Why had the boys wandered off during the storm? He had trained Nate what to do in bad weather and how to survive it, but when faced with the stark reality of the boys being missing, Bob had to admit that he'd fallen short.

Nate and Josh would pay the price for his failure.

"You want the ranger station to contact your wife?" Childers asked.

At the mention of his wife, Bob got yanked from his misery into a different kind of hurt.

"What?"

"Once the weather clears and the helicopter takes off, the media might find out," the man said. "It'll only be a mat-ter of time before reporters make contact with Jackie."

Bob turned his face toward the summit and shut his eyes. His throat wedged tight when he thought about his family. Mike Childers was right. Jackie and Zoey needed to know what happened before they heard it on the local news or from an overzealous reporter. He couldn't put off telling them any longer.

"If they can patch me through, I want to be the one who tells her."

Childers grabbed his arm and said, "You got it."

After the man left, Bob heard him update Joe and Stan,

but he only half listened. With memories of his son haunting him, he raged against the impotence that threatened to choke him. He felt powerless to help his family and now there was little he could do except wait for the ranger station to mobilize. Bob had no idea what to tell Jackie. Without knowing where the boys were, he felt as helpless as she'd be, waiting for news.

He didn't want to accept that, but he had to. The lives of Nate and Josh would be in someone else's hands soon.

Abbey

Near Healy, Alaska

When Dad knocked on my bedroom door to ask if I wanted to take the canoe across the lake with him, I gave his invite serious thought. On a normal day, parting with my mattress so early wasn't my usual thing. Unless Dad made me or I had my own weird reason, I rarely did it. After what happened last night, I seriously could have used the distraction, but something made me stay in bed.

Spending time with Nate had changed me and I had no desire to pretend to be normal.

After sneaking back into the cabin at dawn, I'd tried to sleep, but my mind only let me get as far as dream limbo, the tortured sleep of those with a guilty conscience. Out of the blue, the collision that killed my mother bombarded me in cruel flashes. With Nate pressuring me to talk about my mom, that must have stirred something I'd pushed deep inside, an ugly reality that lurked beneath my paper-thin skin when it came to her.

Screeching tires, broken glass and the smell of gasoline

battered me in the safety of my bedroom. In my sleep, I felt vulnerable. In a frightening rush that horrible moment happened again. In the stillness after the crash, when I remembered waiting to die, I squinted into the intense light of that memory. But instead of seeing the beautiful boy made of clouds with the unforgettable blue eyes—and feeling his gentle warmth—I saw Nate staring back at me through the broken windshield. He looked scared and when he opened his mouth and screamed my name, his perfect face shattered into shards of bloody glass.

"No!" I jumped up in bed, gasping. I caught the tail end of my scream and gulped it down like nasty-tasting medicine. "Damn it."

I collapsed back onto my mattress—a pathetic puddle—shaking and covered in sweat. All of it felt too real. Seeing Nate invade my memories of the crash confused me. Since we didn't know each other five years ago, I had no idea what his being in my nightmare meant. Seeing him made me feel like he'd intruded on something very personal and private. Or maybe his being there had been my doing—his sudden and unexpected appearance held a meaning that I hadn't figured out yet. Nate either had the power to invade my dreams or I'd chosen him to sabotage my life and dredge up a past I would be better off not remembering.

Either way spelled trouble for me. Once I opened my eyes, I couldn't go back to sleep. I stared at the ceiling of my bedroom for what felt like an eternity. When that got ridiculous, I got up and looked out my window, gazing at my mountain and wondering what Nate was doing.

Fantasizing about him had become almost second nature to me.

Before this trip to the cabin, he'd been the maraschino

cherry that topped off my chocolate sundae, the special treat that I gave myself when life sucked worse than usual. Having him in my head had made things tolerable—good, even. But after meeting him for real and kissing him and talking for hours last night by the fire—something about him had burrowed deeper under my skin and rooted there. His voice had become a favorite song that I wanted to play over and over in my head. Every time I looked out my bedroom window and stared up the mountain, I pictured him on the ridge—and I felt guilty for keeping him waiting.

After yesterday, Nate Holden wasn't just a nice daydream. He haunted me.

Maybe it was being at the cabin, when all I thought about was him because I had little else to distract me. After that kiss, I tipped the scale toward being a woman for the first time and it felt good. I wanted him to kiss me again, but something dark kept me from racing up that hill and looking for him.

Not all of my newfound feelings for Nate were good.

In a million years, I never would have thought that he could scare me, but he did. That kiss had been everything I'd dreamed of and yet something felt off about it…and Nate. Being alone with him, knowing my dad wouldn't approve, had been an exhilarating part of that fear. But my hesitation came more from how fast and in how many ways he could shake me up.

He was painfully targeted on death and how I felt about my mother dying. Except for my dad, I hadn't talked about that with anyone who didn't charge by the hour. Nate seemed to sense my vulnerability and seized on it, but why? Did he have a cruel streak that he disguised or was the compassion on his face genuine? I knew what I wanted that answer to be, but I wasn't sure if I was only being gullible. If I trusted him, would I open myself up for the biggest hurt since my mother died? Meeting Nate for real wasn't what I had expected—and that drove me crazy.

But what happened last night before I left him had petrified me the most. Nate had lost it. When he grabbed my arm, he hadn't been in control. It looked as if he had a split personality or something had possessed him. I felt sorry for him. He had to be desperate if he'd come to *me* for help, like I was the only one he had left. The fear that edged his voice had worried me ever since.

I must have been insane to even think about seeing Nate again, but I couldn't turn my back on him. This time when I looked out my window, all I saw was the urgency in his eyes as his voice echoed in my head, the way he had begged me. I had to see him. Rushing to the bathroom, I got ready in a flash. In ten minutes, I headed out the door.

If Nate had something wrong with him, I had to know, even if he scared me.

On Denali

When Josh moaned, Nate heard the sound as if it came from inside a deep barrel. At first he couldn't place it. After he opened his eyes, he found it hard to move a muscle until Josh groaned again. With great effort, Nate lifted his head, triggering a worsening bout with nausea and a head that threatened to explode.

"Ah," he gasped.

In the murky darkness, seconds ticked by before Nate remembered where he was. The wall of ice surrounding him billowed and shifted in the gloom as if it had a life of its own. His dizziness had breathed life into them and played tricks on his mind. He fumbled his hands over the ice, feeling for the flashlight. When he found it, he turned the beam on and let the dim glow cast shadowy fingers into the cavern, but Nate had only a few seconds to let his eyes focus.

After bile rose hot from his belly, he barely had enough time to react. He rolled to his hands and knees and heaved until he didn't have anything left in his stomach. He felt weaker and with his head tight, that put a strain on his eyesight. Spots spiraled before his eyes and with every pinpoint of light, he thought the creature had come back to take over his body again.

"Josh?" he whispered and crawled toward his friend.

What he saw made his heart lurch. Josh looked dead. Dark circles made his eyes appear sunken and his breaths were shallow. His skin looked gray as if every drop of blood had been drained from him and his lips were dark blue with bits of skin peeling off.

Despite his own pain, Nate yanked off his gloves and grabbed snow in his hands, rubbing it until it melted. Cupping his hands over Josh, Nate let every drop of melted snow target his friend's mouth. Josh needed water. Nate knew that exposing his hands to the cold wasn't the smartest move, but letting cold snow melt in Josh's mouth would only chill his core and bring on hypothermia faster.

When Josh felt the water drip into his mouth, he opened his eyes and ran his tongue over his parched lips and coughed. The effort looked painful.

"Th—thanks," he choked. "My leg. It doesn't hurt… anymore."

Nate forced a weak smile, but inside he was miserable. If

Josh's leg felt better, that only meant his body had grown numb from the worsening cold—a very bad sign. His extremities were shutting down. He wanted to keep Josh awake and force him to talk—to fight for his life. Sleeping would be giving in to the cold, letting it win an inch at a time. But when Nate couldn't come up with an argument for prolonging the inevitable, it pained him to wish his friend would simply shut his eyes and let it happen.

They were trapped. No one would come for them. It'd be easy for Nate to close his eyes and let death happen, but a fire to live still burned in him. He couldn't give in and he didn't want Josh to do it, either.

"Stay with me, Josh. Talk to me…about anything." He grabbed his friend by the collar and shook him, enough to make him wince. Pain meant he was alive. "Tell me about your date with Heather, the time you guys went to the prom last year."

"W-what?" Josh winced. "Can't…remember."

The memory of prom felt absurd and distant, given what had happened, but it had been the first thing he thought of.

"Sure you can. Just talk to me. And don't stop." He fixed his friend's collar, zipping it tighter around his neck to keep him warm. "How did Heather look? Do you remember?"

"Heather…she looked so…pretty. I r-ran out of gas…not my fault." When Josh shut his eyes, he quit talking.

"Come on, Josh. Don't…" He shook his friend again, but this time he had lost consciousness. "Oh, God."

Seeing Josh passed out left Nate hurting for company. He didn't want to die alone, but with Josh in bad shape, he didn't have the heart to wake him. His friend would mercifully shut his eyes and drift into a forever sleep. He wouldn't know what hit him, but that wouldn't be the case for him.

Nate knew he'd see death coming. He'd feel every inch of it and he'd be alone when it happened.

His body would do what it had to. As his core temperature dropped, his veins would collapse to keep blood flowing to his vital organs. Like Josh, his exposed skin and lips would turn a deathlike blue. But once his organs shut down one by one, he'd die a slow death. His body would go first before his brain would finally stop. The essence of who he was would flicker out last, trapped inside his dying body.

At his age, Nate hadn't given much thought to dying.

Even now he refused to dwell on it. He focused on survival and drank what remained of the melted snow before he put on his gloves. When he tried to stand, dizziness made him sick again, but he pushed through it. He shined the flashlight through the cavern, looking for a way out. Even though he had no idea which way to go, he had to try.

With all his strength, he hoisted his body up a wall of snow and ice, using his crampons to dig his boots into the ice. He leaned into the formation to steady himself. After he got high enough with his perilous balancing act, he dug into the snow with both hands. Every move hurt and with his strained breathing, he choked with his mounting effort to dig. He risked suffocation if the snow caved in on them, but accepting their fate without doing anything wasn't an option.

For both of them, Nate had to fight back.

There was no way he could dig his way out of where they were. His only hope would be if the snow caved in, enough to create a sinkhole on the outside that could signal where they were. Nate shut his eyes and heaved a sigh in prayer, hoping he wouldn't make things worse by bringing the whole house of cards down on their heads.

He leaned as far as he could and scooped out large chunks, shoving them away from where Josh lay below. It didn't take long for the snow to break free. Heavy slabs buckled and fell to the floor of the cavern. When the icy ceiling gave way, it collapsed a section of packed snow that had wedged into the crevasse.

With the rumble of falling snow, Nate cringed, hoping he wouldn't smother them both. Every controlled movement of displaced snow made him feel like he had done something, but too much could end their fight to survive in minutes.

Sweating and out of breath, Nate worked without much thought to his numb fingers or the pain that shot through him with every move. But as the crevasse filled with a ghostly light behind him—enough for him to see his own shadow on a wall of ice—Nate knew he and Josh weren't alone anymore. When he looked over his shoulder, the sight of the creature made him lose his balance—and he fell, hard. The jarring blow, of hitting ice with the force of his body, sent a jolt of pain through him.

"D-damn it," he cursed.

Panting for air, Nate struggled to his feet and came within a few yards of the strange being that had returned to torture him. He stumbled and edged away, not taking his eyes off the brilliant pulsing light. When the filmy blue body of energy followed his move and drew closer, Nate did the only thing he could.

He talked to it.

"Who's that girl…Abbey?" he blurted out. To his surprise, the creature stopped and hovered over him. "She's special to you, isn't she? Why is that?"

At the mention of Abbey's name, the pulsating light slowed and the entity shifted into a steady soft glow that was easier on Nate's eyes. A blue light, the color of the sky, shimmered in its body with tufts of white drifting through it, like clouds. For the first time, Nate thought the entity looked peaceful…*and beautiful.*

"What are you?" Nate really wanted to know, but he kept his distance and inched back as far as he could until his shoulders hit ice. "Where do you go when you're not here…with us?"

He didn't know if the entity could speak or understand him, but he had to try and reason with it, for both their sakes.

"Help us. Please. Josh has a family, a mom and baby brother. My parents and little sister, Zoey, are waiting for me to come home, too," he pleaded. "Does that mean anything to you?"

What he said had an effect on the entity, but not what he hoped for. After Nate pleaded for help, the spirit swelled and its light erupted to pierce the shell of its body. Nate squinted and raised a hand to shield his eyes. Every shadow disappeared in the crevasse and melded into dazzling white. In his condition, Nate felt sick and dizzy as the brightness wreaked havoc on his equilibrium. When the intense light blinded him, it gave him a splitting headache.

Nate knew the creature wouldn't listen anymore. Out of options with nothing to lose, he was done playing nice.

"What the hell are you? Why are you using me?" he shouted. When the thing kept coming, he shouted, "I won't let you do this, not without a fight. If it's the last thing I do, Abbey's gonna know what you did. You hear me?"

With his threat, the creature slowed down, but it didn't stop. It had come to take over his body again. Every time that happened, he lost consciousness, losing any opportunity he'd have to keep him and Josh alive. Being trained for mountain rescue, Nate needed to focus on their survival, but battling for control of his own body took all his energy—and brought both of them closer to dying.

"Every time you take me from Josh, he gets worse and so do I," he yelled. "You're killing us."

In Nate's weakened condition, he didn't have the strength to resist. The fierce stab of light intensified and dazed him into a stupor as it came closer. When it forced its way into him, Nate felt a strange warmth as his mind flooded with picture postcard images of a mountain clearing overlooking a valley of evergreen trees covered in snow.

The last thing he remembered seeing—before he felt his body collapse hard to the snow—was Abbey's face.

Abbey

Near Healy, Alaska

When I climbed the snowy mountain trail to the upper ridge, I fought the urge to run. My heart couldn't wait to see Nate, but my brain held me back and reminded me that he could hurt me in a way no one else could.

When I finally got to the fire pit, I felt out of breath. I'd expected to see him right away like the other times, but when that didn't happen, I couldn't hide how I felt. The cold fire pit made me feel lonely. Not even the memories of my mother and marshmallows filled the void that Nate had left.

He'd promised to be there. Even as strange as that promise had been, I hadn't realized how much I'd counted on it. I slumped onto a fallen log, feeling the full weight of my disappointment. The only evidence of our time together from the other night had been Dad's flashlight. It lay on the ground, covered by a thin dusting of snow, right where I'd left it. Last night, I'd raced off the mountain and forgot it. I reached over and held it in my hands, letting the metal chill my fingers.

But the shiver that skittered through my body had been for Nate.

Doubt made me scared that I'd never see him again. Yeah, that wasn't rational, I know. I'd probably stalk him over the summer in town or I'd catch him in the fall when school started again, but a nagging sensation mired me in dark thoughts, compounded by my deepening and protective feelings for him.

"He's not coming," I whispered. Saying it aloud made it real. "Get over it."

But when I heard the rasping caw of a raven and saw the black flash of wing in a tree, I knew I was wrong. Nate had come. He had an undeniable connection to those creatures in a way that I didn't understand, but had accepted. When I heard a crunch of snow behind me and saw something dark move in the trees, I fought to calm my pounding heart. I stood and turned with a grin on my face.

"Nate?" I called out. "Where were you? I thought you weren't..."

I couldn't finish. Seeing him took my breath away. His face looked ghastly white and his skin was as blanched as a corpse. The dark circles under his beautiful blue eyes made him look sick. What he had on looked strange, too. He was dressed in layers of winter stuff—too much for this time of year in Healy—and he was harnessed in mountaineering gear as if he'd just come off Denali.

"What happened?"

When he stumbled forward, he reached out a hand for me and I took it. I wedged my shoulder under his arm to ease him down before he fell.

"What's wrong, Nate?" I pleaded, holding him in my arms and touching his cold cheek. "Please...talk to me."

Nate's eyes closed. He looked sick. *Really sick.* And I had no idea why.

chapter 10

Palmer, Alaska

"Oh, Bob, no."

Jackie Holden choked back a gasp with tears stinging her eyes. Holding the phone in her trembling hand, she collapsed onto her living-room sofa, feeling weak in the knees and numb.

"How did it happen?" she asked.

"We woke up this morning and both of them were gone."

"But why? That makes no sense. Nate knows better."

"I know. That question has been killing me." His sigh mixed with a wavering swell of static from the radio transmission. "We've been looking…storm wiped out their tracks. The boys must have wandered off during the night…for some reason…never found their way back, but Nate… took his beacon."

"What about help from the ranger station?"

She plugged an ear and shut her eyes, straining to con-

centrate on every word he said when all she really wanted
to do was scream.

"They're on it. We have to wait for the weather…but
that should be…a helicopter…in an hour."

"Has someone contacted Josh's parents?"

A long hiss on the line made her think he hadn't heard
her, but eventually he answered.

"Sarah is my next call."

Jackie shut her eyes tight and fought a wave of nausea,
her misery compounded by what Sarah Poole would be going through soon. A single mom, Sarah was very close to
her two boys. She'd weathered a rough divorce with the
help of her oldest son, Josh. Her little one, Kevin, had always been a ball of energy that took his share of her time.
But Sarah had dedicated her life to taking care of her boys,
making up for the ugly chapter in their lives when a con-
tentious divorce threatened to drag them through hell.

"After you break the news, I'll call her and invite her to
stay here," she said. "She shouldn't be alone at a time like
this. She could probably use the help with her youngest."

"That's—"

"What? You cut out. I didn't hear you."

"I said…good idea."

The high winds on Denali and the erratic hiss of the radio transmission made it hard for Jackie to hear her husband
on their landline connection, but his pain came through
loud and clear. If there was anything as bad as hearing the
devastating news about a missing son, it would be breaking
that same news to another mother. Jackie couldn't imagine
being the one to make that call.

She hadn't seen Bob cry many times, but she heard something broken in his voice now. Despite the distance be-

tween them, she felt the connection they had always shared. They'd built a life and a family together. They'd been partners in everything, including the decision they both had made about allowing Nate to join Bob's spring expedition to Denali.

Jackie couldn't help but second-guess that choice. She wanted her son home. Pressing a fist to her lips, she fought an aching emptiness inside her. When she could speak again, she had one question.

"What should I tell Zoey?"

Silence. She heard Bob clear his throat, but she knew what was really happening on his end of the conversation.

"Where is she?" he asked.

"She's still sleeping."

"That's not like her."

"Well, she had a rough night, something about a bad dream."

Thinking of her daughter made the tears come faster. The hardest thing she had to do right now was fight back the urge to get angry and blame Bob for what happened. The way he led his life, on the edge, had influenced Nate to follow in his footsteps, but blaming her husband wouldn't get Nate back and crossing over that line now would only tear her family apart.

"She's a smart kid," he said. "If you keep this from her, she'll know...when this hits the TV news, she may see... You've got to find a way to tell her."

"Tell her what?" When she heard the anger in her voice, she fought it. "I'm sorry. I didn't mean to..."

"I know you're angry. I am, too...with myself. He's missing because of me."

Jackie shut her eyes and breathed in deep. There was

plenty of guilt to go around, but now wasn't the time to lash out.

"We don't know why he's missing, Bob. You said so yourself, but right now he needs you. We all do."

This time when she heard his ragged breaths over the phone, all she wanted to do was hold him.

"You'll find them, honey. When you do, both those boys will need your strength." Fresh tears drained down her cheeks. "Call me, no matter what happens. I have to know."

"Yeah...I w-will."

With the agony in his voice unmistakable, she had only one thing left to say to him.

"I...l-love you."

"I love you, too."

After Jackie hung up the phone, she went to Nate's room. For a long moment, she stood at the threshold, unable to step inside. It felt wrong, as if her aching sorrow would taint her memories of the boy she'd seen grow up within these four walls. Yet she couldn't stay out, either. She felt a strong unbearable urge to connect with him. In stunned silence, she walked to his closet and looked inside, unsure what she searched for until she found it.

His varsity jacket.

She slipped it off the hanger and put it on, wrapping her arms around it like a hug. When nausea struck again, she looked for a place to collapse. Sinking onto Nate's bed, she grabbed his pillow and clutched it to her chest, breathing in the scent of her only son. Through her husband, she'd heard the frightening stories of mountain rescues over the years and knew how precious every minute would be—and how quickly a rescue could turn into a body recovery operation.

"Nate," she whispered. In the stillness of his room, her son's name sounded like a prayer.

"Why are you crying, Mommy?"

Jackie jumped at the sound of her daughter's small voice. When she turned, she saw Zoey at the door. Dressed in pink cotton pajamas, the little girl wiped sleep from her eyes with her stuffed moose clutched to her chest.

What would she say to Zoey?

Abbey

Near Healy, Alaska

I held Nate in my arms, too shocked to move. With him looking sick, I realized how stupid I'd been. I never thought about where he stayed in Healy and how he'd found me. Questions raced through my mind without any answers. I clutched him to me and brushed back his hair, feeling his forehead and cheeks with my hand. He felt ice-cold and he looked as pale as one of Dad's "clients."

When he moaned and moved his head, I blew out a sigh of relief.

"Nate? Can you hear me?" I raised my voice and patted his cheek. "Come on. I'm right here. Open your eyes."

After his lashes fluttered, he opened his eyes and it took a long moment before he could focus on me. When he did, I smiled.

"Hey." I cupped a hand to his cheek and kissed his forehead, fighting back the lump of emotion in my throat. "I thought you were...never mind."

I could have held him forever. Our intimacy felt normal, like we'd done this before. Even though Nate looked coherent enough to sit up, he didn't try. He let me hold him, but I had too many questions to pretend this wasn't strange.

"Your skin is cold. And your face, you look...frozen." I cradled his head in my arms. "What's wrong with you?"

He gave me a weak smile before he reached for my hand and kissed it. "I had no idea how fatal envy could be."

"Envy? I don't understand." I grimaced. "Is there anything I can do to help?"

"I'm afraid there's nothing. This is all my doing. I've set something in motion and I'm not sure I can change it."

"What are you talking about?" I asked. "And why are you dressed like this?"

Nate glanced down at his mountaineering gear with a puzzled look on his face before he shifted his gaze back to me. He looked stumped on what to say. After he took a deep breath, he pulled away from my arms and propped his back against a fallen tree near the fire pit. At first I thought he wanted distance between us, but after he reached for my hand, I moved close to him.

"Abbey, I'm losing control...something I'm not used to." He couldn't look me in the eye. "I don't know how to fix it."

"Losing control over what?"

"I never intended to hurt you, but I'm afraid that I will," he said, ignoring my question.

He looked as if every word he uttered put a strain on him, but when I opened my mouth, he placed a finger to my lips.

"That day when I first met you here, I had to talk to you," he went on. "I didn't want you to be frightened when you saw me, but I'm afraid what I've done…it was a stupid thing. Maybe it's too late to make things right."

"I wasn't afraid that day. Confused maybe, but not scared." I let my fingers trail through his mussed hair. We were so close, I felt his sweet breath on my face. "But I have to admit that you scared me when you talked about my mother. Why did you do that, Nate?"

"Because I know…I mean, I sense how much she means to you…even still. I wanted you to trust me…to confide in me."

With effort, he raised shaky fingers to my face. I grabbed his hand and kissed it.

"But you pushed too hard and trust takes time. It's been hard for me to talk to…anyone, especially about my mom."

"You're right. I rushed you. That's my fault, but now we've…run out of time, something I didn't…expect."

I ached with regret when he talked about running out of time. For some strange reason, I had felt an urgency between us, too, like a clock ticked down whenever we were together. I held on to him as if I could keep him with me forever.

"Run out of time…why? Are you leaving Healy?"

A sad smile nudged his lips. "Yes, guess you could say I'm leaving."

"But I'll see you in Palmer, right?"

With a faint smile, he tucked a loose strand of my hair behind my ear. "I know I haven't been fair, but I had to know what it would be like…"

"For what?"

"Kiss me, Abbey." The tenderness in his eyes almost made me cry. "Kiss me and make it last forever."

I knew what Nate meant about forever. His kiss had

marked me, too. We shared something hard to deny, even if I didn't understand it. I wanted to kiss him as badly as he needed me to.

This time I didn't close my eyes.

When my lips touched his, I breathed him in and let the sweet tang of his skin fill me up. His chill made my face and fingertips tingle, but after my shyness faded, I felt a soothing heat as I nuzzled into his chest and kissed him harder. Loving the feel of his arms around me, I closed my eyes and let go. It felt as if I had fallen, but I wasn't afraid, not with Nate. I'd become a soft white feather adrift in a warm breeze, not wanting the sensation to end.

When his tongue touched mine, it felt natural. And with my hand cupped to his face, the ice of his skin melted and I imagined the quiet pulse of our hearts in my ear. In my mind, I drifted into a warm summer day with clouds dappling a beautiful pale blue sky, the way I had always pictured the perfect day would be.

Nate made me feel all of that.

Being with him felt like we were two stories, one leading into the next, picking up where the other left off. The story began with me, but ended with him. The hard part to accept was that our story went on without me whenever we were apart. That's how I imagined love to be. It was that sweet torture of needing him so much that I only felt whole when I was with him, that the joys in my life wouldn't be the same without him to share them.

For the first time, I thought I understood how crushing and wonderful love could be with a special boy. I never wanted that feeling to end, but when Nate pulled from me, I snapped out of my euphoria and the world came rushing back to separate us. His soft gasps melded into my own and with his forehead pressed against mine, he spoke in a low breathless voice meant for only me.

"I want you to know…that being here with you…has meant everything to me. You've given me a gift, one that I will…always treasure."

His words carried a familiar ache. I opened my eyes and kissed his cheek. "You act like you're saying goodbye."

"In my zeal to embrace life, I have underestimated the human spirit to do the same. I find that quite ironic." He breathed in deep as if he savored something amazing. "Because I have a newfound conscience, I know now that what I'm doing is…wrong."

"What are you doing that's so bad, Nate? Tell me." I laid my hand to his chest.

"I can't." He couldn't look me in the eye. "If I tell you everything now, I don't think I could take it if you chose sides. That would hurt too much."

"You think I'd go against you?" I shook my head and didn't wait for his answer. "What's going on? Why are you talking like this?"

I pressed him for answers I wasn't sure I wanted to hear.

"Because even if you don't understand what I'm telling you now, I want you to really listen and remember what I said, without filtering my words through…your anger. Believe me when I say that I thought I'd have a choice to make—to do the right thing—but I'm afraid it's not up to me anymore."

"You're right. I don't understand anything of this."

"I know. And for that, I'm truly sorry." He laced his fingers in mine. "But I'm afraid if you understood everything, you'd hate me. And that would break…this heart I've stolen."

"Okay, now you're really scaring me. Why are you telling me this? I need you to spell it out for me, 'cause I'm not getting it."

"I came today because I didn't want to break my promise to you, when I said that I'd be here, but I can't stay." Nate kissed my cheek and got up. He stood on unsteady legs and looked down at me. "There's something very important I must do…and I pray that I'm not too late."

Nate didn't wait for me to say anything. He turned his back and headed for a stand of trees higher up the mountain. There was nothing up there. Strange that he didn't use the trail that led down toward the lake and the main road.

Where was he going?

"Will I see you…after?" I called to him, but Nate didn't turn around.

By the time I jumped to my feet, he had already become nothing more than a hazy shadow under the dense canopy of trees. I thought about chasing after him, but something made me stay—like I didn't belong with him—not now. In a strange way, I sensed him all around me even though I couldn't see him.

You may not want to see me again…but if you do, I will be here.

His voice faded to a low whisper by my ear, as if he was still with me. I shut my eyes and listened with my heart.

If you come to me, I will be here, Abbey.

I opened my eyes wide and cried out, "Please don't do this, Nate."

I didn't know what I was asking of him or why I thought he could hear me. I just knew that I didn't want things to change, but Nate wasn't giving me that choice. He didn't want me to choose sides. Thinking back over what he'd told me, I hadn't understood much, but his pain over what he'd done had been plain to see. He felt plagued by something terrible—something he knew was wrong.

"Oh, Nate," I whispered. "What did you do?"

Even though I lost sight of him, I ran into the forest after Nate, fighting my instincts to let him be. I wanted to see him, but I sensed that this time he wouldn't let me. Stumbling over the snow, I ran through the trees, gasping for air. In the morning cold, my lungs burned and my breaths had become vapor as tears chilled my face. I felt him and yet there was an eerie stillness that I'd never experienced before. The birds had stopped chattering and even though I still saw the wind stirring the trees, I couldn't hear the sound of the leaves rustling.

Nate had gone, leaving me empty and numb. I had a bad feeling that if I saw him again, it would be for the last time.

Palmer, Alaska

Jackie Holden hadn't gotten much sleep since her husband and son had left for Denali, but last night had been the worst. Zoey came to her room, telling her that she had a bad dream, without any other explanation. Normally her daughter told her everything, but it took effort to calm her down and get her back to sleep. With just the two of them in the house, Jackie drew comfort from hearing her daughter's quiet breaths in the dark. Even if the reason Zoey came to her bedroom had been a nightmare too scary to talk about, Jackie needed to feel the weight and the warmth of her youngest child in her arms.

Now this.

She broke the bad news about Nate to her daughter and

waited for the girl's reaction. Although Zoey's eyes welled with tears, she hadn't said anything. She looked visibly shaken, but Jackie knew something else was wrong. She'd expected more from a child so attached to her older brother.

It was as if Zoey already knew.

"Is Nate dead, Mommy?"

"No...*no*, why would you...?" Jackie was surprised at how fast she answered Zoey, telling her "No." She had no idea if what she'd said was a lie or not. She only knew that she was unwilling to accept the alternative. Yet with child-like innocence, Zoey asked the question and made it all too real, like Nate was beyond help.

Hearing Zoey say it felt like getting hit in the stomach.

"He's missing, Zoey. That's all we know right now. Daddy is looking for him. Lots of people are."

Jackie pulled her daughter into her arms and rocked her with eyes shut tight, desperately clinging to the hope that her son was still alive.

"I think I saw him," her daughter whispered, "last night."

"Saw who?" Jackie grimaced and pulled away from Zoey, gripping the girl by the shoulders. "Who did you see?"

"I saw Nate, Mommy."

"That's not possible, honey. You know that. Your brother is on Denali...with Daddy."

"I know. That's what I thought, too. But I saw him, Mommy."

Jackie stared at Zoey, trying to figure out what to do. Clearly her daughter had been more traumatized by the bad news about Nate than she'd let on. She had to be careful and not make things worse for her daughter....if that was even possible.

"Did you see him in a dream?" She forced a weak smile. "Dreams aren't real. You know that, right?"

"But I *wasn't* sleeping." A tear rolled down her daughter's cheek. The sight of it broke Jackie's heart. "I heard a bird outside my window. It made a loud noise…at nighttime, so I got up and looked out. It was a big black one."

She'd been ready to dismiss her daughter's story and chalk it up to the worry the girl had for her brother's safety, but when Jackie heard about the big black bird, a gasp caught in her throat. Zoey could have seen a raven, like the one outside Nate's window on the night before he left for Denali. Holding her daughter by her thin arms, Jackie let out a deep breath.

"Is that why you came to my room last night? You said you had a bad dream, Zoey." Jackie didn't know what to believe, but one thing was certain. Her daughter was hurting. "Tell me everything, honey. What did you see?"

"It was dark, but I saw Nate. He was on our driveway, standing there." When the tears came heavier, Zoey shrank into her arms.

"Why didn't you tell me about this last night?" She held her daughter and cradled the back of her head in her hand. "We could have talked about it."

"I didn't want to make you sad."

"Why would you seeing Nate make me sad, honey? You could have seen him because you miss your brother, that's all."

"Because I think…he was crying, Mommy. Nate was crying."

Jackie clung to her little girl, fighting back her own tears. Although she didn't want to believe that her daughter had actually seen anything, listening to Zoey tell her about Nate felt too much like a terrible omen. Her daughter wouldn't have lied about seeing him and the detail of the black bird didn't feel like a coincidence. That had been bad enough, but another frightening thought gripped her.

Nate could have already been missing—*or dead*—when Zoey had seen something on their driveway. No matter how hard Jackie wanted to shake the eerie feeling, one question took hold and wouldn't let her go.

Had her only son come home one last time...*to say good-bye?*

chapter 11

Palmer, Alaska
Two hours later

"Tanner?" His mother called from downstairs, her voice muffled by the sound of the living-room television. "You should see this."

"I'll be down in a minute," he yelled from his bedroom as he scrolled through another query on the internet.

"No, it'll be over by then."

Tanner grimaced at his mom's persistence. All he heard was the doubt in her voice that he could make it downstairs in time. That sounded like a challenge. He wheeled his chair toward the hall, prepared to make record time using the mechanized lift that his father had installed in their house, one that got him and his wheels between floors. But before he got far, his mother's voice took all the fun out of his race to prove her wrong.

"Turn on channel 9. It's breaking news," she insisted. "Hurry."

Breaking news always got his mom's attention. Even if the TV was on mute, she had a sixth sense about breaking news.

Oh, brother. What now?

With an eye roll, Tanner reached for the TV remote that he'd tossed on his bed. He hit the power button and flipped the channel to the local station, catching the tail end of a story about climbers missing on Denali. No names were given until next of kin could be notified, but the description of two missing locals had been enough for him to imagine the worst. After he heard the guys attended Palmer High, it didn't take much for him to make a connection to Nate and Josh.

No, this can't be happening.

Rolling his wheelchair toward his new radio setup, he hit the power switch and scanned the static for a solid signal. After he zeroed in on a channel, he listened for any updates on the missing climbers.

Damn it! He felt like such a loser.

He'd been so wrapped up in computer code and spending a few days out of pocket with Jason Cheevers in Anchorage that he'd totally forgotten about Nate Holden's trip with his buddy Josh Poole. Tanner thought he'd been helping Abbey, but after she found out that he'd dropped the ball on keeping track of Holden by radio—and the guy went missing on his watch—she'd never forget that. Abbey hadn't asked him to babysit Holden. Tanner just felt responsible, that's all. Now anything he would tell her, about why he'd been distracted while she'd been gone, would sound like a pathetic excuse, especially if he couldn't get word to her.

None of what he'd done about the cyber-bullies would matter now.

"Did you hear it?" His mother had come upstairs and now stood at his door. Her voice had nearly given him a heart attack, but he downplayed his reaction and acted like he'd meant for his hand to jump.

"Yeah, enough."

"Well? Do you know them? That reporter said they go to your school. I figured you might know who they are."

"I don't know. Maybe." Avoiding direct eye contact, he pretended to go back to his computer.

"You think they'd mention those names on that radio of yours?" she asked.

Barely looking over his shoulder, Tanner shrugged. "Maybe."

"Aren't you even curious? They could be someone you know, Tanner."

She made him sound heartless, like he didn't care, when nothing could be further from the truth. He'd kept the reason he wanted the radio a secret—for Abbey's sake—but if his mom got even a hint that he knew something for real, she'd never let it go. She was like a pit bull on a bone when it came to getting the inside scoop on other people's misery. At first, he didn't understand how she got off on stuff like that, but after a while he figured she needed to feel the commiseration that someone else had a worse tragedy than coping with a paralyzed kid. He couldn't fault her for that.

"I'm still helping Jason with his computer, but if I hear something, I'll let you know."

His mother didn't say anything for a long time. Her silence almost made him look up, but eventually she backed off.

"Well...okay." She sighed and headed back downstairs,

muttering, "I bet those boys' parents are going through hell, poor things."

Tanner hated not telling her everything, but letting his mom in on what he knew felt like a betrayal to Abbey. He didn't want to talk about it with anyone but her. His mom had a skill for prying. If he even gave her an opening, she'd zero in on Abbey's reason for taking an interest in Holden. She might also take a guess at why he wanted to track the climb with his new radio. His mom always pressed him for girls he liked and Abbey had become top of her hit parade. If his mother knew about Abbey's crush on Holden, that would make him look like a pathetic loser. After listening to the radio and not hearing anything new, he grabbed his cell phone off his charger and tried Abbey one more time.

"Come on, Abbs," he said under his breath. "Pick up, please."

Tanner listened until the ring of her cell turned into a very familiar message that her phone was "out of service." If he was going to reach her—and redeem himself in her eyes—he had to get more creative.

On Denali
13,500 feet

The sun emerged from the storm and burned off the last of the clouds over Windy Corner. Reflecting off the sparkling snow, the sunlight was blinding, even with protective eyewear on. Bob Holden squinted into the stark white horizon set against a startling blue sky as he worked alongside his men, looking for signs of Nate and Josh.

His team was roped together for safety and used shovels, ice axes, and wand markers to prod through the snow of the slab avalanche. He instructed his team to search along the line of flow and the bottom run out where debris could be found. If they got close to Nate's beacon, their digital trackers would flash red. An active signal would start with a slow steady beep that would end with a high-pitched rapid sound as they drew closer. To investigate the avalanche higher up the steep pitch would be too risky. They'd have to wait for the Park Service helicopter and the mountain rescue rangers for that kind of help.

Childers had received word that a B3 AStar helicopter had been deployed from the ranger station at 7,200 feet, heading for their location. As Bob worked his wand into the snow, searching for breaks in the ice underneath, he listened for the sound of a thumping rotor on the wind. A craft like a B3 AStar had a solid reputation of handling high altitudes while carrying a larger payload, with one known to have touched down on the summit of Mount Everest at just over 29,000 feet. The Park Service had one on call every climbing season. Bob used the service once before, after one of his climbers busted his ankle.

But he'd never been as grateful for help from the Park Service as he was today. The sun made it easier to believe Nate and Josh were still alive. With help coming, he indulged in the hope they wouldn't be too late, but with each passing minute, a sense of urgency made that harder to do.

"Will you look at that?" The voice of Mike Childers broke Bob's concentration, forcing him to look up.

Childers pointed to a raven circling above their heads. "Seeing them here at this altitude always surprises me."

"Yeah, I know…" Bob didn't get to finish. A coughing jag took hold of him.

Without the high winds, communicating with the others

had become easier, but Bob's voice had already turned raspy and threatened to cut out on him altogether. He shook his head at Childers, without saying another word, and grabbed his water. With the others working, he took a gulp to hydrate and watched the raven's aerial show. The large black bird cocked its head and made a sharp cut through the sky. It targeted something higher on the mountain.

At this altitude—especially after the devastating storm— Bob couldn't imagine what the bird spotted, but something made him stop and watch the creature. Maneuvering with ease on velvet wings, the raven swooped down in a powerful rush, zeroing in on something only it could see. In a show of control, the bird landed with pinpoint accuracy on a mound of snow that jutted out of the avalanche, a spot higher up the mountain.

Ah, hell no!

Bob wasn't sure why he had taken such an interest in the raven, but now he was angry. Like Mike Childers, he had noticed the birds on Denali, mostly because they seemed like a stroke of bad luck the way a black cat crossing someone's path would be. Things were bad enough, but seeing the raven messed with his head and he lost it.

"Git!" he yelled as loud as he could and waved a hand. "Damned scavenger!"

When the bird didn't react, Bob took a step up the steep grade and stopped. The raven strutted across the ice and jammed its large beak into the snow, pecking at something beneath the surface. But when Bob realized what might be happening, he didn't have time to explain to his team.

He had to move. *Now!*

"I'm going up. Don't follow me. Brace yourselves, in case I fall."

If he got sucked into a crevasse, he didn't want the rest of his team to suffer the same fate. Harnessed together, the others could help him if he fell through, but Bob had to see what the raven had found—before the bird took off with it.

Kicking up snow and stumbling across the chunks of ice, Bob ran toward the raven, keeping an eye on the creature, looking for glimpses of what the bird had found. His lungs were on fire and the lactic acid in his legs made them feel wobbly, but he trudged on, struggling through the steep climb with his harness on. When he got close enough, the raven fought for its prize and squawked a complaint over his intrusion before it bounded across the snow and lifted off the mountain with ease.

Oh, no… No!

His heart sank when he saw the bird fly away. Had it taken anything? Bob stared at the creature as it circled above him, until he lost sight of it in the intense glare of the sun. He couldn't see if the bird had anything in its beak, but as he approached the snow where the raven had landed, he found its tracks around a hole it had dug.

A glint of metal caught his eye.

Bob dropped to his knees, gasping for air. He reached down into the snow to pull out a silver clover-leaf charm. It dangled from a bracelet that he recognized.

The bracelet Zoey had made for Nate.

Bob held the bracelet in a gloved hand and raised it toward the sun, but behind his sunglasses, a tear slid down his weathered cheek. Nate and Josh had been in this very spot. Knowing that made things worse after his tracker flashed red with a slow steady beep. From all indications, it looked as if the boys had been caught in the avalanche they were searching. In a disaster like that, with the first fifteen minutes being highly critical, every second counted. Victims suffocated in minutes.

Too much time had passed for the news to be good.

Even with the droning sound of the rescue helicopter in the distance and his tracker beeping, Bob felt the last of his hope vanishing as he looked down at the tiny bracelet clutched in his shaking hand. This time he didn't hold back. He couldn't fight his dark thoughts any longer as he knelt slump-shouldered in the snow. Every pent-up emotion came in a rush and hit him hard.

Bob let everything go.

With the helicopter approaching, Mike Childers called to him, "You got a signal?"

He couldn't answer. He'd seen what Denali could do to the dead.

Soon he'd be digging to retrieve the body of his only son and his boy's best friend. He couldn't shake the haunting picture of Nate's lifeless eyes, clouded by death. That image would overshadow a lifetime of memories that he had of the good-natured glint in his boy's eyes when he laughed. Nate's skin would feel ice-cold, too. He'd never again feel the warmth of his son's body when he hugged him. Nothing would prepare him for what could come next.

Nothing.

When he could finally move, he stuck his flagged wand deep into the snow to mark a boundary where they should look. Most people would have taken the discovery of Zoey's four-leaf clover as a sign of good luck, but Bob only feared the worst after crossing paths with the raven. He didn't consider himself a superstitious man, but if Nate and Josh had been trapped under an avalanche all this time, he was experienced enough to know what to expect.

The best they could hope for would be closure to an ordeal no parent should have to face.

Abbey

Near Healy, Alaska

After my last strange encounter with Nate, I talked Dad into taking me to town for a late lunch. He needed a caffeine fix and I needed to snoop into where Nate was staying. Healy wasn't much to see, even on a good day. Guess I was desperate, but hanging out at the cabin would have driven me crazier than usual, especially with Nate being the only thing on my mind. I had been obsessed with him before, but after spending time with him on the mountain, he wasn't a fantasy anymore.

Nate was real and it felt good to keep him all to myself—like a beautiful secret.

If he stayed near Healy, someone in town might know his family. The tricky part about stalking him in such a small town would be asking questions without arousing curiosity, especially Dad's.

Set against a breathtaking backdrop of snow-covered mountains, Healy had a main drag lined with real folksy-looking log-cabin buildings decked with colorful signs that lured tourists to spend money on souvenirs. Parts of it looked like an old gold-rush town, like the kind shown in Westerns or on that TV show, *Northern Exposure*. In Healy, Alaskan Ulu knives, walrus oosiks, homegrown jams and jellies, smoked salmon, reindeer sausage and jewelry made from moose droppings were hot commodities during the summer.

On the edge of town, the Miner's Market and Deli sold gas and quick eats. Down the road were more tourist traps like the Three Bears Gallery, a river-rafting outfit and Rose's Café, Dad's personal favorite. During this time of year, the usual horde of RVs and trucks with out-of-state plates were conspicuously missing, which was fine by me. That meant we got a good place to park outside Rose's. Next to Motel Nord Haven off the Parks Highway, the café was a red building with a metal roof that looked more like a warehouse than a café with a hand-painted sign in red and white out front.

"I smell a grizzly cheeseburger that's got my name on it," Dad said as he got out of our SUV and slammed the door. "What about you?"

"Nope. I'm getting a chili cheeseburger with fries." My mouth watered already. "Don't try to change my mind."

"Wouldn't think of it."

When Dad opened the café door, a rush of noise and smells hit me—the clank of plates, loud laughter and conversations, and a whiff off the deep fryer.

"Hey, Graham," Rose yelled from behind the counter with a big grin on her face. "It's good to see you. Heard you and Abbey were in town. Coffee?"

"Yeah, that works." He nodded.

Rose and her husband, Bill, owned the family-run café and knew my dad well. After we found a place to sit near a window, she brought two waters, forks wrapped in paper napkins and a coffee mug with a pot of fresh coffee, ready to pour.

"Come to see if I still had your photo hanging?" the dark haired woman joked.

On the café wall hung a picture of my dad. His local

claim to fame came after he ate one of Rose's one-pound burgers, topped with an egg, a slice of ham, with a side order of fries. Not one of his best moments, and alcohol may have been involved, but it had been good enough to immortalize him on Rose's wall, along with countless others.

"Actually I was hoping you'd retire that photo, make room for someone else."

"Not on your life." She grinned. "What can I get you two?"

After we chatted Rose up, she placed our order and it didn't take long to get our food. The platters were brimming over. As we ate, Dad got in a chatty mood. He did all the talking and that worked for me. It gave me time to scope the place out, looking for new people in town and watching the traffic drive by.

"Who are you lookin' for?" my dad asked.

"What?" I narrowed my eyes and shook my head, like I didn't understand. "I'm not... I'm just..."

"No rush." Rose saved me from lying by dropping off the bill and refilling Dad's coffee. "Good seein' you two. Be sure to stop by before you head out."

"Will do." After Dad finished his coffee, he stood and got out his wallet to pay up.

"We in a hurry?" I asked. "I got things to pick up at Miner's."

"Like what? I just bought enough snacks to..."

"Woman stuff."

Those two words worked every time. Dad stared at me in stunned male silence, letting what I said sink in.

"No problem. Finish your fries. I'll be back."

Voila! Dad quit asking questions and went to pay the bill. With him gone, it gave me alone time with Rose, a local who knew everyone. She came to wipe down our table and pick up the dirty dishes.

"Hey, Rose, you know the Holden family? Nate Holden goes to Palmer High with me. And his dad, Robert Holden, has a Denali expedition service called Stellar Mountaineering. Ever heard of them?"

"I heard that Stellar guide service is a good outfit, but I've never met the owner." She shrugged. "They own property near here?"

"I think so. Or maybe they're renting somewhere close," I told her. "I thought that I saw Nate in town this week, but I couldn't be sure."

"Rentals are slow. Only the hard cores come this early in spring." Rose cocked her head and pursed her lips. "Well, you got me, if they own a place near here. Want me to ask around?"

"Naw, that's okay. No big deal." I scrunched my face. "I was just curious."

"Is he cute?" She grinned and winked. "That one you go to school with?"

Wide-eyed, I flapped my lips and sucked air like a beached salmon. When my cheeks flushed hot, I knew my face had turned bright red. Not cool.

"Don't worry. Your secret is safe with me, honey." She shook her head and chuckled as she headed back for the counter. "If I hear anything on your new boyfriend, I'll let you know."

"He's not my..."

Rose never let me finish. She left me stammering in the wake of her throaty laugh. I had a feeling that no matter what I said, she wouldn't buy it. In a small town, rumors were as good as facts. Better, even. I heaved a sigh

ON A DARK WING

and made a mental note to play it smarter when I hit the Miner's Market.

Within minutes, we had pulled into Miner's parking lot. While Dad filled our SUV with gas, I popped inside the store, fortified with the money he'd given me for my "woman stuff." (Money was another side benefit of using those two magical words.)

Even off season, the place was hopping. Outside, Dad had to wait in line to fill up. The clerk behind the counter, Jake Edenshaw, was a guy I'd first met three summers ago. He had a small line in front of him, but that didn't stop the guy from glancing at the TV mounted on the wall near the register. Even with the sound off, Jake had captions running and looked as if he had an interest for something on the local news.

Using the cash Dad gave me, I replenished my stash of Kit Kats and planned to buy one token box of "woman stuff," but changed my mind. With Jake behind the counter, no way I'd embarrass myself on purpose. I kept an eye on the checkout line, waiting to make my move when things slowed down. I needed time to talk to Jake, without anyone listening in. When he had a break, I walked up and put my junk on the counter.

"Hey, Jake."

"Hey, Abbey. Saw your dad in here the other day." He grinned and nodded his head. "When I saw he bought your usual stash of munchies, I figured you were in town. How's it going?"

Jake was a tall skinny guy with long dark hair and an intense way of staring that made anyone believe he had plenty going on inside his head—but they'd be wrong.

"Good. You guys are busy as usual." I shrugged as he

rang up my stuff and I paid him. "I bet you see everyone in town eventually, huh?"

"Yeah, pretty much. Gas and food, the necessities of a full life." Jake had a quiet voice and was real laid-back. "Hey, that reminds me."

Without any further explanation, Jake ducked below the counter, looking for something. Jake had one consistent quality. No one could rush him. The guy would come up for air when he felt good and ready. While he dug through stuff under the counter, searching for whatever, I kept talking.

"You know the Holden family? Nate Holden goes to my high school in Palmer. His dad has a Denali guide service, Stellar Mountaineering. Ever hear of them?"

Prairie dogging it, Jake popped his head up and said, "Yeah, I heard of his dad's trekking company, but never met the actual dude."

I was encouraged that Jake knew Nate's dad by reputation. At least that was something.

"Do the Holdens have property around Healy? I thought I saw Nate in town and I wondered."

"I've never heard that, but could be. You never know, right?" When he straightened up, he had a torn scrap of paper in his hand. "Got it."

"What's that?"

"Some guy called for you. I wrote down what he told me. Here."

The wad of paper was wrinkled, as if it had been thrown away...maybe more than once. Although Jake's handwriting was terrible, I eventually figured out what he'd written. Tanner had called the Miner's Market, trying to reach me.

To the untrained eye—any amateur in the ways of Tanner Lange—that note didn't make much sense.

> *Have news about Silver Scorpion. Call me ASAP.*
> *Tanner*

"Weird, right?" Jake smirked like he knew something I didn't. *A very scary thought.* "Dude told me *Silver Scorpion* was a comic book, but I never heard of it."

"Yeah, it's new."

"Wow, cutting edge." Jake raised an eyebrow and nodded real slow.

"Yeah, Jake. Hot off the press." I smiled. "Thanks for the message."

"Cool."

Tanner's message about the comic looked like a diversion. I figured he wanted me to call him, but if anyone got curious and asked questions about why he'd sent up a flare in Healy, he'd given me an out. I could make up something about him having a bizarre obsessive thing for graphic novels. I liked how intuitive my relationship with Tanner was. We didn't have to spell things out. We both just knew.

Like I knew that whatever Tanner called me about had to be important or else he would've waited until I got back to town. He acted like a low-maintenance uncomplicated guy, but he had plenty of noteworthy layers. The accident that paralyzed him might have clipped his free-spirit wings a little, but he still had an outlaw soul. Tanner was never boring.

But with everything that had been happening with Nate in Healy, I'd been totally distracted and had quit worrying about my cell and its lack of bars. With my stash of candy in a bag, I went to the back of the store toward the pay phones to give my best friend a shout out. Using the change I got from Jake, I placed a call to Tanner. He answered on the third ring, without even saying hello.

"Man, I've been trying to call you. I left messages in Healy."

"Yeah, I got the one you left at Miner's, Silver Scorpion." Smiling, I pictured Tanner decked out in shiny silver armor and mind-melding with metal.

"Guess you weren't kidding about the cell service sucking up there," he said. "You didn't get any of my text messages, either?"

"No, and I forgot my damned battery charger, like an idiot." I slumped against the wall. "What's up?"

After a long silence and a heavy sigh on the other end of the line, I knew the news wouldn't be good.

"What's going on, Tanner?"

"It's about Nate Holden. I mean, maybe I'm jumping the gun and this is nothing, but…"

When I heard Nate's name, I breathed a sigh of relief.

"Yeah, I heard. His Denali climb got delayed, something about bad weather."

"Where did you hear that?" Tanner asked.

"From Nate. He's here in Healy." I couldn't hide the smile in my voice. I knew Tanner would understand, but when he didn't say anything, I had to ask, "Tanner, you still there?"

"Oh, man, I was worried. It's all over the news, but they haven't released the names yet. Guess I was wrong."

"Wrong about what?" I asked. "What are you talking about?"

"If you heard that news from Holden himself, there's nothing to worry about. That's just...great."

Blocking out the noise in the store, I plugged an ear and listened as Tanner told me about the missing climbers on Denali. While he talked, my gaze shifted to the big-screen TV the store had mounted on the wall near the cash register. Set on mute, the captions were working. When a breaking news alert came on the screen after a commercial, I did a double take and knew what Jake Edenshaw had been interested in.

Reading the captions for the latest on the missing guys, two names scrolled over the TV screen. Even with Tanner telling me reporters hadn't yet identified the climbers, I saw something different on the news. When the names of the missing boys flashed across the screen, I wanted to throw up. I clenched my teeth and glared at the screen, even as a twinge of doubt gnarled deep in my belly.

With other people in the store watching the news unfolding, Jake took the TV off mute and a reporter identified the missing guys again, along with the Denali guide service company they had used, Stellar Mountaineering. Even if I wanted to believe the TV news got the names wrong, Stellar Mountaineering was run by Nate's father. With the reporter stating they'd been following the breaking story since early that morning, how could they still have it wrong?

The whole thing was there on the screen, playing out in front of my eyes. The news reported Nate Holden and Josh Poole were missing on Denali, but I knew differently— *didn't I?*

"Tanner, I gotta...go." I turned my back on the TV, gripping the phone so hard that my fingers ached.

"You want me to call if—"

"No, just..." I cut him off, but couldn't finish. "Sorry, there's something I gotta do. I can't..."

I hung up the pay phone and leaned my head against it, still gripping the receiver with my eyes shut. All I wanted to do was get somewhere quiet to think. I had to hang up on Tanner. He knew me too well. Hearing something in my voice, he'd never let me brush him off, not without prodding me for more. Tanner was too smart and I couldn't face that. Not now. I took a deep breath and rushed for the door with everything in a blur.

"Hey, Abbey." Jake called to me. "Don't you go to Palmer High?"

"Yeah, Jake." I didn't wait for him to ask me any more questions. Without stopping, I shoved open the glass door as Jake yelled after me.

"Hey, you forgot your candy."

When I hit the cold air outside, I breathed it in as if I'd been suffocating and had come up for air for the first time. I ran from the store, fighting a rush of emotion that hit me like a nasty punch to the gut. After I saw my father waiting in the car, I knew by his expression that I couldn't hide what I felt.

Dad already knew something was up.

"What's wrong with you? You look like you've seen a ghost." When I didn't answer, he said, "I thought you went in to buy something."

"They were out."

"But…"

"Don't worry about it, Dad. Please." I softened my tone and slid down in my seat with my arms crossed. "I'm okay. I just need… Can we go?"

"Yeah, okay."

My father started the car without another word, heading back to the cabin. I acted like a jerk and knew it, but I couldn't look at him. He probably chalked up my mood to hormones and I let him think that. I wasn't ready to give him the deets on what bothered me by playing twenty questions.

All I could think about was Nate. Everything he'd said, everything I'd seen—all of it replayed in my head like a waking nightmare. The way we kissed had been real. I felt sure of it…and we'd talked all night. Most of that had been really good, until it wasn't. But all the good stuff got over-shadowed by my undeniable suspicions. I had no idea what any of this had to do with the death of my mother, yet I knew it was connected somehow.

This whole thing was insane!

How could the TV station get their breaking news story wrong and air such tragic details without verifying them? Couldn't they get sued? And why hadn't the Holden family or someone else come forward? Even if Nate's parents were out of town, someone who knew the truth should have seen the story and contacted the news station by now, to set them straight.

The more I questioned what I knew, the more I feared that something was terribly wrong.

Remembering Nate dressed in weird mountaineering gear the last time I'd seen him—looking frozen and nearly dead—was an image I couldn't explain away or shake from my mind. The way he'd grabbed me before, begging for my help in a voice I barely recognized as his, all of my growing doubts came rushing to the surface until I heard him in my head again—making me a promise that I hoped he'd keep one more time.

If you come to me, I will be here, Abbey.

If Nate had been on Denali for almost a week, who the hell had I been talking to?

chapter 12

On Denali

Once the Park Service helicopter lowered a team of mountain rescue rangers by hoist, near the spot where Bob Holden stood, one ranger came over and took charge. Until today, Bob had never met Ranger Virgil Lewis, but now this man would commandeer the search for his son and Josh.

"I picked up a beacon signal, where I found something in the snow belonging to my son, Nate." Pointing up the mountain, Bob raised his voice so he could be heard above the sound of the helicopter. "I marked that spot with a wand. The beep was slow and steady, so I only got a piece of it."

"Good job. You saved us time," the ranger said. "Narrowing down the search grid helps."

"That's my son up there. Maybe his friend is with him… or nearby." Bob fixed his gaze on the ranger. "If there's anything I can do…"

"I understand, sir. I know this can't be easy." Ranger Lewis bent over to adjust his harness as he talked. "But my team needs to do their jobs and we work faster on our own. I hope you understand."

Bob nodded and didn't say anything more. He moved aside, standing apart from Mike Childers and the rest of his climbing team as he watched the rangers work the mountain. His jaw clenched tight enough for his teeth to hurt.

The pilot kept in communication with Lewis who guided his team, narrowing the search along the perimeter of the avalanche near Bob's flag using probe poles and transceivers to track Nate's beacon. The rangers set ice screws and used snow pickets to secure high-angle snow areas, allowing them to work safely. But once the rescue team hit on a series of steady tracking signals that they could triangulate off of, the rangers converged on a section of the avalanche and moved in. After they tightened the search radius, Lewis waved off the helicopter to allow his men to hear their transceivers and call out coordinates. The helicopter did a second pass overhead before the pilot found a flat section to land and wait for further orders, down trail.

Bob's heart raced, beating as fast as the digital signals he heard on the wind. Each man called out coordinates. With the signals turning into high-pitched rapid beats, they narrowed the search grid to a central location.

Bob knew they'd found Nate. Without Josh carrying a beacon, it was impossible to tell if they'd find the boys together, but if he knew Nate, Bob felt certain they would. He didn't want to think of Nate and Josh being separated, suffering through their ordeal scared and alone.

"We have a sunken break in the snow. It looks fresh, not iced over." Lewis called to his men, pointing to a section of the avalanche where the snow looked uneven and concave. "We may have a crevasse below, covered by the avalanche. Use your probes to find the edge of the ice."

When Bob heard about the possibility of a crevasse and that Nate's signal had been isolated in the middle of it, he shut his eyes tight and prayed. If luck was on his side, there'd be a chance the boys had found a pocket of air to breathe, for a while. But if the crevasse was really deep, there'd be a possibility they might never recover them.

Bob wanted to feel like a lucky man.

Palmer, Alaska

After Abbey hung up on him, Tanner sat slumped in his wheelchair and replayed their brief conversation in his head. *What the hell just happened?* She'd cut him off, midsentence. Then there had been the actual hang-up. Their call could have disconnected by accident, but since she hadn't called him back, that would make him a delusional pathetic moron to think that. No, Abbey Chandler had hung up on him, abso-frickin-lutely. Since that wasn't like her, she must've had a really solid reason. His Abbey never would've done that, not while talking about her favorite subject, Nate Holden.

Something had definitely been up with her.

"Were you watching the news?"

His mom rushed to his bedroom with her face flushed from her scramble up the stairs. She had a Palmer High yearbook in her hand.

"They reported the names of those missing boys," she said. "Do you know Nate Holden and Josh Poole?"

Tanner couldn't keep the surprise off his face. Even if he

wanted to keep things secret from his mom, she already had her answer.

"So you *do* know them? I got their pictures right here."

After she took a corner of his unmade bed, she flipped open the yearbook to pages she'd marked and showed him the class pictures of Holden and Poole.

"Uh, yeah." He nodded. "They look familiar, I guess."

Although he heard the words coming from his mouth, the voice didn't sound like his. He still had his mind on Abbey and their conversation. One minute, she'd been happy talking about Nate. The next, she'd pulled a 180 and ditched him by hanging up the phone.

"When did you hear the names, Mom?" Tanner went on the offensive before his mother quizzed him on everything he knew about Holden and Poole.

"Just now. All the local stations are covering the story, but channel 9 announced the names, not five minutes ago. Why?"

"No reason. I hadn't heard the latest, that's all." He shrugged.

Maybe Abbey had seen the same news, but if she'd been with Nate, why hadn't she told him that the news had it wrong? That would've been really cool to have the inside scoop before the news people did. Her fifteen minutes of fame had called and apparently she'd ignored it, but something in her voice triggered his concern for her.

That he couldn't ignore.

"It's a real shame." His mother sighed, unable to take her eyes off those photos. "Both are such good-looking boys, too."

Tanner stared at his mom. She had no idea how that sounded to a guy like him, like good looks was a magnet for great things and a promising future. What did that say about him? He'd found out the hard way that shit happened. After it did, a guy had to deal with it. He didn't have a choice. Taking a deep breath, he shut his eyes and let the moment pass, without saying a word.

"Oh, before I forget. I told Marta Kennedy, down the street, that I'd help her make snacks for our book club tomorrow. I won't be gone long." She tossed the yearbook on his bed as she stood and ran fingers through his hair—being a mom. "If you get hungry, I've got those pizza things in the freezer. That should hold you until I get back to make dinner."

His mother sounded like everything had turned back to normal, but that's not how she looked. She stared down at him for a long time, looking as if she would cry. When that moment came and went, without her saying anything more, she leaned down to kiss him on his forehead.

"I love you, Tanner." She smiled and stroked his cheek.

"Love you, too."

Later, when Tanner would think back on that exchange with his mother and wonder what had gone on in his head, he'd have no idea what had flipped his switch. Yet something definitely happened. He'd gotten it in his mind to help Abbey, even though he didn't have a clue how he'd do that—or even why he felt the strong urge to. She'd always shut him down whenever he brought up the death of her mother. Maybe something else was at play in Healy, something other than her crush on Nate.

He waited until his mom left the house and shut the front door behind her. He even let ten minutes go by— enough time for her to walk down the street to the neighbor's house—before he decided to cross a line. *A very big line* with his parents. Something was up with Abbey and from the sound of her voice, it had to be epic.

He couldn't—*or wouldn't*—let her go through it alone. In truth, he didn't need an excuse. He wanted to be with her, enough said.

After he tossed stuff in a knapsack, he changed into warmer gear and printed out the directions to Abbey's cabin, the ones he'd saved a few years ago. He didn't even know exactly what he would do, but when he kept going without hesitation, he realized that he wouldn't back down. Not now.

He would break the law...for the second time this week.

"Lange, you're an idiot," he muttered, but when he checked his computer before he took off, something he read online made him grin and he thought of Abbey again.

"Awesome!"

His high didn't last long. Tanner headed downstairs to leave his parents a vague note, so they wouldn't worry more than usual.

Knowing he'd get grounded for life—*and beyond*—he bolstered his courage by picturing the Silver Scorpion. He grabbed the extra set of keys hanging by the door out to the garage—keys to his mother's van, the vehicle adapted for him to drive. If he got stopped by the troopers without an adult with him, he'd have his beginner's permit yanked, but that would be the least of his worries. Whether he got pulled over or not, his mom and dad would come up with something much more inventive to punish him. He wouldn't talk his way out of it. *No chance in hell.*

There would be a price to pay for what he was about to do, but it would be a self-inflicted wound and he was good with that. Something had happened in Healy. He felt it and it wasn't in his nature to sit on the sidelines.

"When I find you, Abbey, please don't make me feel like more of a major jerk wad than I already do."

Abbey

Near Healy, Alaska

When we got back to the cabin, I knew what I had to do—but knowing it and doing it were two very different things. I wanted to believe that Nate would be waiting at the fire pit for me, with a perfectly rational explanation for everything that had gone on, but a part of me suspected that wouldn't happen.

That's what scared me. I couldn't deal with it. Yet I had to, and I had to do it alone.

I told my dad that I wasn't feeling well and went to my room and locked the door. That hadn't been a total lie. I sacked out on my bed—hashing things over in my head—until shadows crept into my room. With the sun sinking low on the horizon, a clock in my head ticked louder. If I confronted Nate at our usual spot, I didn't want to do it in the dark. Not this time. He had enough of an advantage.

I wasn't ready to do this. I never would be, but I didn't have a choice.

I put on my jacket and opened my bedroom door, ready to face Dad and the questions I knew he'd have. I found him in the kitchen staring into the fridge with a book in his hand. When he saw me, he closed the door and turned to face me.

Right off, I could tell by the look on his face that he'd

ask me easy stuff, like if I wanted dinner after our burger overload, but he must have changed his mind after he saw me. Dad sometimes had a weird sense about what to ask. He could zero in on what really mattered.

"Where are you going?" he asked.

A direct question like that almost always resulted in me telling him a lie. I didn't even have to think about it. That's just how my brain was wired. I could have said that I wanted to walk off our big lunch. That wouldn't have been a lie, exactly. But Dad might ask to come along. *No way!* I could have said that I wanted to check my cell bars again, but he'd only ask why I hadn't thought to use a pay phone in town. All these thoughts and more flashed through my head, but what came out of my mouth was something I hadn't been prepared for.

An element of the truth.

A hard truth that involved the death of my mother— the role I had played in it—and the terrible memories that wouldn't leave me.

"I'd like some time alone so I'm going for a walk," I told him. "I've been thinking about Mom. Guess I have things to sort out."

I never even saw that coming. I'd chosen to trust my father with a gem of the truth and waited to see what he'd do. He stared at me for a long moment. Behind his dark eyes, I could tell this trust thing wasn't easy for him, either. There were times—like now—that I connected with him best, when we didn't use words at all. Don't get me wrong. I still didn't have a clue what was in his head or what he might say.

But in that moment, I sensed his love for me and felt a different connection to him. With everything that had happened, I felt closer to him than I ever had before, and not just our father-daughter thing. We were two people dealing with grief and finding our way through it. Maybe that was enough to know for now.

"I'll be here when you get back," he finally said. "If you feel like it, maybe we can talk."

What he said felt as good as a hug. My throat wedged tight and I felt the burn of tears behind my eyes.

"Thanks, Dad."

I stepped outside and closed the door to the cabin behind me, taking a deep breath of the cool mountain air. When I started up the narrow trail to the upper ridge, for the first time I didn't want to go. I knew there was a reason that Nate had talked about my mother and maybe I wasn't ready to hear it. For all the guilt I had over her death, was I really ready to face what had happened? Is that what this was all about…something inside me that had to come out so I could move on? Or had my mom's death become a crutch that I needed more than the truth?

Every step up that mountain had consequences.

When I got to the lower ridge, ready to make the turn toward the clearing above, I heard the caw of a raven. It grated on my nerves like the truth I didn't feel ready to hear. In the fading sun, I caught a glimpse of the bird's shadow—a dark streak that crossed my path. If I had any doubts about Nate being there this time, they vanished like the raven's elusive shadow.

With the sun low in the sky, the clearing took on a chill that didn't have much to do with the weather. The fire pit that held memories of my mother looked colorless. Its dead ashes swirled in the faint breeze. I wanted to remember her laughter, but I heard the haunting flutter of wings instead.

I never saw the raven.

Although the clearing looked empty, I felt him as if he stood in the deepening shade of the evergreens, beyond my sight. He didn't speak inside my head, but I felt him— *watching me.*

"I know you're here." My breaths puffed icy vapors. "You p-promised you'd be."

Even after I heard the crunch of snow behind me, I didn't turn around. It took every fragment of courage I had to stand my ground and act as if I had every right to be there with him. My skin rippled with wave after wave of goose bumps and the swelling thud of my heart came from inside my ears, the enduring echo from a lifetime of nightmares.

Forcing myself to move, I turned to see Nate. This time he took my breath away for very different reasons. He moved as effortlessly as the wind and emerged from the trees, at first no more than a murky shadow that took shape into the boy I had come to see. Yet for the first time I saw him as a stranger. He came in a familiar package, one I'd obsessed over for years, but now I felt certain everything had been...*a lie.*

I had to face that.

"Who are...y-you?" My voice trembled.

I swear, my whole body shook and my legs felt as if they could betray me. I stood firm and acted tough, but inside I looked for any excuse to cut and run. Even if I faked it and pretended this Nate was real, the very fact that I asked— *who are you?*—that question said it all about what I knew in my heart.

This *thing* that stood before me had Nate's beautiful blue eyes and his perfect lips, but Nate wasn't with me now.

He stared as if he studied me. I resented his intrusion into my most intimate thoughts about a boy I'd become infatuated with. He'd made me believe that Nate shared those feelings. He'd tapped into my fears and invaded the unending pain I had over my mother's death, using the love I had for her to entice me to be with him.

Why?

All these feelings swelled inside me—my darkest suspicions, my countless questions, and my bruised pride—and threatened to suffocate me as I stood in front of him. Yet one consistent reason kept me from totally losing it.

He had Nate's face, a frightening reminder that the real Nate was in trouble.

Like a reflection in a mirror that told a morbid dark future, this Nate looked as if he could barely stand. Still wearing mountaineering gear, he had ghostly dark circles under his pained eyes, a telling sign that the pretense was over. To see him sad and sick tugged at my heart, but when he stood there and didn't say anything, I had too many questions to let him get away with that. I had to know what happened to the real Nate and figure out how this thing had connections to my mother.

"Answer me," I insisted. "You owe me that much."

When he took a step toward me, I jumped back. With a sideways glance, I looked for the trail down the mountain, the one that would lead me back to the cabin—and Dad—even though I wasn't sure this Nate would let me go.

"Surely you know who I am…" He cocked his head and blinked with Nate's eyes. "Don't you?"

His voice sounded different. It was softer than before, but it had a gripping undertone that kept me on edge. The other times we'd met at the fire pit, he'd sounded like Nate, but now his voice hooked me on a deeper level. I heard it echo in my head and it resonated under my skin like a disturbing yet tantalizing shiver.

His hypnotic voice held me where I stood.

I couldn't move. And worse, I didn't want to.

"I thought you were the answer man," I challenged. "You promised to be here and you are, but why hold back? Answer me, straight up. No more riddles."

"Come on, Abbey. If you think real hard, you'll know we've met before." He blinked and ran his tongue over those flawless lips. "I met your mother that day, too."

"Quit talking about her. Leave my mother out of this."

"I can't do that, Abbey. It's not an accident that I chose this spot to meet you. This ridge and that stone fire pit meant something to both you and your mother."

The way he looked, with his voice barely a whisper, grabbed hold of my sympathy. Without warning, I felt bathed in a profound sadness that radiated off him. When he cast his eyes down, to look at the cold stones in the fire pit, he never even raised a finger.

In a sudden rush, a raging fire erupted in the stone pit. Flames leapt from nowhere. I screamed and jumped, cowering in the shadows for a place to hide. I wanted to run, but something made me stay. He stood still as a stone, watching me. Not blinking. When I heard the soft, warm laughter of my mother, and smelled the burning sweetness of marshmallows on the wind, tears welled in my eyes and I couldn't stop crying.

"Why are you doing this to me?"

"Your mother is why I'm here, Abbey."

His shadow flickered onto the trees behind him. And the raven that I had heard, but hadn't yet seen until now, flew out from the deepening shadows and fluttered onto a branch to land near him. Its slick black wings reflected the fire and glimmered iridescent color.

"She did this to me. Your mother," he said. "I think it's time you know what really happened the day she died."

abbey   chapter 13

With hisses and pops off the crackling fire making me
edgy, I stood in front of the boy who looked like Nate.
Dead Nate. He wore out-of-place mountaineering gear
with pale gray skin and deepening bruises under his eyes
that made him look more like a ghost than real flesh and
blood. Perched on a crooked pine branch, his raven cocked
its tufted head and stared down at me with onyx eyes,
flaunting its secrets.

Your mother is why I'm here, Abbey.

His words stung me as if I'd stuck my hand in the fire.
With the sun about to drop below the horizon, I could already feel everything closing in on me with a suffocating
darkness. Whatever torment I felt would only get worse.
But even in broad daylight, seeing him in this place would
never be the same again. Any memories I had of him would
be tainted. From the first moment I saw him on my mountain, he mesmerized and controlled me even from a dis-

tance. Now the danger of being with him oozed from every pore of my body, yet I had to come.

Nothing could have stopped me from seeing him one last time.

"You asked who I am," he said. "Look into my eyes, Abbey. You tell me."

This time when he stepped closer, I let him come nearer without jumping out of my skin. I wanted to see Nate beyond those eyes, but I didn't sense him...*or his fear.* The real Nate was gone or too weak to fight back anymore. That made me feel even more alone.

"Abbey, please look at me. Don't be afraid."

He reached out his hand and touched a finger to my chin, forcing me to look him in the eye. When I did, something strange happened.

Flashes of the accident that I must have blocked from my mind emerged from the gloom of my memory to punish me. I heard my mother scream, felt the bones crunch in my chest, and tasted the coppery venom of too much blood in my mouth. Those new memories choked me. When those harsh visions stopped, once again I experienced the eerie stillness after the crash as if I'd really been there. And a familiar heat gave me comfort when an ethereal boy, made of clouds and sky, gave me his hand—the boy who had taken away my pain and freed me from my damaged body.

"No. You can't be him." My breaths came too shallow. When I couldn't get enough air, I felt light-headed. "That b–boy. You were there, the d–day of the accident."

"Yes." When he smiled, the gesture looked sad and distant, and it didn't last. "I reached out my hand and you took it. Do you remember?"

I shut my eyes and let memories of encountering that

strange boy wash over me. If it was even possible, the memory became more vivid. I felt it and wanted that feeling to stay. *Yes, I remember,* I thought. When I opened my eyes, he nodded as if he'd heard me say those words aloud.

"Is that how you look?" I asked. "When you're not… human?"

"I am different for every soul. Part of my duty is to ease the burden for a human being to make the transition into Death. When I take a soul, I separate it from its human body and try to bring comfort by whatever means. With you, I reflected a beautiful summer sky with cloud animals. Even though I didn't realize it at the time, I know now that being with you and easing your pain made me happy. You stirred something in me that I didn't understand until I became…human."

"If you were there, the day of the accident, that means you must be…" I couldn't bring myself to say it, but inside I knew.

Death.

"Death," he said it the same time as I thought it. "In different cultures and faiths, I am called by many names. Azrael, the Angel of Death, Sariel, the Grim Reaper, Thanatos, Morana."

Slowly, he walked around the fire, keeping his eyes on me. In the spiraling smoke between us, his face blurred and made it easier to see the ancient being he was.

When he stopped next to me, he smiled and said, "And to you, I am…Nate."

Hearing his many names and finally knowing who and what he was, I had a hard time seeing only Nate. I knew enough not to doubt him—*I felt it*—but with his skin the color of a gloomy storm cloud and the shadows under his eyes getting darker, a chill radiated off his body that made me shiver even in front of a blazing fire.

Being close to him now, I felt the unbroken stillness of eternity. It was far too easy to imagine Nate already dead.

"The day you died and I took your hand, you looked into my eyes," he said.

When he touched my cheek, I felt him reach me beyond his touch. I knew there would be something more Death wanted me to see.

"Clear your mind and remember, Abbey."

This time when I met his gaze, memories flooded me. The blue of his eyes once again triggered that familiar image of the icy depths of the ocean, a color that I'd conjured in my mind at the accident. But experiencing that vision a second time made me realize that I'd seen something more that day—and it came back to me in a sudden rush after he'd touched my cheek with his cold fingertips.

That vision flashed through my mind, only this time I saw what lay beyond the serene beauty of his eyes—what had always and would forever be there. Every soul he had ever taken resided within him in a vast undulating ocean. Together yet alone, each soul drifted in peace, waiting for whatever came next.

The pieces to my faulty memory came together with what he wanted me to understand.

When people survive an encounter with Death, they often talk about an out-of-body experience where they see a glimmer shining through a tunnel. The soothing light comforts them and at the end of that tunnel they describe seeing the shadows of people who have come before them. That's what I saw that day, but the light and the passageway filled with shadow people, I knew now that wasn't heaven or any concept of an afterlife. With Death's touch, he let me see beyond the vision that most people experienced when they died.

What I had actually seen had been a glimpse into Death's eyes—his ocean of souls—and I knew what he tried to make me understand.

I gasped, feeling the sting of tears as I called out to him from the shadows of that painful memory, "Why are you showing me this?"

Death made that image vanish in one blink of his beautiful blue eyes. In an instant, I shot back to the clearing, feeling the heat of the fire and looking up at his raven perched on a branch.

I wasn't ready for the truth, but it was coming.

"Did I...die?"

"Yes."

The part of him that wasn't human answered without hesitation and without an inkling of remorse.

"When I took your hand, that's when it happened, didn't it?" I asked.

"Yes, I came to collect a soul."

When he brushed a strand of hair from my eyes, his touch felt like nothing more than the wind's embrace.

"I had come for you, Abbey."

On Denali

Bob Holden watched as the Park Service mountain rescue team anchored their harnesses. Everything had to be secure and safe enough for them to dig through the avalanche over an area where Nate's tracking beacon gave the strongest

signal. Ranger Lewis and his men had marked the edge of
the crevasse where the snow looked deep-set and sunken.

Now it would only be a matter of time.

"They've located a tracking beacon. They're digging
now." Using his radio transceiver, Bob raised his voice to
be heard above the wind and the static. His transmission to
the ranger station had been patched through to the landline
at his home where his wife and Josh's mother, Sarah Poole,
were waiting for news.

Bob told them only what was happening. The dark spec-
ulations that plagued him, about what they might find in
the crevasse, he kept to himself.

"One beacon?" Jackie asked.

"Yeah, one." Bob took a deep breath before he went on.
"I wouldn't say anything to Sarah until we know something for sure, but Nate brought his tracking beacon with
him. For some reason, Josh left his behind. If we don't find
them together, we'll keep looking for Josh."

The sound of static swelled on the other end of the line,
but Bob knew his wife well enough. There wasn't much
for her to say, not with Sarah within earshot.

"I know that sounds bad, but I'd put money on those
boys being together. They're connected at the hip, you
know that." For Jackie's sake, Bob forced a smile and let
his wife hear it in his voice. "From what the rangers have
found, I think the boys have a fighting chance."

He wanted to believe what he'd said. Jackie and Sarah
and his daughter, Zoey, and little Kevin, needed hope. If
bad news was coming, it would happen soon enough. If
there would be an outside chance the boys had a pocket
of air to breathe, no sense torturing two mothers with the
worst-case scenario.

"I'll call you when…" Bob stopped when a loud rumble echoed across the mountain. Under his boots, he felt Denali shake.

"Falling!" one of the rangers yelled. One minute the man was there, the next he wasn't.

When the mountain rescue team scrambled along the slope, Bob gripped his radio transceiver and said, "Look, Jackie. I gotta go. I'll call soon."

"But, Bob…"

Even with his wife still talking, Bob Holden ended the transmission. He didn't have the heart to tell her what happened.

There'd been a cave-in and one of the rescuers had fallen into the crevasse.

Abbey

Near Healy, Alaska

With Death's fingers still in my hair, I fought the urge to see him as Nate, a boy I'd grown to love even more because of Death's interference. If that cruel manipulation wasn't enough, now he talked about my mother and the day she died—and used Nate's face to do it. That felt beyond brutal.

"But if my mother and I both died, why am I still here?"

"A mother's love for her child can be a powerful thing," he said, something he had talked about before I'd been ready to listen. "Her love for you and your protective instincts are the only explanation for how she saw me that day. Somehow she knew that I had come for you."

He stared into the fire as if he still puzzled things out and remembered.

"What are you talking about?" I grimaced. "Wouldn't she have seen you like I did...because she died?"

"She called your name and you heard it, even after you grabbed my hand. Remarkable." Distracted, he ignored my question as if he hadn't heard me.

"A-Abbey?" *My mother's voice.*

Death conjured the memory of my mother's voice as easily as he controlled the ravens. I heard her again in my mind as if she was with me now. She spoke my name like she'd done on the day she died.

I shut my eyes to make the memory stay.

"Yes, I...remember," I whispered.

After I'd taken Death's hand at the accident, my mother had called my name and broken his connection with my soul. Until now, that's all I remembered, but Death's version of what really happened would not be rushed. He had his reasons for telling me everything.

"*Dying.* The word is...almost beautiful, isn't it? It sounds very much like it is—that one final breath," he said.

He had drawn out the word on his lips to show me what he meant.

"There are those who believe that I will be the last to die," he said.

I tried to grasp the magnitude of what he'd shared with me, but I couldn't come close to imagining it. An eternity of collecting and caring for human souls until the end of time—*alone*—was beyond my comprehension.

"You've seen my burden now, with your own eyes. My spirit harvests countless souls that I look after and hold in my embrace for all of eternity, until it will no longer be my responsibility. And before you ask—yes, I remember each one. It is my duty…and my privilege to remember. Every human soul leaves a mark on me."

The fire shed light on his face that warmed his expression, making the deathlike pallor of his skin disappear. Or maybe—because he talked about my mother—I needed him to look human again.

"Your mother was special," he told me. "The good ones, like your mother, are light. Their souls weigh no more than a feather. I thought you should know that you're still alive because she made a bargain…with me."

"A bargain? What bargain?"

"I had come to take one soul and she gave me hers. She took your place, Abbey."

"No, that can't be." I shook my head. "How is that even possible? If I was the one who should have died, how can you make a deal like that? It should have been me."

"Perhaps, but that's not what happened."

"You took my mother from me. How could you do that?" I felt the heat rush to my face and heard the anger in my voice. I didn't even know what I'd said.

"If you had died that day, she still would have been separated from you." He presented his logic without emotion, but whenever he talked about my mother, I saw a change in him.

"When she gave her life so you could live, I harvested her soul and she became a part of me, a part I've never forgotten," he said. "Feeling the love she had for you, and seeing her sacrifice, that spawned something in me that I have never felt before. Sometimes when someone dies, the love stays…in me, Abbey. I had to know what it felt like."

"To be human?"

"To be loved." His eyes welled with tears that glistened in the firelight until one trickled down his cheek.

"Your mother gave her life for you. That was her wish and I believe her sacrifice had purpose. Celebrate her life and the way she loved you…*still* loves you."

I took a deep breath and let what he'd said settle into my brain. I did want to celebrate Mom's life, but I couldn't do it at the expense of Nate. My mother had died. She wasn't coming back. Accepting what she'd done for me would take time. But no matter how Death justified what he'd done to be with me—and experience what it felt like to become human—nothing would excuse the way he'd highjacked an innocent life.

That wasn't…*human*. Not even a little.

"What about Nate?"

"The human capacity for love was the very reason I chose him." He raised his chin like he'd bestowed an honor. "You already had feelings for the boy. I knew you'd let me near you if I looked like him."

"But that was wrong. How could you ruin his life, because of me?" I shook my head. "Did you have something to do with what happened to him?"

When he didn't answer, I crossed my arms and forced myself to look him in the eye. I had to be strong, for Nate.

"You told me once, when we were talking about suicide, that to squander a life was…a waste. Was that just bullshit?" I didn't wait for him to answer. "Because the way I see it, you messed with Nate's life. You took his body like you had a right to it. If you're the keeper of souls, and every one of them is precious to you, why is it easy for you to take his life like it doesn't matter? He's not a pawn for you to play with. This isn't a game."

"I didn't know any of this would happen. I thought I could control everything. But can't you see? I had to do it, even if it was only for a blink of an eye in time. Love is the most powerful emotion humans possess. Until your mother planted a seed of it in me, I could only glimpse it from the outside."

He reached for my arm and wouldn't let me go.

"I came here to see you again, Abbey. Having your mother's soul within me, I knew if I came to you, that you would trigger her love for you, inside me. And you did."

For the first time, Death grinned, but I couldn't be happy for him. All I felt was profound sadness for Nate.

"In this body…" He opened his arms and looked down. "I had hopes that you might feel the same love…for me. I had to know both sides of love. Don't you see? I thought I could control everything."

This time when he raised his hand to stroke my hair, I flinched. I couldn't forget I was in the company of Death, even if he did look like Nate Holden. When he saw my reaction, he took a step back and clenched his jaw.

"But you didn't control it. Nate's in trouble, isn't he?" I urged, not waiting for his answer. "You have to do something. You can't let him die."

When I reached for his arm to beg for Nate's life, he turned toward the fire and shut me down cold. Any connection we had, when he'd talked with respect for my mother, was gone now—and from the look on his sickly face, he felt it, too.

"If you're Death and you're supposed to live until there's no one else, what's wrong with you? You look…sick and weak. How can that be?" I had a bad feeling about the way he looked and I couldn't ignore it anymore. "You're dying too, aren't you? What happens to you if Nate dies? Tell me."

"I honestly don't know."

"No, that's not possible," I argued. "What about your duty? You're the guardian of souls, an angel. What would happen to all the souls you have inside? What would happen to my mother's soul if you...died?"

"What I did—taking control of a living body—that's never happened before. I fully expect to be punished for what I did. It may not be up to me anymore." He shook his head. "I never intended to hurt Nate, but I fear that I have. It may be too late to do anything about it."

"Why are you saying that? I know Nate is trapped on Denali. What's happening to him?"

"He's dying."

"No, you can't let that happen. You can fix it. You're an angel."

"I wish it was that simple." He gazed into the darkness beyond the fire, as if he saw past the clearing and the growing darkness. "Right now, rescuers are digging him out of a crevasse. If they find his body without its soul, he'll be dead. After they discover him like that, I won't be able to bring him back. He's dead, because to them, that's what they see."

"Then switch back." Even though I heard the anger in my voice again, I didn't stop. "Let him have his life back. It's his life, not yours."

Death looked at me as if I betrayed him. I asked him to give back Nate's body as if that was as simple as swapping jackets. That's when his own words came back to me, when he'd said that he envied humans and that his greatest fear would be enduring an existence of feeling nothing. That's what I'd asked him to do, to go back to that reality and give up being human, something he wanted with all his heart—something he'd learned from my mother.

Now that he'd tasted what it meant to be human, I couldn't help but wonder if it would have been more merciful if he'd never known those feelings at all? For him to experience being flesh and blood, only to have that taken away now, felt beyond cruel.

But so was getting robbed of your life—and that's what had happened to Nate. *How could Death expect me not to*—

"You said before that you were afraid of me choosing sides," I said. "I didn't understand what you meant, but I think I do now. I choose Nate, the *real* Nate."

"Abbey, don't do this."

"I have to. No one is speaking for him."

"But I've told you. It might already be too late. Everything is out of my control."

"No, I can't accept that. I won't."

I realized how stupid I sounded. I was a kid, arguing with Death like I had something real to say. But by the look on his face, nothing had gotten through. I had to get his attention and I had to mean every word.

Nate's life depended on it.

"You're the one who bargained with my mother. You took her life instead, because you can do that."

Wringing my cold trembling fingers, I took a shaky breath before I said the only thing left to say to Death.

"If you need a soul to collect, take my soul instead."

On Denali

After he heard a loud crack and the rumble of heavy snow crashing down into a breach, Bob looked up the slope and squinted into the dying light as the mountain rescue crew raced for a dark opening in the snow. On instinct, he followed the men with barely a glance over his shoulder, calling out orders to Mike Childers.

"Mike, stay put. I'm going up," he yelled.

Even over the noise of the wind, Bob heard the zing of ropes that had snapped to a stop. Cool under fire and well trained, each member of the mountain rescue team carried out their assignments without saying much.

"I got tension," one man called out as he dug in and gripped his rope.

With his gear working as it should, the man who had fallen through was held in place, swinging by his climbing harness and belay loop. By the time Bob got to the dark chasm, he saw the fallen ranger waving his hand, giving his thumbs-up signal to Lewis.

"I'm okay."

Layers of snow formed a solid wall of ice where the ranger had fallen through, but beneath those layers was a dark expanse that the waning sunlight couldn't reach. Bob peered through the shadows, hoping for a glimpse of Nate and Josh, but it was too dark to see anything except the suspended ranger in his red parka, swaying by his lifeline.

After the ranger in charge saw his man was safe, he stared into the deep fissure, smiling at his guy. The worried look on Lewis's face, that had been there only seconds earlier, had vanished.

"You always were an overachiever, Nelson," Lewis said.

"You know it, sir." The guy, who looked to be in his twenties, grinned as he swung from his harness like a child on a swing. His voice magnified and reverberated within the cavern below. "If I'm good to go, you can lower me.

No sense wasting this great vantage point. I can do a little recon."

"That was my plan. Nice of you to fall on the sword."

"Anytime, sir."

With the angle of the sun, only shadows stretched into the hole. There wasn't enough light for Bob to see beyond the young ranger as he dangled and swung across the tight opening.

"We're gonna lower Nelson down to check things out." Lewis grabbed Bob's shoulder and fixed his gaze on him. "Your boy's beacon is stronger now. Can you hear that?"

Bob hadn't noticed, but Lewis was right. Hearing that the rapid-fire beeping had grown more intense, he couldn't help but react. His heart raced way too fast and his breathing at this high altitude made his lungs burn. When one of the rangers readied first-aid gear and two rescue gurneys, nothing could keep Bob from hoping that his son and Josh were together and alive.

Using a series of Prusik rope knots and Munter hitches tied to a system of karabiners and pulleys, Lewis's team worked fast to secure and anchor Nelson's tie line before they set up a transfer-load escape system. To handle the ranger's suspended body weight and keep the ropes from cutting into the ice, the men wedged a knapsack between the tie line and the edge of the crevasse to act as a buffer.

Now with Nelson cinched tight and the other rangers lowering him, Bob watched as a flashlight beam moved in the growing darkness. The young ranger looked for any sign of the boys.

"Give me slack," he called up with his voice echoing from the hole, "until I yell stop."

The incessant beeping of the tracking beacon would have

gotten on Bob's frayed nerves, but that noise meant they'd found the boys. To Bob, he couldn't remembering hearing a sweeter sound.

"*Stop!* I see something."

When Nelson yelled from the icy chasm, Bob held his next breath and waited.

"Yeah, I see a glove…and a boot under some snow," he called out. "I think I got him."

Him? Bob's throat wedged tight. He prayed they'd found both boys.

"You see two of 'em?" Lewis must have read his mind.

"Can't tell, sir. Lower me down. There's a ledge. I can swing over."

With a stern face, Lewis gave a nod to his team and they strained to lower his man a few more yards. As the rope hissed over the canvas knapsack, Bob shut his eyes and prayed, listening to every sound coming from the cavern. When the rope went slack and the tension loosened on the metal pulleys, he heard that clacking sound and opened his eyes.

Ranger Lewis called down to his man, "Is the boy alive? Are they both there?"

After a long silence, Nelson's deflated voice came back up the hole.

"I found both of them, sir. One's got a compound leg fracture. He's in bad shape." As Nelson moved, every sound he made magnified and welled up through the breach. "I'm not finding a pulse on the other one."

"Let's get those boys out of there," Ranger Lewis said, ordering his team into action with a wave of his arm.

Lewis told Bob that both boys would get medical attention at Fairbanks Memorial, the nearest acute-care facility, but his reassurance got lost. With Bob being in shock and numb, not much of what Ranger Lewis had said sunk in.

Not after Bob heard that one of the boys didn't have a pulse.

Abbey

Standing before Death with my offer to him still ringing in my head—*"take my soul instead"*—I wanted to look sure and brave, but all I had inside me was tapioca pudding. I didn't want to die and I'd never had a death wish, not even after Mom died. (Well, maybe that's a lie, but I got through that.) Now my future would be in Death's hands. I suddenly knew how my mother felt. The decision she made had been an impossible one, but I understood it because Death hadn't left me a choice, either.

I already knew what it felt like to live with the guilt of causing someone to die and I was tired of carrying that burden. Death helped me see that, so the irony wasn't missed on me that Death had watched me paint myself in that corner again. Only this time, Nate's life hung in the balance and I was the only one who could bargain for him.

I would gamble on Death's brand-new humanity and the love I felt certain he had for me—*my mother's love*—that he wouldn't take me up on my offer. But if he did, I wouldn't back down. My mother showed her love for me with a sacrifice only she could make. How could I let Nate die and do nothing?

If that happened, my life and her death would mean nothing. I waited for him to offer his hand to me. When he did, I would take it.

"Whatever happens…after tonight, we will not see each

other," he said. After he glimpsed my face, he turned to-ward the fire. "I know your tears aren't for me, but maybe one day I won't be beyond your forgiveness."

He repeated the words about forgiveness that he'd said to me before, when I didn't understand what he'd meant. Now I did. The hurt in his voice gripped my heart in a way that I knew would never let go. When I met his gaze, I didn't see Nate anymore.

I saw someone different—a boy I would miss.

"I want you to know. The time I've spent with you has meant everything to me. Whether I face an eternity of nothing or it all ends tonight..." He looked up from the fire and fixed his beautiful blue eyes on me. "You were worth the risk, Abbey."

Without saying anything more, he vanished in the split second it took me to blink. Like the embers off the fire, he splintered into pieces that spiraled through the smoke. After he disappeared into the darkening sky, he left me alone with an aching emptiness.

I had no idea what Death had decided.

All I knew was that he didn't offer me his hand. He and his raven were gone, but if one human boy's life was truly beyond his control, that terrified me. In the deepening shadows of dusk, I started down the mountain with my mind a total fog, except for one thing.

I had to know what happened to Nate.

abbey   # chapter 14

Near Healy, Alaska

I raced down the steep trail through the switchbacks and when I got closer to our cabin, I was breathless and had a stitch in my side. The crisp mountain air that smelled of pine, my halfway boulder landmarks and every glimpse I usually took of the lake between the snow-covered evergreens—my entire trip down the mountain had gone by in a blur.

I didn't know what I would tell my dad, but whatever happened next, I knew I couldn't do it alone. Nate was in trouble on Denali and without me having a TV, or a landline phone, or a juiced cell with bars, I had few choices to get news on the rescue. Since staying at the cabin without word would drive me crazy, Dad would be my only option. I'd have to tell him why I needed his help.

But as I ran around the corner of our cabin, I skidded to a stop on the gravel. Like an answer to my prayers, Tanner

Lange sat behind the wheel of his mother's van, talking to my dad in our driveway. In an instant, it hit me.

I realized how much I'd missed him.

Tanner was a real friend, someone I didn't have to ask for help. I don't know what clued him in that I needed him, but somehow he knew. When I walked up to his car, he and Dad turned toward me. All I saw when I looked at Tanner's smiling face was...

The Silver Scorpion.

When I needed him most, Tanner Lange made me a believer. Picturing him as his superhero alter-ego wasn't a stretch, but something more clicked in me when I saw him. It made my face flush hot. *Oh, my, God!* I had a strong urge to kiss him.

When that strange impulse flashed through my mind, it lingered as if it had every right to stay. I couldn't *unthink* it and I couldn't stop myself from imagining what kissing him might feel like. That toasty feeling for my friend Tanner hung there in my brain like someone else planted it there.

But the only one who could've done that—*was me.*

"Hey, Tanner." I waved.

With my chest still heaving for air, I felt a wet trickle down my spine under layers of clothes and my jacket, but not even sweating could stop me from grinning. I desperately wanted to talk to my best friend alone, but Dad stared at both of us like he'd figured something was up.

"Tanner was just about to tell me why he's driving alone. If memory serves, that violates his driver's permit." With crossed arms, my father said under his breath, "This should be interesting."

From the look on Dad's face, he fully expected Tanner

to lie and come up with a really lame excuse, but my father didn't know Tanner.

"I stole my mother's car, sir. Seemed like a good idea at the time. So in light of being charged with grand-theft auto, violating my permit pales in comparison…sir."

Dad raised an eyebrow and glanced at me before he finally said, "You're gonna have to do better than that, son. You better come inside."

"Can I have a moment alone with your daughter, sir?"

Before Dad gave his answer, Tanner turned off his engine and held out his car keys to my father.

"A show of good faith, Mr. Chandler."

Dad had always liked Tanner. According to my father, the kid had a brain that he used once in a while and he showed respect toward adults, something Tanner picked up from his military dad. Although my father probably hoped those good qualities would have rubbed off on me, somewhere he'd given up on that notion and made peace with his disappointment. I had to admit there were times I wondered why Tanner had stayed my friend, too.

But as my father stared at the keys dangling in front of him, I watched the boy behind the steering wheel. Imagining the man he'd become wasn't much of a stretch. Tanner could've made a different choice about what he'd told my father. He could've told him about the rescue attempt on Denali and that the fate of two boys from our school was being played out on the news.

Knowing my dad, he would've definitely had more sympathy for Tanner if he thought his trip had been urgent. Who wouldn't get caught up in a high-profile news story about two Palmer kids, happening near Healy, right? But Tanner had kept my father focused on his illegal driving and his first felony—coming off like a criminal—for one reason.

He was being a good friend. Whatever I wanted to tell my father, Tanner would leave that up to me, because that's what a good wingman did. He had my back. Pretty clever for a comic-book, reality-show freak. Despite being in the dark, Tanner had broken the law, pissed off his parents and risked his whole summer—*for me.* I should have felt bad about the nasty stuff heading his way, but a little ember burning inside me never let that happen. Inside I smiled.

And inside smiles were best of all.

"You've got five minutes," he told Tanner as he grabbed his car keys. After he shifted his gaze to me, he added, "I'll be keeping track."

"Thanks, Dad."

My father looked stern, but I could tell he was oddly amused. After I kissed his cheek, I waited until he went inside the cabin and closed the front door before I ran to the passenger side and climbed in. Tanner wasted no time in telling me the latest.

"Heard on the radio driving up here, they found 'em, Abbey. A helicopter is taking them to Fairbanks Memorial, but there's no real word on their condition."

I felt a smile coming on. Nate and Josh were rescued, but when Tanner couldn't look me in the eye, my grin faded fast.

"What's wrong? That should have been decent news. There's more, isn't there?"

Tanner gripped his steering wheel and sighed.

"They reported that one of them had a compound leg fracture and other injuries, but that the other guy was unresponsive. That's not good news, Abbey."

"They didn't say which one?"

"Nope, they never said." He clenched his jaw and stared out his windshield.

I had a bad feeling the unresponsive one was Nate, the boy with the jacked-up soul. When I heard Tanner's news, I flashed back to that night by the fire pit when Nate seemed out of control as he grabbed me and begged for my help. At the time, I didn't understand what had happened to him, but I had a better idea now—and that scared the hell out of me. The real Nate had sounded very far away, and even now, when I felt the phantom touch of his hand on my arm, a sick feeling swept over me.

The only reason Death had found him was because of me. I had let Nate down.

Listening to the pings of Tanner's cold engine, I felt the outside chill invade his van. I had a terrible feeling that even though Nate had been found and rescued, that wouldn't be good enough. Something clicked inside me and I knew what I had to do.

"I've got to see him," I said.

"Yeah, guess I knew that was coming." Tanner turned toward me, not even asking who or what I meant.

"But, Abbey, I gotta say this. I'm doing my best to forget about you telling me Holden was here in Healy when that clearly wasn't the case. Why would you…?" Avoiding my eyes, he raised both hands off the steering wheel and stopped himself. "No, I'm not gonna ask. Guess you'll tell me the truth when you're ready, because that's what… friends do. They trust each other."

Trust. I knew Tanner wasn't only talking about him trusting me. Trust worked better if it went both ways. From what I saw in his eyes, he thought I had lied to him…and that I didn't trust him enough to tell him the truth. But telling him about my hanging out with the Angel of Death, that wasn't exactly a five-minute conversation. With my dad watching us from the cabin, it wasn't the best time to explain to Tanner what really went on, even if I understood it myself.

"I know I haven't been a very good friend lately," I began. "But for the record, what I said on the phone about seeing Nate, I didn't lie to you. I can totally see why you'd think that, but that's not what happened."

"Then what *did* happen?" he asked. "Why can't you tell me?"

He didn't even try to hide the hurt in his voice. Most guys would have given attitude to cover how they really felt, but not Tanner. He wasn't afraid to be himself with me, but that made it harder. I wanted to say, "Please trust me," but if I were in his boots, I'd have a hard time believing that, too. As much as I loved having him in my life that was the very reason I needed time to think things through.

Telling Tanner that ravens had connected me to memories of my dead mother and that I'd kissed the Grim Reaper, those weren't things that rolled off the tongue without consequences. Since my mom's death, Tanner had been the one constant in my life that made all the bad stuff tolerable. Even imagining him calling it quits made me ache inside.

Tanner's questions still hung in the air, without an answer from me. He stared at me, trying to hide the betrayal I knew he had every right to feel. But when I met his gaze, I felt a rush of intimacy that I'd never felt with him before.

I'd crossed a line that I hadn't seen coming and there was no going back, not even if I wanted to.

Tanner and I shared something that went beyond friendship. He knew the real me—would *always* know the real me—and he kept coming back for more. Being loners might have drawn us together out of necessity, but it was our friendship that had made us strong enough to come out on the other side. Being alone with my best friend—a guy who made it easy to love him—it felt like I was on a high wire without a safety net, balancing between being a kid and wanting to be more.

"Something is h-happening…" Looking down, I let my fingers fumble with a zipper on his jacket sleeve. "With Nate, I mean, something I can't explain, not in five minutes. Hell, I'm not sure I could explain it in five years, but I promise you. I will tell you everything."

When my fingers brushed the back of his hand, I felt a rush of heat shoot to my face and I jerked my hand away. *Way to go, idiot!*

"What's going on, Abbey?" He narrowed his eyes. "You're acting all nervous and stuff."

"Yeah, well…I'm worried." I nodded. "Over Nate."

"What are you gonna tell your dad?"

Good question. And boy, did I appreciate the distraction of Tanner asking about my dad. I heaved a sigh and shook my head. Telling my dad that I wanted to see an injured friend wasn't the problem. It was the part that would come after I got to the hospital that bothered me. If Nate's life hung by a fragile thread, how far would I have to go to help him?

"Well, whatever you tell your dad, I'll back you up," he promised. "But maybe it wouldn't hurt to start with a little of the truth."

The truth? Tanner had no idea what he'd asked me to do, but I did know one thing. I had to find a way to tell my best friend everything. He deserved to know the truth—*the whole truth.*

"That boy took his mother's car and drove all the way from Palmer. Guess he thought he had a pretty good reason," Dad said as he cocked his head with a raised eyebrow.

My father stared at me as we sat at the kitchen table. He only half bought what I hoped to sell him.

"And you're saying he did it, just to give you the news about those missing boys?" he asked. "That's very CNN of him."

Hearing it come from Dad's mouth, I didn't buy it, either. Tanner had risked too much to see me. I grimaced and took a deep breath, giving him a shrug with only a point-five degree of difficulty. The marginal shrug gave me time to think.

Days ago, I might have been tempted to say "well, yeah" and felt okay about lying to my dad, but my normal instinct to keep him in the dark came and went, leaving me to deal with the glaring silence that had built between us. I felt too antsy to let that go on forever.

"Not...exactly," I said.

I told Dad that I'd seen the TV news story at Miner's. That's why I'd been so upset. I called Tanner on a pay phone to find out if he knew more. No way would I tell him about my crush on Nate. My extravagance with a coin-operated phone had been the extent of my honesty. My turning over a new leaf, when it came to dealing with my father, would be only a quick chapter in my life.

Baby steps, I solidly believed in baby steps.

"Did Tanner drive up here, because you asked him to?"

"No. He came on his own." I shrugged. "Guess he got worried..." *About me*, I wanted to say, but didn't. "And he couldn't reach me."

My father sighed and ran a hand through his hair, glancing out our window at Tanner. He had his poker face on, the one he'd taught me. The one I often reflected back to him like a mirror.

"He took his mother's car, Abbey...without permission. That's not right. You can't expect me to allow you to leave with him."

"I know, Dad. That's not what either of us expects, believe me." I looked my father straight in the eye. "But this is important. I have to know what happened to...those boys. I can't go on like everything's okay, not when we're this close to Fairbanks. It's like two hours or something, right?"

"A little longer than that this time of year, but...close enough." My dad narrowed his eyes and met my gaze. After another parental sigh, he finally nodded. "Okay, but I'm going with you."

Even though I kept my face as serious as I could, inside I felt happy for the first time in a long while. My heart busted a chest-poppin' Krump move that I'd practiced in my bedroom mirror and couldn't even do in my dreams, but I knew Dad wasn't done. The guy practically invented the word *conditions*.

"That would be great. What else?" I asked.

"I ride shotgun."

"You're letting Tanner drive?" No way. I couldn't believe it.

I shot Dad my trademark crooked smirk that I sometimes practiced in my bathroom mirror and immortalized with my cell camera to post to my Ditz Face album on Facebook. Whenever Tanner posted something bizarre as his status— which was like *always*—I'd hit him hard with one of those babies. Dad got the real thing, full on.

"He got this far, didn't he? And someone's got to keep him legal," Dad said. "But I'm reserving the right to pull the plug if he sucks."

Dad didn't use the word *sucks* every day. It was one of his special words that usually snagged my attention. He got sneaky like that sometimes.

"Tanner's got to call his parents…and I want to talk to them, too. If he's got a working cell, we'll call them from the car on the way to Fairbanks. No arguments."

"Okay."

Dad explained something about our cabin in Healy being between Fairbanks and Palmer and how the logistics would work if Tanner's parents got all balled up about what he'd done. I didn't exactly listen, but I knew what to say when he got done talking.

"Sounds like a plan." I stood up and kissed him on the cheek, saying, "Thanks, Dad."

With a hard-to-stop grin on my face, I ran to my room to grab my fanny pack. That zippered pouch carried all the stuff I couldn't live without—my stash of candy, money and my cool shades. But my smile left in a flash when I took a look in the mirror and grimaced. After I splashed water on my face, I brushed my hair and took a shot at looking girly—*a very long shot.*

By the time I came out of my bedroom, Dad stood at the front door with Tanner's keys in his hand. He looked as if he had more questions and held back on purpose. At least, I hoped he'd hold off. Head down, I bolted by him without a word and flashed Tanner a secret thumbs-up when I got outside. With Dad playing it cool and Tanner going way beyond the call of a friend, I didn't feel alone anymore.

I felt lucky, but Nate Holden sure wasn't.

Just thinking about the real Nate made me realize that I didn't really know him. We'd never met or talked to each other. Even though I knew what it felt like to kiss him—really kiss him—if he saw me, he wouldn't even know my name.

This whole thing had become seriously messed up.

With Death done talking to me, I didn't stand much of a chance to save Nate, either. I only knew that I had to try. I had a bad feeling that his fate might be decided by a flip of Death's coin and I knew I had to find him. I couldn't just stay in Healy with my fingers crossed.

I had to see the real Nate with my own eyes. Maybe then I'd know what to do.

Fairbanks Memorial Hospital
Fairbanks, Alaska

Fairbanks Memorial Hospital was located on Cowles Street off Airport Road, not far from Fort Wainwright. As Tanner turned his van into the medical complex, I got a closer glimpse of the hospital and my stomach twisted into a tight knot. I thought I could handle this. Guess I was wrong. I hadn't been in a hospital since the accident for a reason. That had been the worst time of my life. Plugged into machines and tubes, I'd been in pain and couldn't move much, which left me with nothing to do but think of Mom…and miss her.

Damn it! I really didn't want to step foot inside, but I had to.

After we found a parking spot near the E.R., my dad offered to help Tanner with his wheelchair.

"No, sir. I got it, but thanks."

I'd only seen Tanner off his wheels a few times. His upper-body strength always surprised me. His chest, shoulders and arms were rock-solid muscle and his routine of getting in and out of the van was quick, efficient and amazing. After he got situated, he locked the van and headed for the hospital entrance. He didn't need me to push him, but I knew that he liked me to. It was *our thing.* I climbed on back of his wheelchair and scooted across the parking lot, not saying much until he broke the ice.

"You gonna be okay?" he asked in a low voice.

Typical Tanner. Even though he had his own reason for hating hospitals, he knew how much I despised them and focused on me. When Dad was out of earshot, Tanner looked back over his shoulder to make sure I'd be okay.

"Not really..." I said. "But I don't have a choice."

Without making a big deal, Tanner raised a hand for me to take it. Since we'd never held hands before, that really got to me. I felt a lump in my throat close down like a vise. I couldn't have said anything if I tried, but before he saw me get all gushy, Tanner distracted me.

"Check it." He nudged his head toward the parking lot. "The buzzards are circling."

Near the E.R. entrance, a news van had parked and a reporter and camera guy were getting ready for a broadcast. Before long, others would show up and complicate things for the families of Nate and Josh. Getting a glimpse of this side of the story made me realize that Dad had probably gone through something very similar.

"Bad news is good news," I muttered.

"Yeah, for some."

Once we got inside, Dad took over. He talked to a nurse at the admittance desk and got the 411. After I heard the nurse mention "surgery" and "ICU," I knew to brace for bad news. When Dad got the lowdown, he came to tell us what he found out.

"She didn't tell me much." My father shrugged. "One of the boys is being prepped for surgery, the other is in ICU. She wouldn't confirm names or give me their conditions. The parents are on their way from Palmer. They should be here soon."

A strong twist in my gut told me who would be in ICU and it was more than a good hunch.

"Is there a place for us to wait near ICU?" I asked him.

"We'd have a better shot at getting information on the boy waiting for surgery," Dad said. What he said made sense, but sense had nothing to do with this.

"I know, but…" I sighed. "I'd like to try ICU first."

I didn't bother to explain why I'd insisted on dogging the Intensive Care Unit, but Dad didn't argue.

"Yeah, okay, but they have rules in ICU."

As my father rattled off what the nurse had told him, I only half listened. I knew only family would be allowed behind the secured doors of the ICU on a limited basis. That drill I knew firsthand. The best we could hope for would be a butt-numbing seat outside the Intensive Care Unit in a waiting area.

"Bottom line is…" Dad said. "Only family will be allowed in."

My father looked as if he wanted to know how far I would push this. At some point, I knew he'd eventually press me for that answer, especially with both boys being off-limits. But for now, he looked willing to help.

"I know, Dad, but I have to be here. It's important...to me."

If Nate was the one in ICU, that meant he'd be in bad shape. It would be life...or Death. Because of me, Death had crossed his path. He'd be a boy without a soul. How could I fix that? *How could anyone?* I'd have to fight for his soul, but I couldn't think of a single reason his parents or the hospital staff would even let me near him. If I told anyone the real reason I was there, I'd be fitted for a straitjacket and sent to the psych ward for evaluation.

My odds of seeing Nate were less than zero and from the look on my father's face, he knew it, too.

"I know this sucks for you, Dad."

My father shrugged and pretended that being here didn't bother him, but I knew better. If I had terrible flashbacks about being in a hospital again, I couldn't imagine what Dad felt. He stared at me before he shifted his gaze to Tanner, trying hard not to show that he'd rather be anywhere else, but I saw the conflict in his eyes.

"Okay, if we're gonna do this thing, let's go." My father headed for the elevators following the instructions he'd gotten from the admittance nurse.

Without Dad noticing, Tanner grabbed my hand again, at least until we got to the elevator. Once we were on board, I let go, but I kept my fingers on his neck, not letting Dad see. Even though my hand was ice-cold and shaking, Tanner let me touch him without flinching. Having a connection with him calmed me.

All hospitals were the same to me. They stank of medicines, cleaning stuff, stale coffee and cafeteria food that got mixed up with other smells I didn't want identified. When I remembered being at the lowest point of my life, completely miserable, any hospital staffers who smiled or had fun at their job made me angry.

Every laugh got on my nerves. Every cheery face made me want to hurl. I wanted everything to be as black as I felt, but when that didn't happen, I hated it. I didn't want to know that life went on...*for some.*

When we got to the Intensive Care Unit, I had to take deep breaths. ICU was never a good place to be. I shut my eyes to block out the memories that threatened to come back, but the clank of metal bed rails, the beep of the heart monitors, and the low moans of someone in pain took hold of me and brought everything back in a rush. After being in the critical care unit for so long, I suffered from ICU psychosis, my dad said. The activity at all hours, the noise, the painful cries of other patients, and a complete loss of time brought on hallucinations that made everything worse. To this day, the sights and sounds of any hospital triggered those nightmares and I had no idea what had been real or not.

Even if I filled my ears with Lady Gaga, seeing my father brought those awful memories back, too. I felt like such a slug for putting him through this. Like looking in a mirror, he was a reflection of what I felt. I watched him and when he thought I wasn't looking, my father watched me back. He looked antsy. (That gene I'd inherited.) Even though there were chairs for him to sit, he stood off to the side and fidgeted until the waiting got too much and he had to pace.

I knew it wouldn't be long before he found another excuse to stretch his legs.

"I'm gonna hit the head, maybe go looking for the cafeteria. You guys want anything?"

"No, thanks," I said.

Surprisingly Tanner turned Dad down, too. "No, thanks. I'm good."

Tanner was always hungry and for the past hour, I'd been listening to his stomach growl, but he stayed with me, waiting for my father to leave us alone. After Dad left, he leaned closer.

"So what's the plan?" He glanced at me, showing a flash of his dimples. "You have one, right?"

"I'm working on it. I can't just sit here, not knowing what's goin' on in there."

Being a member of the walking wounded like me, Tanner knew about hospitals, too. We both knew that ICU staff watched the door that gave access to the patients and that there were rules about visiting hours. Some hospitals even assigned code words to family members to let nurses know they were authorized to see the patient, but from the conspiratorial look on Tanner's face, none of that intimidated him. My *"gangsta on wheels"*—my friend who was never boring—had outlaw blood flowing through his veins. I knew that Tanner would back my play no matter what I decided to do.

"We'll probably only get one shot," I whispered.

None of this was a game. Not any part of it. With precious time counting down, I felt the mounting urgency of Nate's situation. Behind secured ICU doors, I had no idea what was going on. Doctors could pronounce Nate dead and I'd never get a chance to help him, but I wasn't there to sit and wait for whatever Death had decided.

My instincts were telling me that I had to do something. *Now.*

But before I hatched a plan, the elevator doors opened down the hall and a frantic woman and a little girl rushed into the waiting area. If I had any doubts about which boy had gone to ICU, they vanished the second I recognized Nate's mother. She had the raw glassy-eyed look of a woman pushed over the brink, and beside her stood Nate's little sister, Zoey.

I'd overheard Nate talk about Zoey with Josh and I'd seen her a few times around Palmer, but when I looked into the eyes of that confused and scared little girl, she tore my heart to shreds. On the outside, she may have been a kid, but behind those eyes I saw something no child should have to know. I knew what that felt like—because I'd been there, too.

This was far from a game and I had a bad feeling that every second would count.

abbey　　　　　　　　　**chapter 15**

Fairbanks Memorial Hospital
Fairbanks, Alaska

"My name is Jackie Holden. I'm here to see my son, Nathan. A rescue helicopter brought him in, off Denali."

"Yes, ma'am. Your husband is with him, but—" The nurse looked down at Zoey.

Not waiting for the woman to finish, I heard Mrs. Holden interrupt her in a shaky voice.

"I know there must be rules about children, but I had to bring his sister. I couldn't leave her. They're so close. Nate would want to see her."

"I'm sorry. We have a strict policy. No children under the age of twelve," the nurse said. "With their level of immunity, children have a risk for infection. An ICU visit can be traumatic for a child, too. I hope you understand."

Mrs. Holden nodded and took a ragged breath. She looked as if she had frayed on the edges and didn't want to break down in front of her little girl. I knew she wanted to find Nate and be with him, something we had in common.

The last thing she'd want to deal with—would be someone like me.

I don't know what made me do it, but I got out of my seat and walked toward her anyway. I never even looked at Tanner. I approached Nate's mom after I'd seen Zoey looking lost and scared and her mother unraveling in front of my eyes. I wanted to puke and my knees felt shaky. The reason Nate got targeted by Death was because of me. Now his family would be touched by my connection to the dark angel.

I hated intruding on his mother's pain, but I knew that if she disappeared behind the double doors into ICU, I'd be shut out from any news on Nate. I didn't know if my belief that I could do something came from wishful thinking or a real conviction that it would be true, but for Nate's sake, I had to try. Although Death had made me a believer in an existence beyond my understanding, Nate didn't belong there. At least, not yet—and not on my account.

While Mrs. Holden stood at the ICU desk, talking to the nurse about Nate and figuring out what to do with Zoey, I stepped closer. Feeling the pressure of knowing that my dad would be back any minute, I ran on instinct now. I had no idea what I needed to do, but I had to make a connection with Nate's family. As I neared the ICU desk, I overheard Mrs. Holden.

"Where's his doctor? Can I speak to him?" Nate's mother grabbed a tissue from the box and dabbed her eyes.

"Yes, ma'am. We were expecting you. I'll let the doctor know you're here." The nurse turned her back and picked up the phone.

I waited until Nate's mom finished with the nurse before I spoke up.

"Mrs. Holden?" I didn't recognize my own voice. I sounded older, like someone else talked for me.

When she turned, Nate's mom looked as if she hadn't heard me, like I'd been a disturbing noise that got on her nerves. Zoey clung to her mother's hand as if it were her only lifeline.

"Sorry to bother you, but my name is Abbey Chandler. I go to Nate's school. When I heard the news, I had to come."

She stared at me with watery eyes and her mouth open like she had a question buzzing in her head that she couldn't quite grasp. Underneath the worry, she looked really pretty and something in her eyes seemed familiar. I'd seen Nate's father in a newspaper article once. Nate definitely took after his dad. Yet after seeing Mrs. Holden's vulnerability up close, I thought he had inherited the soft compassion in his mother's eyes, too. Before Mrs. Holden said anything to me, the nurse broke in.

"Ma'am? I talked to your son's doctor. He's on his way. He'll be here in ten minutes."

"Ah, thank you. And my husband? Does he know we're here?"

"I'll tell him." The nurse nodded. "Please, have a seat."

After the nurse headed through the double doors, Mrs. Holden turned toward me again, looking even more confused.

"I'm sorry. What did you say again?"

She hadn't heard me, but looking into her eyes, I knew why. All she had on her mind was her son and that was how I would reach her.

"I know Nate. I go to school with him. He's so…special. If there's anything I can do, I'll be here."

"Oh…thank you. I don't know what to say." She sighed and clutched the hand of her daughter tighter. "I just got here."

"I know…and I won't keep you. I just…if you could let me know about Nate. I'm so worried."

Staring into her eyes, I realized how ridiculous I sounded. I was a stranger. Why would she tell me anything? And forget about letting me see him. That wouldn't happen. If I got in to see Nate, I'd have to come up with my own plan. It would have to be off-the-wall, out-of-the-box crazy.

"Thank you for coming." She squeezed my hand and forced a faint smile that came and went. "I've got to take Zoey to the bathroom before the doctor comes. We left the house so fast that she never got a chance to go."

After she let go of my hand, Mrs. Holden took Zoey down the hall and I watched them leave. I'd been an idiot. What did I expect? Nate's doctor would be here any minute. The last thing on Mrs. Holden's mind would be keeping me in the loop on her son's condition, but the urgency I'd been feeling to see Nate had come to a head. Every sound, every conversation between doctors and nurses left me on edge and seeing Mrs. Holden and Zoey made things worse.

I didn't want them to lose Nate, but I wasn't sure how or even if, I could help.

When I heard the soft ding of the elevator, the doors slid open and the echo of footsteps came down the corridor. I thought it would be the doctor, but it was my dad. He had a small paper bag in his hand.

"I know you didn't ask for anything, but I brought snacks for later." Dad raised the sack and asked, "What did I miss?"

I shrugged and said, "Not much. Thanks for the munchies. Tanner will be happy."

Dad had prepped for a long stay, but I couldn't afford to think like that. In my head, a clock ticked down. Steady persistent beats had become abrasive white noise to my memory of Nate's pleas for help and the feel of his hand on my arm, back at the clearing.

Those memories were in me, as vivid as if they had just happened, but Nate wasn't with me now. I didn't feel him and that made it easy to believe that fate had taken over. I might already be too late.

Minutes later

Down the corridor, I saw a grim-faced doctor in scrubs walking toward the ICU nurses' station. In a low voice, he spoke to the uniformed woman who gave him a patient's chart. I stood too far away to hear what they said, but with Mrs. Holden and Zoey still in the bathroom, I knew they were almost done. I heard their voices behind the restroom door. Zoey was washing her hands. They'd be out soon.

"I bet that's him, Nate's doctor. I can't hear what he's saying, can you?" I asked Tanner. After he shook his head, I mumbled, "I can't sit here like this. It's driving me crazy."

"Fortunately for you, that's a short trip…and you'd get frequent-flyer miles."

Looking deep in thought, Tanner didn't blink, didn't even turn his head. He stared at the doctor and nurse as if he could read their minds. I could never be that still. My body and brain didn't function that way, especially now.

Inside I bubbled over like a kettle on high heat. Every second that went by magnified the worry I felt for Nate.

All I needed was to see him. I knew that if I did, I'd have a better shot at figuring out what to do. My dad sat across the room, giving us space, but he would look up from his magazine every time I moved. It'd be only a matter of time before he'd push me for answers. He'd want to know how close I was to these boys and why I felt strongly about hanging out in the ICU when I'd never be allowed to see Nate.

Now his doctor stood at the ICU desk and he'd be my best chance at finding out what was going on.

"Wish I was a fly on the wall," I muttered, sitting slouched in my seat next to Tanner. "I'd love to hear what's happening."

"A fly on the wall, huh?" Barely looking over, Tanner reached into his pocket for his phone. "Think I've got an app for that."

"Not funny, Lange."

Without saying anything else, Tanner punched his smartphone with his thumbs, completely oblivious. Normally he was a pretty funny guy to hang with, but when he got uncomfortable—like loitering in an ICU when he'd rather be anywhere else—he grew more cynical. Humor helped him deal with tough things, so I cut him slack.

"You know, you should aspire to something a little higher on the food chain than a fly, Abbey," Tanner said. "Besides, even if flies could talk, why trust 'em? They think a warm cow patty is a choice meal."

Okay, he had a point—and he almost made me laugh—but I wasn't in the mood to hear his views on the wild kingdom or the nutritional value of cow dung. Time counted down in my head and when Tanner grabbed his cell, acting like he had better things to do, I lost it.

"Hello. I'm freakin' out here." I slumped lower in my chair and crossed my arms. "I gotta find out what's going on. What's so important with your phone?"

"This." With a sly grin, he held up his phone. "Voilà! Instant fly. Wall optional."

"What's that?" I sat straight up and grabbed his cell, staring at the display. I thought he'd been goofing off, but when I saw what he had, I gasped.

"Oh. My. God. This is a…"

"A recorder, yeah. High quality MP3…with decent range." He smirked. "Cool, huh?"

"But how would it work? Wouldn't we have to…?"

"Leave that to me." He grinned.

I stared at him until I figured out what he had in mind. The nurses' station was the hub of activity for the ICU. Doctors, nurses and visitors congregated there. If some genius hid a recording device on the counter, disguised as a potted plant or behind a tissue box, I wouldn't need to enlist the help of a fly.

"Brilliant, Tanner. Remind me not to piss you off."

"If I have to remind you, I'm not tryin' hard enough."

"Good point."

Before I said anything more, Tanner rolled toward the counter and chatted up one of the nurses before he grabbed a tissue. When the nurse turned her back, he pulled a sleight-of-hand trick with his cell that Criss Angel, *Mindfreak*, would've been proud of. After he came back, Tanner handed me the tissue.

"You better make this last," he said.

"Yeah, thanks." I snatched the tissue from his hand and leaned in, whispering, "I never saw. Where did you put it?"

"I could tell ya, but then I'd have to snuff you." He shifted his gaze toward the ICU desk. "Dead air isn't the goal. We need something worth recording. Cross fingers, toes, anything that works. We could use a lucky break."

"Yeah, come on, Mrs. Holden. Please?" I crossed my fingers and waited.

"By the way, I found out from the nurse that the night shift is coming on soon...and the O.R. is on the tenth floor," he whispered. "Information is power."

"What?"

I didn't know why Tanner asked the nurse about shift changes and the operating room, but I didn't get to ask him. Seconds later, Nate's father rushed through the ICU doors. Having come off Denali, Mr. Holden looked wind-blown and his face had chafed from the harsh weather. He'd stripped out of his heavier climbing gear, down to the layers he wore underneath. His eyes searched the waiting room, looking for his wife and child.

When he saw them come out of the restroom, I thought I'd lose it.

Without saying a word, he rushed for his wife and buried his face in her neck. Her sobs muffled in his shoulder as he cradled the back of her head in his hand. My fingers went to my lips as I fought the lump in my throat. When everything blurred, from the tears filling my eyes, I turned to Tanner and my father. If I was any judge, we were all affected, especially when Zoey huddled next to her parents and hugged their legs with her arms.

"Oh, God," I whispered.

Those words came out of my mouth, even though I tried

to stay still. Without saying anything, Tanner grabbed my hand. This time, he didn't hide it from my dad. Both of us watched as the doctor approached the Holdens. From where we were sitting, we couldn't hear what they said, but we'd soon know word for word, thanks to Tanner's app...*and Zoey.*

If Mrs. Holden hadn't brought Zoey, she would have been inside the ICU with Nate and her husband, and not standing at the nurses' station talking with the doctor. Tanner's cell-phone app would have been useless. The way I figured it, Zoey had been the real reason Tanner's brilliance came in handy. The love she had for her big brother and the closeness of Nate's family gave me a fighting chance at seeing him.

When the doctor took Mrs. Holden in to see Nate, Zoey went with her dad. Mr. Holden held his daughter in his arms as they waited for the elevator, but before the doors opened, the little girl looked at me. I wasn't sure she really saw me, but I lifted a finger to wave. As the elevator doors opened, she waved back, a sad gesture that I knew would stay with me. The tissue that Tanner had given me came in handy after all.

But when I turned to look for my friend, he was already on retrieval mode. Tanner grabbed his cell and punched a few buttons while the nurses were busy. Without returning to where I sat, he looked over his shoulder and said, "Forgot something in my car. You wanna come?"

Tanner said that for my dad's benefit. He didn't have to tell me anything. I would've shadowed him. He'd given us an excuse for leaving ICU to listen to the recording.

"Yeah. I could use some fresh air," I said before I turned to my father. "Dad, we'll be right back, unless we stop at the gift shop. Can you call me on my cell if anything happens?"

"Sure." My father nodded, but I could tell his fuse burned on the short side. He didn't like being here any more than I did and waiting around, with no end in sight, would soon wear thin. He'd push me for answers that I couldn't afford to tell him.

Whatever came next, I had to do it fast.

Minutes later

Nothing prepared Jackie Holden for seeing her son, Nate, in his glass room in the ICU. Taped to her boy's sweet lips was a ventilator tube that hissed breath into his lungs through a machine. It'd been bad enough to see all the equipment monitoring his condition and the tubes in his arms that were keeping him alive. But every intrusion of the incessant beeping and the hum of equipment wore on her fragile nerves. Even though she knew the tubes in him delivered medicine and fluids to his body, they wouldn't allow her to hold him the way her arms ached to do.

"We're monitoring your son's condition very closely. That's why…" The doctor's voice faded from her mind as she stepped closer to Nate's bed and clutched the cold bed rails.

Before Jackie actually saw her son, the doctor described how Nate would look, so she'd know what to expect, but she only half listened. Rationally, her mind knew what she'd see, but nothing would have prepared her heart.

She'd blocked out the doctor's words, only wanting to see her Nathan. That's all that mattered…*until now.* Standing over him, she noticed his skin looked deathly pale and the shadows under his beautiful eyes scared her. Nate looked dead. Machines kept his body alive.

If his condition grew worse, what the doctor proposed felt like a last resort.

After the doctor left her alone with Nate, Jackie knew that the ICU nurse had been right about the trauma to a child. It had been hard enough for her to see him this way, but Zoey wouldn't understand. She'd be more scared for her brother and Jackie couldn't do that to her little girl, even if it meant she wouldn't see him before his heart stopped beating.

"Zoey can't see you like this, Nathan," she whispered. "She wouldn't understand, honey."

She talked to him as if he heard her and stroked his cheek as if he felt the touch of her shaking fingers.

"But I'm here with your father…and Zoey sends you butterfly kisses." Her eyes brimmed with fresh tears. "We all love you…so very much."

Jackie leaned down and kissed his forehead, breathing in the smell of her son's skin—never feeling so helpless in her whole life.

After I rolled Tanner into the elevator, I reached for the ground-floor button, but he stopped me and punched ten instead.

"Where are we going?" I asked.

"I wanna check out the O.R. before the ICU night shift comes on duty. You may not remember much after your accident, but I felt like Humpty Dumpty. I saw the operating room plenty and it got me thinking."

"About what?"

Before he answered, Tanner reached into his pocket and

pulled out his cell and earplugs he used for music. We'd both hear what he'd recorded from the conversation the Holdens had with Nate's doctor, without anyone listening in.

"ICUs always have a service elevator that bypasses the public," he said. "They don't bring patients through the waiting area and doctors use the back way to avoid the families' usual questions."

"That makes sense."

"It'll take time for the night shift to get up to speed. The way I see it, we may have a small window of opportunity to sneak into ICU during shift change."

I narrowed my eyes. "I see you've given this thought."

"I want to help you, Abbey." When he looked up at me, I saw an edge of hurt in his eyes. Unlike his usual way, Tanner turned stone-cold serious. "I may not know why you're doing this, but I'm your friend. If you ever need someone to bail you out of jail and not post your booking photos on the internet, I'd be *that* guy."

I truly didn't deserve a friend like Tanner, but since I had him alone in the elevator, I did the one thing that I'd wanted to do since he drove to Healy in his mom's stolen car. Standing in front of him I leaned down, planted my hands on the armrests to his wheelchair—and I kissed him. His lips tasted yummy like Reese's Peanut Butter Cups, something I could thank my dad for…if I ever lost my mind. After Tanner jerked back in surprise—guess he hadn't expected me to go PDA on him—he totally kissed me back.

When the elevator door opened, I pulled away and opened my eyes. Our faces were only inches apart.

"No booking photos," I whispered and smiled. "Check."

Tanner looked stunned and he didn't say anything. He

only stared at me until I got on the back of his wheels and pushed us out the elevator on the tenth floor.

I wanted to feel like the cool flirty chick that I'd always secretly envied, but the heat rushing to my cheeks gave me away. I wasn't cool. I'd never be *that* girl and I had no idea how to get a guy's attention, but at that moment, I didn't care. I'd kissed my best friend, Tanner Lange.

My knees felt like Jell-O. Lime, my personal favorite.

"Abbey?"

After we hit the tenth floor, people noise made it hard to hear Tanner until I found a quiet spot for us to talk. I took a knee in front of him and waited for him to finish what he had to say. Seeing the blush of pink on his cheeks up close made me feel better. Both of us were rookies at this whole kissing thing.

"Can we…do that again sometime? I mean, when I'm actually ready," he said. "Because I…could do better."

I thought Tanner was kidding, but from the serious expression on his face, I realized that he wasn't.

"Yeah. I'd like that." I smiled. "Now what's on the recording, Romeo?"

With full-on dimples and a second wave of color to his cheeks, Tanner shot me a grin as he set up his cell to play back the MP3 recording. He plugged his earbuds into his phone and handed me one so we could both listen. The recording sounded primo, especially the doctor's voice. He came in loud and clear. I shut my eyes and listened, plugging my other ear with a finger so I wouldn't miss a word. As the doctor told the Holdens about Nate, I gritted my teeth. It was worse than I thought.

Nate suffered from cerebral edema. His brain was swelling. The doctor guessed that the condition must have hap-

pened after he received a blow to the head when he fell
into a crevasse. Apparently he had a concussion and it had
gotten worse. Something about hypothermia and the high
altitude complicated things, too.

But the doctor said it would be important to monitor
and control every bodily function. That's why he was in
ICU on a ventilator with his blood pressure and other vital functions being watched. He explained the medical options to Nate's parents, saying they could drain fluid off his
brain to relieve the pressure and that surgery might also be
an option. But his recommendation was to induce a coma
in Nate, giving him really strong meds that would put him
into a deep sleep that might allow his body to heal.

"Oh, my God. They can't do that, Tanner," I whispered,
putting a hand over my mouth and shaking my head.

I wanted to ask, "What if you can't get the swelling
down?" but I knew that question was the one neither parent could ask, at least not in front of Zoey.

I wasn't a doctor, but after meeting Death—twice—I
knew outcomes weren't always determined by medical sci-
ence. I had a bad feeling that if Nate got induced into a
coma by strong drugs, that would put him out of my reach.
If he was still in his body, somewhere, I wouldn't reach
him—on any level—if he were drugged. If I couldn't pull
him from the brink of where Death had him, Nate's life
would be in the hands of the collector of souls.

I couldn't let that happen.

"But, Abbey, they have to do something," Tanner said.
"If they can't relieve the pressure on his brain, he could
die...or worse."

"What's worse than dying?"

"He could become a vegetable. His body might function, but his brain would be useless. Or the doctor might declare him brain-dead and his parents would have to make the worst decision of their lives—to pull the plug on their son. Man, this really blows. I don't see how you're gonna get in to see him now."

I pulled the earbud out and sat back on my haunches in front of his wheelchair, feeling drained.

"But I have to try, Tanner." I shook my head. "This is my fault. You don't understand."

"How could it be your fault, Abbey? He was on Denali, you were in Healy. That makes no sense. Yeah, this is bad, but I don't understand why you feel responsible."

I made an offer to Death on the mountain—my soul for Nate's—and the Angel of Death didn't give me his hand. He'd refused my bargain. What would it take for me to save Nate now?

"Help me get in to see him, before they dose him with coma juice, and I'll tell you everything."

Tanner stared at me as if I'd lost my mind.

Maybe I had.

abbey   chapter 16

Breaking in to an Intensive Care Unit wouldn't be easy, but with Tanner, I had a fighting chance. In a med facility, being with a guy in a wheelchair would be like having an open hall pass. People expected us to be there and didn't gawk sideways like they did in the real world, where we usually stood out. I say "us" and "we" because when I hung out with Tanner, I saw how some people treated him.

Most of the time, he got stares behind his back when jerks thought he wasn't looking. Or for whatever reason, people would strike up lame conversations with him. They thought that because he sat in a wheelchair, he should know everybody in Alaska on wheels, like they all hung out together and had secret handshakes. Or sometimes they went out of their way to "help" or be "friendly" to him—even when they obviously weren't into it—just to play nice with the handicapped guy and rack up brownie points in heaven, like God couldn't see through their fake smiles.

But at Fairbanks Memorial, we fit in. I think that's why Tanner came with me. I would've gone down in flames—the odds totally sucked, like a gazillion to none—but my best friend gave me a sliver of hope.

He made me a believer—in him—*and in us.*

"What now, genius?" I asked.

"Watch and learn, grasshoppa."

Tanner navigated the corridors of the tenth floor, acting like he knew where to go. Of course, he faked it for my benefit, but once he got on track, we were golden.

"Here, that's what I need," he whispered and nudged his head to a hallway ahead. Avoiding direct eye contact with anyone, I rounded the corner as Tanner said, "These are patient changing rooms. You know, where you get naked... and everyone's cool with it?"

I rolled my eyes, trying to remember that he came to help.

"We'll find what we need here," he said.

I wanted to ask him what he was talking about, but he'd gotten me this far, why would I question him now? Some of the doors down the corridor were shut, but a few were wide open. He rolled up to the nearest unlocked door where the room had lights off inside, a room with a threshold wide enough for his wheelchair. With a glance down the hall, I made sure no one saw us make our move.

"This one." He shoved the door wider with his footrests and when we got inside, he said, "Shut the door."

Once we had privacy, I breathed a sigh of relief. We were finally alone and could talk without anyone watching.

"Patients use these rooms to change into hospital gowns," he said.

Before I knew it, Tanner rolled closer to a tall bin that

had discarded cotton hospital gowns inside. He pulled out one after another, tossing garments aside.

"What are you looking for?" I asked.

When he found what he needed, Tanner grinned and tossed me something that looked like a blue cotton shower-cap thingie and a plain white gown that tied in back.

"Oh, no. I'm not hanging my ass out of this thing." I shook my head.

"You won't have to. That's my job."

"Oh, this, I've got to see." I smirked.

Without hesitating, Tanner stripped out of his jacket and yanked off his T-shirt. My face flushed with heat. I'd never seen him without a shirt on. I swallowed, hard, and I tried not to look, but I couldn't help it. Tanner's body was hard to ignore. His chest and abs were as muscled as I'd ever seen and his arms were perfect.

Seeing him like this—and being in a small room that got smaller by the second—I forgot to breathe.

"If this is gonna work," he said, "I need you to take off my pants."

Wide-eyed, I gulped when I heard his zipper and froze with my mouth open. *What the hell?*

"Tight quarters, Chandler. I could use your help?"

"Oh…right."

When Tanner looked at me again, his soft chuckle made me smile.

I pointed a finger and said, "You better not be laughing at me, dude. That's all I'm sayin'."

"Never, Abbey. Trust me." He grinned, gifting me with his dimples. "If I'm gonna look like a patient, jeans and boots won't cut it. I can keep my socks and boxers on, but the rest goes."

Okay, so I stripped off Tanner's pants. No biggie, right? I tried not to look. I seriously did, but you know, things happen and I'm not exactly blind. I helped him stash his clothes and boots in a knapsack he always had attached to his chair for school stuff. By the time we left, Tanner looked like a real patient wearing hospital garb with his bare legs showing. He helped me get into my disguise and flipped the white gown around, making it look like a uniform. After I tucked my hair into the blue elastic cap, I took a look at myself in a mirror that hung on the wall. I looked like an orderly who took patients from the O.R. to their rooms… or to ICU.

"What do you think?" I asked Tanner after I turned around.

"You look kind of…" He looked at me, top to bottom.

"Kind of what, Tanner?"

"Kind of…hot, actually."

"Oh, brother." I rolled my eyes and scooted around him to reach for the door handle. I acted like he annoyed me, but inside I grinned.

"Abbey?" Tanner stopped me from opening the door by touching my arm. His expression had changed and he had a hard time looking at me. "I know you promised to tell me everything later, but I gotta ask one thing. Do you… have feelings for this guy? Is that why…?"

He didn't finish. Still avoiding my eyes, he stopped and waited for me to say something. That's when the silence in the room got real loud.

My feelings for Nate were…*complicated*. I'd obsessed over him for so long that I mistakenly believed those feelings were love. When he kissed me on the mountain, I thought he felt the same, but now I knew that wasn't true. Death had kissed me, and all because of the love he had inside him, a gift he cherished from my mother. The real Nate—the one dying inside ICU—wouldn't know me at all.

Something had been off about my kiss with Nate for many reasons, but maybe one of those reasons had been Tanner. I wanted to be with a boy and feel loved. I thought Nate could give me that, but now I realized I'd been wrong. Nate had always been a fantasy. He wasn't real.

But Tanner was real and just now, when he looked at me—blushing like a shy boy—I could tell why he asked and I knelt in front of him.

"I had a crush on Nate Holden, but that's all it was. Feelings like that are one-sided. They're not real. I see that now, but Nate's in trouble, Tanner. Real trouble…and I don't have time to explain."

"Right…no time." He nodded, without looking up at me. "Did you know that time was invented so everything didn't happen at once?"

I narrowed my eyes at him and smiled.

"I'm glad you're with me, Tanner." I touched his cheek and when his lips nudged into a lazy grin, I said, "I think there's a difference between crushing on someone and feeling the real deal. Right now, this is only a theory. I'm not exactly loaded with experience on the topic."

When I shrugged, Tanner leaned down and kissed me. With a gasp in my throat, I cupped his face with my hands and breathed him in. I didn't know if Tanner felt the same way that most boys did about girls, since he was paralyzed from the waist down, but he made me want to find out. I had a strong feeling that my best friend would be different from most boys—*period*—not because he had a wheelchair, but because he would be the kind of guy who fell in love with his mind and his heart, too. The wrong girl could really hurt him, bad. But with the right one, he'd give her a precious key to open everything about him.

Yet even as I kissed him, I didn't know if that girl could ever be me. I didn't feel good enough. With that harsh reality invading my mind, I opened my eyes and pulled back from him.

"Ah, sorry. I, ah…we gotta go."

"Yeah." He nodded. "You're right."

Tanner leaned back in his chair and waited for me to stand and open the door. After that kiss, and with every other feeling of doubt spiraling through me, I felt more on edge than ever as we walked through the tenth floor. I became an obvious example of what *not* to do. I avoided casual glances like eyeballs were equipped with lasers that could disintegrate me with a look. And the way I fidgeted, I must have seemed like a jacked-up druggie between fixes. I white-knuckled the grips on Tanner's wheelchair, stone-cold scared we'd get caught and lose my one shot at helping Nate.

But Tanner picked up on my nervous-wreckage routine and talked me off the ledge with his calm voice, telling me where to go on the tenth floor. He reminded me to stay calm and not push his ride like we were in a race. I took a deep breath and shook my hands before I started over.

Everywhere we went, I saw the night shift coming on duty. New faces reported in, manned desks and took over from the day crew. Tanner's plan came together and although he didn't know any more about this hospital than any other, I trusted him. He went by feel and navigated the halls like he knew what was what. That worked for me. It didn't take long to figure out what he looked for.

An orderly wheeled a patient on a gurney from the O.R. and Tanner told me to follow him. When we got to a bank of elevators that didn't look open to the public, I smiled at the guy and acted like I knew what I was doing—until Tanner opened his mouth and I nearly lost it.

"I'm visiting my dad in Intensive Care," he told the guy. "Is this the right elevator? I think my driver's lost, but won't admit it."

When the orderly shot me a questioning stare, I raised both my eyebrows and said, "It's my first day. I got turned around."

"It happens," the orderly replied. "Yeah, this is the right elevator. The button panel on the inside will tell you which floor, but I'm goin' to ICU. You can follow me."

"Thanks, but there may not be enough room. We can catch the next one." I forced a smile.

"No, I really don't want to wait," Tanner contradicted me. "You mind if we jump your ride? It might be a tight fit, but I'd really like to see my dad. I'm afraid she could get us lost again, even on an elevator that only goes up and down."

"Yeah, sure. No problem," the uniformed man said.

When the elevator doors opened and the orderly turned his back, I thumped Tanner in the back of his head with my knuckle. He flinched and semi-snorted a laugh that I prayed the other guy didn't catch. But after I thought about it, piggybacking on gurney guy's ride made sense. When he got to ICU with his patient, he'd be a distraction that we could hide behind. Since we didn't know what to expect in ICU, an unconscious patient fresh from the O.R. might give us a shot to scope things out and be a convenient diversion.

I had to give Tanner props for his quick thinking, but the elevator ride with him and gurney guy would only be the calm before the storm. The worst was yet to come.

Once we got to Intensive Care, I knew we'd have to keep a low profile until we got the green light for Nate's room. A stone-faced night nurse could kill the deal and it would take a major stroke of good luck to slip into Nate's room unnoticed with his mom around. As we rode the elevator, all the reasons stacked against me weighed heavy on my mind. I knew that Tanner had done what he could to get me this far.

The rest would be up to me.

Like we'd hoped, the orderly rolled out his patient and went to an attendants' station without even looking over his shoulder. We split in the opposite direction, pronto. Tanner took over his chair and didn't let me push him. Guess he figured it would be less hassle if I didn't have to worry about him. Avoiding the nurses, I kept my head down and didn't look around until Tanner whispered my name.

"Abbey, down here."

He waved his hand, calling me to a glass room on the opposite end of the floor from where the new patient checked in. I stepped up my pace and grabbed onto his wheelchair, until I saw what he'd found.

Nate Holden had a private room. The curtains were open, enough for us to see in, and the lights were dim, but the best part—his mom was nowhere in sight.

"What did I do to deserve this?" I whispered into Tanner's ear.

"Come on. Let's go in." He gripped his wheels and made a move to go in, but I pulled him back.

"Wait. What if she comes back and catches us?" I shook

my hands and shifted my gaze between sick Nate and an insistent Tanner.

My stomach tightened into a fist and I couldn't make my feet move, but I did manage to glance over my shoulder, risking eye contact with the ICU attendants. I finally found Nate's mom. She stood at the nurses' station, looking over a clipboard with a pen in her hands. She hadn't seen me. Since I had no idea what she was doing, I couldn't guess how long she'd be away from Nate.

With her close by, I felt like a low-life slug, sneaking behind her back to see her sick son, but I'd come this far. What were four more tiny steps? That should have been an easy answer, yet for me, it wasn't. My luck was crap and this suddenly felt like an epic mistake. I turned back from watching Nate's mom and looked down at Tanner.

"She's at the desk, doing paperwork," I whispered.

"Come on, then. Let's go, Abbey." Tanner went for the door to Nate's room, but stopped when I didn't follow him. When he looked back at me, he sighed.

"Abbey, this is a gift. He's in there alone. If you give up now, you might not get this chance again. Is he in trouble, or not?"

Shaking head to toe, I swallowed hard. My throat went dry and I felt sick, but Tanner had a point. I finally nodded and pushed him into Nate's ICU room with both of us shutting the drapes to hide what we were about to do. With the curtains drawn, I held my breath. I swear, I expected someone to call security and for alarms to go off, but when nothing happened, I turned toward Nate—with Tanner watching every move I made.

No pressure…no pressure at all.

★ ★ ★

When I saw Nate—the real Nate—for the first time, see-ing him in his hospital bed only reminded me what a fool I'd been. Death had conned me and now Nate would pay the price. Reality hit me hard. The last time I'd seen him, Nate was at school with his buddy Josh making plans for the big climb—his dream of a lifetime—before I messed everything up for them.

Now this.

Seeing him hooked up to machines that breathed for him scared me. I couldn't feel any connection to him. The crush I had on him seemed trivial and unimportant, like my ob-session over him had been a million years ago. Because of those feelings, I had put Nate in danger without knowing it. From the day of the accident that took my mother's life, I felt the dominoes of fate tipping, crashing forward one by one until they brought me here—standing by Nate's ICU bed—and a powerful dark feeling came over me.

Was I too late?

The Nate I crushed on had been a healthy, confident, amazing guy who was gone now. Only a very sick boy had been left behind. *A dying boy.* Even if I dared to dream that he might survive his ordeal, what would he remember? He'd be changed forever, because of me. I'd gone into this blind with no idea what I was doing.

His body could be nothing more than an empty shell. Death might have already taken his soul and robbed him of the essence of who he was and highjacked his memories of the people he cared for most and who loved him back. I touched his cheek and his skin felt cold. The boy with the warm flushed skin that I had kissed on my mountain was only a distant memory. And with the shadows under his eyes, Nate looked like he was beyond my help—or anyone's.

Why did I ever think I could make a difference? I was a joke. *A loser.* I was Necro Girl, queen of the walking wounded. *Why was I even here?*

"It's not fair. You can't let him die, not like this," I whispered as tears rolled down my face. "Not because of me."

"Who are you talking to, Abbey?"

I heard Tanner's voice, but couldn't say anything, or even turn around. I wouldn't take my eyes off Nate, not even for my best friend. There was too much at stake that he didn't understand. Even though my grief-stricken mind reeled with what Death had told me, I struggled to remember everything. I had a feeling it would be important.

The Angel of Death said that his greatest fear had been living an eternity, feeling nothing and that dying might be a welcomed alternative. I didn't know what he meant then, but I did now. The darkest of angels had wanted to know the whole human experience. He'd taken everything from Nate.

Now Death wanted his last breath, too.

"You're still in him, aren't you? You want to know what it's like to die." My throat wedged tight and I felt a new swell of tears. "You once told me that suicide was a profound waste, that it squandered life, yet what do you call this? You're done with immortality, aren't you? If you want to call it quits, no one can stop you, but why take Nate with you? What happens to my mom's soul if you die? Every soul you hold should be precious to you. They're your responsibility. Why have you stopped caring?"

With all Death's talk—of living through infinity feeling nothing—I sensed he grasped for the human experience of dying, too. The longer Nate was possessed by Death, the weaker the dark angel got. I had seen that with my own eyes on the mountain. Although Death had told me that was an outcome he hadn't expected, because no being had ever done what he did before—maybe dying had become something Death craved now...*for himself.*

Who knew what it would be like to exist for an eternity as a collector of souls, only knowing duty and being alone forever? Thinking of him in that way made me ache with sadness. Yet no one would appreciate the quirk of fate more than Death with his dark sense of irony—that in learning how to live, he'd soon know what it would be like to die.

Although he had told me how much he valued human life, he'd made bargains with my mother and had taken over Nate's body to become human...to be with me. So it wasn't hard to believe he'd be willing to sacrifice one human life to end his suffering and escape an eternity of feeling nothing.

I suddenly knew Death wouldn't listen to me. I had to think of another way to stop what was happening.

"Nate? Are you still in there?"

"Abbey, what's going on? You're going Blair Witch on me." Tanner rolled his wheelchair closer. I felt him behind me, but I couldn't stop.

"Look at me, Nate. Open your eyes and really see me," I begged. Reaching for his hand, I squeezed it. I had to know if he was still in there. "I'm here, holding your hand. Reach out like you did before, with your mind. You were strong enough once. I know you can do it again."

The hiss of the ventilator and the beeping of the heart monitor was all I heard. Nate lay stone-cold still. Not even his eyes twitched. Only his chest heaved from the ventilator pumping into him.

"Nate, do it for your family. Zoey needs you. She's here at the hospital. Be strong for her," I pleaded. "My mother traded places with me the day of our accident. She died for me. That's how much she loved me. I've seen that same love in your mother's eyes, Nate. She needs you to fight back. We all do."

Still nothing. I squeezed his hand and laced my fingers in his. Heat rose to my face as an overwhelming sense of panic closed in. Nate was slipping away and I wasn't strong enough. I lowered the bed rail to be closer to him and I touched his chest to make a connection.

When I still felt nothing, I let the words come from my heart, holding nothing back.

"Don't make me have to live with what I've done. I'm not as strong as you. *Please!*"

Shutting my eyes tight, I collapsed on his bed, laying my head on his chest. I heard his heart beating, but I knew machines were helping him do that. It felt as if Nate was already gone and the worst was yet to come. I'd have to deal with what would happen next. All the pain I'd felt since my mother's death, I knew would magnify for every one of Nate's family—especially Zoey.

I didn't know how I would live with that.

"Abbey?"

I heard Tanner's voice like it came from a faraway place.

"Abbey, look at him. Can you see it?" When Tanner finally got through to me, I dared to open my eyes and stare down at Nate.

It took a while before he came into focus, but this time when I saw him, I noticed what Tanner had seen. Nate's

eyes moved under his lids. It felt like he was in there, struggling to open them. With him stirring, monitors beeped
and alerts went off. My alone time with him had run out.
The nurses and doctors would be rushing in.

I didn't know whether to laugh or cry. I thought what I
saw was a good thing—*but I was dead wrong.*

From deep inside Nate's body, a ghostlike image heaved
from his chest and arms, struggling to break free. Nate split
in two and blinding spears of light erupted from him. Covering my eyes, I stumbled back and tripped over Tanner's
wheelchair. When I collapsed onto his lap, he held me tight
and pulled away from the bed. Something massive separated
from Nate's body, cutting through him and splitting him
apart with an intense light.

"What's happening, Abbey?" Tanner yelled. "What the
hell is that thing?"

Through my gapping fingers, I squinted into the light.
My eyes burned and watered, but I couldn't look away. I
had to see it. I had to know for sure.

"Oh, my, God," I gasped. "I was right. He's still here."

"Who is, Abbey?" Tanner grabbed me tighter and rolled
his wheelchair farther away. "What's happening to Nate?"

Before I could explain, the piercing streaks of light jutted
from Nate's body until the ICU room filled with a spiraling
cloud that pulsed and glowed as the energy passed through
him. When I glared into the hovering light, my eyes watered and my hair swept back as if I stood in a strong wind,
until the entity took a familiar shape.

Gone was the gentle boy made of clouds and sky. In his
place rose a powerful being, with energy radiating around
me and through me. Static electricity zapped my body,
making my skin tingle even through my clothes. Jolts of en-

ergy pricked my skin in a million jabs of a needle and when a blaring heart monitor sent out a high-pitched alert, the bed rails rattled from the pressure building in the room. My ears popped and a jarring pain shot down my back. When the light hurt my eyes, I turned away and saw Tanner.

He'd be a sitting duck, another guy I could hurt because of Death's obsession with me.

"Tanner, we gotta get out of here. Move it. *Now!*"

I waved my hands, begging him to open the door and let me back him out of the room. No time to turn his wheelchair around. On instinct, he did as I said, keeping his eyes on the growing light behind me. The fear I saw in Tanner's eyes scared the hell out of me.

After he flung the glass door open, I gripped my hands to his armrests and pushed him backward. With me straddling the threshold of the room, before I let him go, I saw a sea of white running toward us. Nurses and doctors—and Nate's mother—were rushing for his room.

Time had run out. I couldn't hesitate now. I locked my gaze on Tanner and for a split second, I saw the fear in his eyes...*for me*. He knew what I would do.

"I'm sorry," I told him.

It was all I had time to say before I shoved my best friend out of Nate's room with all my strength into the hall.

"Abbey? What are you doing? *No!*" he yelled.

I shut the ICU door behind him and wedged a metal chair under the handle so I'd be alone—the way I knew it had to be.

Only precious seconds remained. With a hand shielding my eyes from the fierce light, I turned to confront my fate. No going back now. If the Angel of Death wanted to take me—to collect my soul in place of Nate's—I'd have no way to stop him.

It'd been the bargain I made and a promise I would keep...*for Nate.*

abbey   chapter 17

Fairbanks Memorial Hospital

Outside the chair barricade that I'd made at Nate's door,
the ICU alarms and hysterical voices made me a gnarly
wad of nerves—stripped raw by an overdose of guilt—but
two people made me cry. The voices of Tanner and Nate's
mother gripped me hard. They made me realize what I'd
be doing to my father, too. I hated what I'd done—_to all
of them_—but my life wouldn't mean much if Nate died. I
couldn't live with that.

Some things were worth dying for and Nate's life would
be my line in the sand.

If things turned out for the worst, my father and my best
friend would pay a price for what I was about to do. They
wouldn't understand why I had to do this and I wouldn't
get a chance to explain, but I couldn't do anything about
that now.

With my shoulder jammed against the door, I felt someone pounding on the other side. It wouldn't take long for

them to muscle aside the chair I had wedged under the doorknob. With every strike of that fist, the hammering sent a shock wave down my spine that mirrored the trembling I felt deep in my bones after I'd turned to see the Angel of Death hovering over Nate's body.

Gone was the boy with amazing blue eyes and an ethereal body that brimmed with a summer's day. In his place soared the darkest of angels embodied in a vile and deadly storm. I wanted to scream, but I couldn't. My throat had wedged tight. In that instant when I didn't believe things could get any worse, they did.

With the terrifying image of Death laying claim to Nate seared into my brain, everything in the room switched to pitch-black. Sudden darkness threw me into a tailspin and made me dizzy. I didn't know if I stood still or had fallen through inky blackness. I felt lost and helpless, with nothing but a ghost image of Nate in trouble to taunt my eyes after the lights went out.

The hospital room had disappeared and the pounding on the door and the incessant alarms drifted into a muffled echo. Those sounds were masked by something worse— the menacing rumble of Death's dark storm-gathering force over my head. Everything around me shifted into murky shadows, leaving only the bluish haze of a turbulent moonlit night.

After my eyes adjusted to the deepening shadows, I fumbled through the dark for Nate and found him still in his hospital bed. As if I was caught in a nightmare, tendrils of lightning pierced the eerie darkness and with every earpiercing crack, I cringed. Cocooned in Death's rage, I had no way to escape. He'd blocked out my world and put up a barrier between me and everything I knew.

I didn't have to be dead to realize this was a very bad sign.

The storm intensified and with every jagged streak of lightning that shot across the emptiness, I saw glimpses of Nate under that maddening strobe. The eruption of light made him look sicker. And when static energy prickled every follicle of my hair, my skin crawled with the sensation of unwanted fingers trailing over my body. I wanted to run, but I had nowhere to go. Death had made escape impossible. I felt cornered with an unconscious Nate in the dark angel's grip.

The immortal had unleashed his power and took control.

When I looked into the eye of that fierce storm, a huge shadow spread its inky black across the void, unfurling its menacing fingers like an oil slick. A pair of black wings ruptured the dark billows of clouds. The feathery shadow magnified and grew as the night sky fractured with lightning to stretch the dark angel's reach across the vast emptiness.

The Angel of Death reminded me who he was.

"Why are you doing this?" I yelled as I grabbed Nate's hand. "You lied when you said you loved me. *You're a liar!*"

Squinting, I turned my face and stared into the ominous, swelling cloud.

"Being inside someone special like Nate, didn't that teach you anything?"

Maybe I had a helluva lot more to lose—dealing with an immortal being who had far too many ways to torture me—but it didn't feel that way. I felt up against it and the odds weren't good that I'd walk away from this.

"You know nothing about my mother and her love for me, not if you can hurt Nate and scare me," I accused. "If you're gonna take my soul, then do it, but I'll fight you for

Nate's life. We had a bargain. Or did you lie about that, too?"

The gravity of what I said hit me hard. If Death had lied about everything, I had no reason to expect him to save the life of an innocent boy. I tightened my grip on Nate's hand and glared into the thunderstorm, but my defiance was all for show. I had nothing to fight with. I'd relied on Death playing fair. *What an idiot I'd been!*

If the dark angel wanted to reap both our souls, he could do it. Death tested any courage I had left, but for Nate's sake, I had to stay strong.

"You're mean and cruel. Nothing but a bully," I screamed. "Whatever made you think you could be human anyway? Being human takes heart and compassion and you don't have it. Maybe you never did."

It hurt me to say these things to him. I still had feelings that were jumbled up in the crush I used to have on Nate. Feelings like that didn't go away overnight, despite what I'd told Tanner. I felt like a hypocrite.

If I thought Death had been mean and cruel, returning the favor didn't feel like a solution. But anger had its grips into me now and I wasn't clever enough to find another way to get through to him. I clutched Nate's hand and shut my eyes. Waiting for Death's final retaliation with a prayer on my lips, I let memories of my mother flood my mind. She was my only comfort now. She always had been.

I love you, Momma. I made my peace with her and thought of my dad as I waited for what would come next.

The minute Abbey had shoved him out of Nate's ICU room, Tanner felt as if something went wrong with his ears. The creature that had risen from Nate's body looked like a ghostly spirit out of a horror flick. Medical alarms went off and the rumble of an approaching storm gained momentum like the quickening undercurrent of the *Jaws* theme song, but once Abbey pushed him into the hall, all the intense commotion stopped at the slam of that door.

What the hell was going on? In the corridor outside Nate's hospital room, it looked as if nothing much had happened. The closed door and shut drapes had gotten attention, but nothing else. Tanner could have sworn that alarms went off. How in the hell didn't anyone hear the noise once that creature hatched out of Nate's body?

He wanted to ask why they hadn't made a big deal about it, but kept his mouth shut after he saw the look on the face of Nate's mother. She looked worried. Why make it worse? Explaining now would only earn him a psych evaluation and a fitting for a straitjacket.

"Why can't I open this door? My son is in there." Mrs. Holden tried the knob again, without success. When she turned, she didn't look for a nurse or doctor. She drilled her gaze at Tanner and he swallowed, hard.

He'd become the one piece of the puzzle that didn't belong in Intensive Care and she'd picked up on that.

"You were with that girl...the one in the waiting area. Is she in there with my son?" Nate's mom honed in on what she remembered of Abbey.

Looking into the woman's eyes, Tanner didn't have the heart to lie to her, not even for Abbey. A mother with a sick son deserved the truth.

"Abbey knows Nate, Mrs. Holden," Tanner said. "She only wants to talk to him for a minute. I swear. She'd never hurt him. She really...cares for the guy."

It pained him to admit that Abbey had real feelings for

Nate, but it was the truth. He hadn't lied. Guys like Nate
would *always* get the girl.

"How did you get into ICU?" This time a nurse took
over the interrogation, but when Tanner didn't answer, the
woman in uniform looked past him to someone else. "Call
security. Now."

Tanner could have left the scene of the crime using all
the fuss as cover. He'd be in enough trouble with his parents, but he wouldn't leave Abbey. Instead, he stayed put
and knocked on the door like he had every right to do it.

"Abbey? Please...open up."

He listened for any sound coming from inside the room.
When he didn't hear anything out of the ordinary, he
looked down at the base of the door. That's when he saw
it. A dark shadow spilled onto the floor like an oil slick under the door. Something bad was happening inside.

And Abbey faced it alone.

"Open the door, Abbey." He pounded with a fist.
"Please!"

Abbey

Seconds later

With my eyes shut tight, I held my breath and waited for
Death to take my soul. Muffling in my ears, the pounding
of my heart was the only thing that told me I still lived. But
in a split second—as I held Nate's hand with thoughts of
my mother flashing through my head—the howling winds
and dark clouds of Death's abuse stopped. An eerie stillness replaced it as if I'd slipped into the eye of a hurricane.

In shock, I opened my eyes with a gasp caught in my throat.

I stood in Nate's ICU room and still held his hand, like nothing had happened. The equipment that kept him alive went back to its normal state, steadily beeping at every beat of his heart and the ventilator continued to breathe for him. Even the thumping at the door, that had mirrored my heart throttling, turned into a persistent knock, instead of a frantic urgent one. From the looks of it, everything that I'd witnessed had been an illusion.

The mind-bending chaos had vanished. Or more likely, Death had made me see and hear what he'd wanted, to scare me. Hard to imagine that the gentle boy who had kissed me on the ridge—and had wanted to know what it felt like to be loved—had tried to hurt me.

"Abbey? Please open the door." Tanner's voice.

"What's happening? I have to see my son," Mrs. Holden begged.

Death's storm had vanished as fast as it had come, but when I looked up from Nate, it surprised me to see that the dark angel was still with me.

He'd turned back into the boy I had always remembered, made of cloud animals adrift in an azure sky. His mesmerizing and ethereal body—that looked as light and as airy as whisper-thin gauze—took shape in front of me. He blinked with wide blue eyes, the color of the deep ocean. Once again, Death filled the room with comforting warmth that drained the last of my fear. A pulse of glimmering light replaced the menacing lightning and looked like the dazzle of the sun on water.

I wanted to believe our ordeal had ended, but the Angel of Death had made a bargain with me—my soul for Nate's life. I waited for him to hold out his hand for me to take it and seal our deal, but he showed me something else in the blue sky that he wore, his precious collection of souls.

I saw the face of my mother. She looked younger than I had remembered and more beautiful, if that was even possible. When she smiled at me, her eyes glistened with tears. She could see me…*really see me.*

"Oh, Momma. I'm sorry," I whispered. "I miss you…so much."

All the feelings I had for my mother welled inside me—things I had never said to her—but as I told her how I felt aloud, she smiled at me again. I wanted to hold her, to hear her voice one more time, but as my fingers reached out for her, something broke my connection.

"No!" Nate choked the only word he could muster. Struggling against his ventilator, he grabbed my arm and stopped me. He gagged on the tube down his throat. When his mother sensed his distress, even from outside his room, she cried out.

"Nate, is that you? Oh, my, God. I hear him. My son's awake." Mrs. Holden sobbed and pounded on the door. "What's going on in there? Please…open the door."

With all his strength, Nate pulled me away from the very being that had stolen his body and almost took his soul. As weak as he looked, he interfered with Death to keep me from touching him.

"I'll get your mom," I promised him. "And a nurse."

Despite what I'd told Nate, I wasn't sure Death would let me help. Nate looked alive for the first time since I'd walked into his hospital room, but would the dark angel let him stay that way? I had an urge to shove aside the chair I'd wedged at the door—and let Nate's mother and the nurses into the room—but something stopped me. If Death wasn't willing to give up Nate, I could get more people in trouble if I opened that door.

So I did the only thing I could. I looked into the angel's blue eyes and said, "Let Nate live. If you still want my soul, I'll go with you." It was the promise I had offered and had always intended to keep.

Death stared at me with his hypnotic eyes and blinked twice. Without Nate, he couldn't speak—or feel—yet the faint expression I saw on his ghostly haunted face made him look sad, as if his fleeting human experience lingered. For his sake, I hoped I was wrong. Death looked at me the way he did on the day of the accident, when he first crossed my path. He stared as if he memorized every detail of my face. It wasn't until he vanished seconds later that I realized.

In the only way he could, Death had said goodbye.

He'd let Nate live and I still breathed…at least until the day I'd inevitably see him again, for real. I stood in the middle of that ICU room, shaking and in shock. Our ordeal had suddenly ended, but Nate needed his mother and medical attention. I rushed to the door and thrust aside the chair I'd shoved under the knob, letting time and reality rush in again.

Mrs. Holden burst through the door first. With only a sideways glance at me—more like a questioning glare—she rushed to Nate. Crying and kissing him, she couldn't keep her hands off his face, not even to let nurses work on him. Eventually his mom stepped away and let others do the job of taking out his ventilator tube and checking his vital signs.

But even from across the room—with the distractions of people and questions—Nate kept his eyes on me. I had to admit, that scared me. I was on Nate's radar…and not in a

good way. I knew I'd have explaining to do—*to everyone*.
Every eye in the room eventually found me, even after I'd
done my best to stay out of the way and keep a low profile.

If I could become smaller, I would have totally done it. I
was back to wishing I were a fly that could buzz away without someone swatting me, but when Tanner rolled close and
reached for my hand, all bets were off.

I completely broke down.

I collapsed onto his lap and hugged him, burying my face
in his neck. Every emotion I'd held back came at me in a
sudden rush. I realized that Tanner had become my anchor,
the guy who kept me connected to what really mattered.
In his arms, I felt safe.

"You did it, Abbey. You really saved him," he whispered
in my ear, only loud enough for me to hear.

As Tanner held me, I swear I felt him crying, too. From
that moment, I knew I'd always have a soft spot for boy
tears—and for guys who did the right thing, even if it hurt.
As I hugged Tanner and cried, I couldn't help but think of
what nearly happened to me…and Nate.

Death eventually did the right thing, but his sacrifice had
come at a price.

The Angel of Death had disappeared and taken my mom
with him. Although he'd left me emptier than I ever felt
before, I wanted to believe that my mother's soul would be
safe in his care. I hoped that's why he let me see her, so I
wouldn't worry. In the end, he'd done the right thing and
letting me see my mother one last time felt like a gift.

For a brief instant of his forever, Death hadn't been perfect or godlike. He'd been vengeful and cruel to Nate and
to me, but had it been more than that? Maybe he raged
against the injustice of an existence that was dominated by

duty and sense of purpose. If he did, who could blame him? I couldn't do his job—completely alone for an eternity—not without lashing out in anger at someone, too. He would be forever looking in from the outside, seeing a world and a life that he envied. Maybe that's why he never intended to have a human heart. Living the life he did would hurt too much for any one soul to endure.

By letting Nate and me live, I wanted to believe that Death had come to the realization that the importance of his duty—being the caretaker of souls—outweighed his need to be loved.

Yet how could I wish that for him...*for anyone?*

From the look on Nate's face as he stared at me from his hospital bed—the strained questioning expression that he reserved only for me—I knew he wouldn't feel the same about Death. The last thing he'd feel was grateful that the dark angel let him live. Nate had every right to be hostile. From the intimidating look in his eyes, the guy had built a good head of steam. I only hoped he didn't believe in guilt by association.

If he did, I would be in deep trouble.

abbey   chapter 18

Near Healy, Alaska
Hours later

After we left Fairbanks Memorial Hospital, it was too late for Tanner to go back to Palmer, even if his parents would have let him, which they didn't. If the one-sided conversation he had with his dad on the phone was any indication, tomorrow would suck for Tanner. Because they'd have two cars to drive back, both his parents were driving to Healy to pick him up. That would *not* be good and Tanner knew it.

His last night of real freedom would be spent with us in our cabin. I made up the couch for him to sleep on. It was the first time I'd had him at the cabin, but if I had anything to say about it, it wouldn't be the last.

To distract Tanner from the misery of facing his parents tomorrow, I stayed up with him, talking by the fire. Dad snored in his bedroom. With a boy in the cabin, my father had good intentions of being a typical dad. He hadn't closed his door when he went to bed. Guess he figured he could spring into action if Tanner went into predator mode with me, but Dad never got the chance to show his stuff. The late night at the hospital and the road trip back to Healy had taken a toll on his parental stamina. After I heard Dad catching his share of Zs, I knew I could really talk to Tanner.

I told him everything.

Saying the angel's name aloud had been the hardest. Hearing the words *Angel of Death* brought a rush of emotions I hadn't seen coming. Even though I covered up the fear I still felt about the nightmare I'd lived through, that scare would shadow me. The wound felt too fresh to make light of it and the other thoughts I had about Death would take longer to figure out. I guess that showed, too. I must've sounded like a delusional psycho to my best friend.

But Tanner surprised me.

I'd expected typical Lange mode, a mix of questions and smart-ass remarks, but that's not what happened. He sat beside me in his wheelchair, staring into the fire, listening to every word I said without interrupting. As I stared at him, telling my crazy version of the truth, I realized something.

I'd let Tanner cross a line that made him more than a friend. I'd kissed him and liked it and I wanted more, but I wasn't sure I deserved a guy like him. Maybe that wouldn't be up to only me. I knew Tanner liked me, too. I mean, really liked me…like a regular girl. But I felt scared that I'd screw up our friendship.

"You're kind of quiet," I said. "What are you thinking, Tanner?"

While I waited for his answer, I took a mental snapshot of him. I always wanted to remember Tanner like this. The flames flickering on his adorable face stirred something in me. Being alone with him, talking like a real guy and girl, poked at my heart in a way I'd never felt before.

"Yeah, well...I've got lots of questions about you facing down the Grim Reaper," he said. "I mean, what the hell were you thinking, seriously?"

Tanner didn't expect an answer and I loved that he totally believed me, without making fun. But when his expression changed, I braced for what I knew would come.

"I'm having a hard time getting past the kiss. You kissed Nate Holden, Abbey."

"He kissed me...first." The minute I said the word *first*, I knew it had been a mistake. Tanner was too damned smart to let that go.

"You kissed him more than once?" He shook his head and couldn't look me in the eye. "I know you've had a crush on the guy. That's not something you can switch on and off. It just...hurts, Abbey. I mean, angels and demons aside, you thought you were kissing Nate Holden and he still goes to our school. I don't think I could deal with—" He didn't finish.

As the silence built up between us—filled by the crackling fire and Dad in the next room—I wanted to say *anything* that would make him feel better, but I had no idea what that would be.

"This is my problem, not yours," he said. "Guess I haven't been very honest. I pretended I didn't care that you liked the guy, but *surprise*." He held up both hands, pretending it was party time, but his eyes sent another message. "I do care, Abbey. I couldn't stand it if you can't shake your feelings for him. I feel like a...*damned jerk*."

I didn't want to smile, but I couldn't help it. Hearing

Tanner's roundabout confession made me feel good, despite the fact that he looked totally miserable.

"Hey, quit calling my best friend a jerk. Only I get to do that." I reached for his hand and laced my fingers in his and he let me.

"Since we're on an honesty bender, it's my turn." I squeezed his hand. "Somewhere I crossed a line with you that I didn't see coming, Tanner. Yeah, I had a crush on Nate, but those feelings weren't anything compared to how I feel about you. Nate was like a wake-up call. He made me realize that I was ready to have a special boy in my life, but you made me see that I already had one. You're not just my best friend. You're more than that, but that's what scares me. I'm afraid of screwing up what we have…and losing you. That would kill me."

"Yeah?"

I nodded.

After a long silence, he smiled and said, "Then we won't screw this up."

We both knew it wouldn't be as easy as that, but for one night, simple worked. No drama felt like a vacation. He told me how much it hurt him that I didn't share my guilt over my mother's death and we talked about his four-wheeler accident, too. He shared things he never told me before, things I always imagined that he'd tell a real girlfriend. He told me how it hurt to find out who his real friends were after the accident and how sometimes, he could still feel his legs. I thought I knew Tanner, but I realized after tonight that I had only scratched the surface of discovering him.

"This reaper guy." Tanner shook his head. "Whenever you talk about him, you act like he's…human, like he's a regular guy, but that's not what I saw. Which is it? Human or the next star of a Wes Craven horror flick?"

"You got a glimpse of something that scared me, too. I guess I'm still sorting through it all, but it's not that simple…for me."

Tanner smiled and leaned over to kiss the back of my hand, not taking his eyes off me.

"I'm real proud of you, Abbey. What you did took guts."

"Well, I don't know about guts, but I sure got a lot of mileage out of pissed." I grinned. "Thanks for trusting me."

Tanner only nodded and teased me with his dimples. When we were done talking, I curled up in his lap and kissed him. The friendship we shared made that easy, yet a part of me felt really scared. We'd stepped over a line that we'd never get back and if something happened between us, I risked losing my best friend and someone I'd made a home for in my heart.

But with his arms around me and the warmth of the fire at my back, it felt easy to love Tanner Lange. I couldn't imagine a planet or an alternative universe where that would ever change, but tomorrow would test the new feelings we were discovering for each other.

After hospital security lost interest in me, my dad made a promise to Mrs. Holden that he'd bring me by the hospital to see Nate tomorrow. I knew Tanner would want to come, but after our big reveal, any time I spent with Nate alone had the potential to weird him out. Tanner told me he understood, but his eyes communicated something his mouth hadn't said. His brain might have understood, but his heart would be another story.

I hoped that by seeing Nate Holden, I'd put an end to

the chapter in my life when my crush on him ruled everything. Ready to move on, I didn't feel like a kid anymore.

Mostly, I prayed that I'd never hurt Tanner again.

Fairbanks Memorial Hospital
The next day

Round after round, doctors came and went, even ones not
involved with Nate's case. He watched them flip every page
of his med chart, looking for a reason that they never found.
"You're a miracle," they told him.

Nate had survived a documented brain swell as if it never
happened. The only thing left behind had been an annoy-
ing headache and a trail of nurses who gave him way too
much attention. Some of them even brought coworkers to
point and stare at him through the glass, whispering as they
shook their heads or smiled and waved.

He felt like he was on the wrong side of a cage at the zoo.

Yeah, he'd been damned lucky, and so had Josh. He
hadn't seen his best friend, but later today hospital staff
promised to bring him for a visit if Josh felt up to it. The
only reason Nate remained in ICU was for observation, but
later he'd be moved to a private room so Zoey could visit.
If things went well, he'd go home soon.

Home. He loved the sound of that word, but something
in him would never be the same again and he knew it. Nate
wanted his life back. He wanted to feel bulletproof again,
but that wouldn't happen. He had almost died and that
changed everything. The strangers in and out of his room
were a reminder of that. He heard the media had covered
his story, too. Because of that, things would be worse when

he got out. He wouldn't get his old life back—at least, not soon enough.

He wanted to be left alone with his family and even though he didn't understand what happened to him, he suspected Abbey Chandler could shed some light. His life and any hope he had of getting back to normal would depend on her.

His mother had arranged for Abbey to visit him. That's why he waited with his eyes on constant alert for any movement outside his room. He'd asked his family to give him space and they'd left the hospital for a bite to eat. He needed to talk to Abbey alone. With the clock ticking down, he got jumpier.

What the hell was wrong with him?

Nate ran a hand through his hair. After he poured a cup of water, he took a gulp as he heard a voice at the door. *A girl's voice.*

"Hey, Nate," she said. "I know I'm early. Is it okay if I come in?"

A chunk of ice went down the wrong way. He nearly gagged.

"Uh, yeah, no p-problem," he choked. "C-come on in."

Abbey Chandler looked prettier than he remembered her. Instead of wearing sweats or oversize clothes like she sometimes wore at school, she had on jeans and a pale pink ski jacket that brought out the color on her cheeks.

But seeing her face-to-face—up close and for real—had turned into a déjà vu Nate didn't know what to make of. He stared at her now, trying to put her face in context to a memory, but all that came up were weird images of seeing her through the eyes of someone else. It took him a moment to realize that he stroked the cut on his hand, the wound that had jolted him into seeing her in the first place, by that fire. He felt trapped, suffocating in a sudden wave of claustrophobia. Glimpses of her reminded him of slasher flicks where the camera shot through the eyes of a predator as it watched its victims.

Why was this happening?

In vague glimpses, he remembered seeing Abbey at school and around Palmer, but it wouldn't be until he got trapped in a crevasse on Denali that her face triggered the best and the worst of what he'd experienced. *Why her?* He hadn't officially met her before she came to the hospital. Why would he conjure her out of thin air, literally? Looking back on what happened to him after the avalanche, he couldn't be sure any of it had been real. Maybe his memories on Denali were nothing more than strange hallucinations.

His head trauma could have caused *everything*.

"Your mom said you wanted to see me." Abbey looked nervous and she had a hard time looking him in the eye.

Truthfully, he felt the same.

"Yeah, I did. I mean, I do." He pointed across the room. "Pull up a chair. If it's okay, maybe we can talk."

"Sure."

He forced polite conversation, stalling. Bizarre things had happened and with his brain still sorting things out, he couldn't be sure what he wanted to say to her.

The ranger who found him on Denali said he didn't have a pulse—that he'd been dead—but Nate knew that the extreme cold might have made his pulse slow to virtually nothing. Doctors later told him that his body had shut down. Like a bear in hibernation, only his essential functions kept going. Every ounce of reserves that he had left went to keeping him alive. After he'd been rescued, his body had been jumpstarted again by paramedics. That's what it must have been.

Telling anyone about the strange creature that had invaded his body—a memory that he still couldn't accept—would have made him sound like a freak. Every kid in school would never let him live it down, especially if Josh couldn't back him up. Hell, even if he could, why would he? Head trauma and his near-death experience had put his mind and body through a wringer. That would be an easier thing to believe and talk about.

Dismissing the weirdness of his ordeal would have been easy except for the one glaring reason looking at him now. Abbey Chandler sat by his hospital bed, staring at him like she knew him. She'd brought him back from wherever he'd been. *That*, he felt pretty sure of, but why he'd been so certain scared him. He always thought that he understood what "normal" meant, but for the first time, he wasn't sure.

For the first time, he didn't feel safe. Before he made his trek up Denali, he had a future ahead of him, but in one dark instant, all that changed. He almost died. Abbey Chandler would always remind him of that.

She could confirm or deny, and tip his world over the edge. In a small town the size of Palmer, she could make his life a living hell if she spilled her guts and cut loose with all the wrong stuff. He didn't know her well enough to trust her. They could both mess each other's lives up, when all he wanted was to be left alone.

Everything hinged on Abbey.

"I remember you from school, but I'm sorry," he said. "I'm kind of hazy on stuff. How did we meet?"

"Well, um. Here's the thing…"

As Abbey talked, Nate only half listened. He'd made up his mind about the girl. For whatever reason—however he would explain it later—he knew one thing remained clear in his memory.

Abbey Chandler had played a part in his ordeal, a very big part. He would always be grateful to her for pulling him through it. Even if he'd been the one who conjured her up, for some strange reason he had latched onto her as his savior, a feeling he'd probably never shake or explain. He may not have remembered much about Abbey Chandler before, but in the blink of an eye, everything had changed.

I see you now, Abbey.

He'd also made up his mind about one other thing. He would never talk about the being that had taken over his body. Not to her. Not to anyone.

Ever.

Abbey

I'd never actually talked to Nate Holden, unless I counted the fantasies I'd had about him. The Nate in my dreams had always been perfect, but the guy who nearly died on Denali looked…vulnerable. After being with Tanner, I knew when someone really listened to me and Nate wasn't. He looked distracted and nervous. I'd never seen him like that before.

But even under the influence of his near-death experience, with the haunting shadows under his eyes from his ordeal, seeing him up close still had an effect on me. I didn't know who I actually saw anymore.

"You look better today," I said.

I forced a smile as my stomach reminded me that I hadn't eaten much. I felt too jacked up to eat my usual cereal.

When his lips curved into a smile, I had to ask, "What?"

"Considering I was practically in a coma, *better* is not exactly a lofty goal."

"Well, when you put it like that..." My chuckle fell flat and sounded strained.

Another awkward silence. I waited for Nate to bring up what he had on his mind without me pulling it from him. I could tell he had something he wanted to ask or say and I wasn't sure how much he remembered.

"Did you drive up from Palmer?" he asked. "I mean, why did you come? How did you know...about me?"

Catching him up on what had happened felt weird. It felt as if he was making fun of me, like he knew more, but was only testing me.

"I was already near Healy. I came with my dad after school let out. We have a cabin there." I nodded. "When I saw the news, I came...to see if I could help."

"Help?" He narrowed his eyes. "How?"

Okay, I hadn't handled that well. If I intended to walk away from Nate and close the chapter of my life that had his name on it, I had to do better. I went on the offensive—to see how much he remembered.

"Honestly, I don't really know. Since we went to school together, I just had to come." I shrugged. "On the news, it sounded really bad. I thought you and Josh had...died."

"Still here." He tried to laugh, but his heart wasn't in it. "Josh got the worst of it. He's the lucky one."

"You both are." I shrugged out of my jacket and laid it on my lap. "Do you remember much...about what happened on Denali, I mean?"

Nate had a hard time meeting my gaze. I knew what it felt like, to survive steep odds that made no sense. As a kid, you never think bad stuff will happen to you. When it does, it knocks you flat on your ass and I swear, you never want to get up again. Eventually you have to and the flip side of your life can either make or break you. The jury was still out on me.

For Nate's sake, I hoped he'd be stronger.

"Not really. All the bad stuff is a blur." Stalling, he grabbed his cup and downed more water.

"But when you saw me here yesterday, you acted like you knew me," I said. "I don't mean how you knew me from school. You looked at me funny, like you knew something I didn't. What was that all about?"

After a long moment, he eventually said, "I don't know. I was pretty out of it. Guess I don't remember."

"You grabbed my arm. You yelled, 'No!' You don't remember what that was for?"

"No, why would I?" he asked. "I had a concussion."

"*Had* a concussion. What? You got over it? How does that happen?" I wasn't angry. I wanted to know if he just played me, or not.

"And what? You couldn't send a get-well card? Why did you make a big deal about seeing me in ICU, Abbey? I mean, we don't even really know each other."

Okay, I deserved that. Thanks to my inner smart-ass, I trod on dangerous ground now.

"You're right. I'm sorry. The last thing you need is crap from me. It's just that I know what it's like to be in here, when you're hurting…and your mind is trippin'. It's not fun. So what are the doctors saying?"

He shrugged.

"Doctors call it a miracle, but…" His voice sounded distant and sad, especially when he said, "I just want my life back."

I remembered what that felt like—to want something that would never happen. Before I knew it, I reached through the bed rail and grabbed his hand. I could tell by the look on his face that I surprised him, but he didn't pull away.

"Five years ago, I was in a really bad car accident. Things happened. Stuff I still don't remember." I wanted to look at him, but I couldn't. Everything I wanted to say felt too personal. "Being a survivor, your mind will play tricks on you. It'll take time to sort it out, but you're a strong guy. You'll get through it."

I told Nate about the car wreck that nearly killed me. Of course, I left out the part about me actually dying…and that Death knew me by my first name now, but it felt natural to share my experience with him. I finally had his full attention. When he squeezed my hand back, I knew we'd connected in a way that may never happen again.

"I guess what I'm saying is, surviving something really bad can change you. The person you were…well, he's done now, you know?" I looked him square in the eye. "But you don't have to let what happened take over your life. You can start fresh. Not many people get a second chance to get it right, you know?"

Nate stared at me. He didn't nod or make a big deal about what I'd said, but I could tell he really heard me. I didn't have the heart to say that the life he'd get back wouldn't be the same life, but he'd realize that soon enough. After he got stronger, he could deal with it.

Okay, I had to admit. It shocked me that I'd given him

advice. I considered myself the poster child for dysfunctional. *Damn.*

I resisted the urge to ask him about our kiss. That kiss hadn't actually been with him. I'd kissed a dark angel, a beautiful blue-eyed boy made of clouds and sky who only wanted to know what it felt like to love and be loved, to feel something beyond a forever of nothing. Death had come to me because of my mother's love—a force within him that he couldn't refuse—that fed his need to feel human. But my mom had something to do with that, too. She came to my rescue, knowing I had to deal with what happened or else I wouldn't have a life at all. And irony of ironies, Death had been her messenger.

But none of that had anything to do with Nate. I knew that now.

My fantasies about him had come from my own needs, but my feelings for Nate had always been made-up and one-sided. What I really wanted was someone to love the real me—the good, the bad and the ugly me—a real boy that didn't have to pretend to be perfect around me, either.

I had that right under my nose—with Tanner.

Now, as I stared at Nate, his blue eyes still got to me, but they looked different now. He'd always be beautiful, but underneath the surface of who he was, I saw a shadow—the glimmer of another boy who carried the soul of my mother in his arms. I'd never see the real Nate the same way again and I was okay with that.

"You look a million miles away. What are you thinking?" he asked.

"Nothing." I shook my head. "It's not…important."

Time flew by after that. Although we talked about a lot of stuff—his love for climbing, his friendship with Josh and the love he had for his little sister—his brush with death and my car accident didn't come up again. When time got short, I made my excuses and stood to leave. I knew we'd have to hit the road soon to see Tanner before he headed home. I'd left him asleep at the cabin, after we'd pulled an all-nighter.

But before I left his hospital room, Nate had something more to say.

"I'm not sure why, but I have a strong urge to…thank you, Abbey."

I grinned as I stared at the boy who had filled my fantasies with so many sweet memories, but inside I felt the bittersweet ache of letting those memories go. Maybe I should have thanked him, for very different reasons.

"You don't owe me anything. Seeing you breathing, that works for me."

I walked out, pretending to be a woman of mystery as I headed for the waiting room where my dad waited. I should have corrected Nate. I was the last person he needed to thank. I only fixed what I'd screwed up.

I wasn't fooling myself that the next time I saw Nate Holden that he'd actually acknowledge knowing me. Guess that was my way of preparing for the worst. If Nate was really a good guy, he could surprise me, but I wasn't counting on us being BFFs. We both had things we'd rather forget and seeing me would only remind him of what almost happened.

Neither of us needed that.

Two hours later

After the hospital moved him to a private room on another floor, Nate felt relieved the room had real walls and no glass. With the door closed, he didn't have the unwanted attention he'd gotten in ICU being miracle boy.

"You up for visitors?" His mother's voice followed a soft knock, but when Nate saw Zoey poke her head into his room, he grinned for real.

"Heck, yeah."

His mother held his face in both her hands and kissed him until his cheeks burned with embarrassment. After she gave him messages from his father who stayed at the motel to sleep, she stood by his bed, finger combing his hair.

"If I can find a vending machine, you want a soda?" His mom grinned, but she looked tired. "I know how you crave stuff after you come off a mountain."

"Yeah, I'd kill for a Pepsi," he said.

"Me, too." Zoey squirmed by a visitor's chair and pulled it closer to his bed.

After his mother left them alone, Zoey crawled onto the chair and used it to climb into his bed. Having Zoey close, Nate breathed in the familiar scent of her hair that smelled of vanilla and flowers, and it made him feel that getting back to normal might be possible.

Most days, Zoey was a real chatterbox, but not today. She kept her eyes on him as if he could disappear and she had to touch him.

"Did Mommy tell you?" Zoey's face turned serious. When she got this way, a little dimple over one eyebrow appeared.

"Tell me what?"

"I saw you. You were supposed to be on that mountain, but you weren't. You came home. I saw you on the drive-way outside my window." She touched his chin with a small finger. "Mommy said I dreamed it, but you were real, Nate. I swear."

His mom had already talked to him about what Zoey saw. She'd asked him about it, as if he could fill in the gaps of what really happened. With his mom, he only shrugged and refused to say much, like his sister had imagined the whole thing. That seemed to make his mom relax. Maybe one day he'd tell her the truth, but now didn't feel like the right time. His mom needed the wound to heal before she could put everything into perspective.

With Zoey, it would be different.

The truth was that he remembered doing it. At the time it felt cruel, but he couldn't help it. He thought about her and the next thing he knew, he stood on the driveway outside his house, looking up at her. He'd thought of his mom, too, but he figured Zoey was the only one who saw him and *believed*.

Telling his sister that she'd only imagined him felt like a betrayal, not after he'd looked her in the eye that night to say goodbye. With her trusting face staring at him now, it changed everything. Lying would have been simpler, but something about that little dimple over her eye felt like a truth serum.

"Were you there, Nate?"

"Yeah, I think I was." He brushed back a strand of her hair and tucked it behind her ear. "After I fell, I hurt my head. I can't remember everything, but, yeah. I saw you, Zoey. Can this be our secret...just you and me?"

"Yeah, okay." She smiled and snuggled closer. "You were crying when I saw you. Were you sad?"

"I thought I might not see you again. Yeah, I was sad."

She looked up and stared into his eyes. "Daddy said they found you because of my bracelet...the one I made for you."

Nate grinned. "Yeah, I heard that. Guess you were my lucky charm. My guardian angel."

When he pulled Zoey into a hug and shut his eyes tight, for the first time since he'd been rescued, Nate cried. He'd come close to losing everything, but Abbey Chandler had been right. He had a second chance.

Despite what happened, maybe he'd been a lucky guy after all.

"I love you, Zoey."

abbey   chapter 19

Near Healy, Alaska

By the time my dad drove me back to the cabin, I had
an hour with Tanner before his parents arrived. With my
father working outside, getting the cabin in shape for our
departure tomorrow, he'd left us alone. Maybe he'd done
that on purpose. I wanted to think that Dad had changed
and suddenly turned chill overnight, but maybe I was the
one who'd changed.

A scary thought.

As we ate cereal together, Tanner got real quiet. He
probably thought that if he asked about Nate, it would send
the message that he felt jealous. But *subtle* wasn't a word I
would ever associate with Tanner.

Nope, that word didn't fit my boy. Or me, either.

"Just so you know, Nate didn't say much," I said. "I figured he either didn't actually remember or he didn't want
to talk about it."

"Well, which is it?" Tanner shoved away his empty cereal bowl across the kitchen table.

I shrugged and said, "I wouldn't want to talk about it, would you?"

"Hell, no." He shook his head. "But if an angel high-jacked *my* body, he'd be really disappointed."

I tried not to laugh, but totally blew it. It felt good to let go with Tanner, until I shifted my gaze around the cabin and thought of my mom and dad.

"It feels like this trip has lasted a lifetime, you know?" I sighed. "But being here hasn't exactly been terrible with my dad. And I really connected with my mother…this time. I still can't believe I got to see her."

Understatement of the century. I felt a lump in my throat when I thought of Death letting me see my mom one last time. He'd given me a gift, for no reason other than he wanted to. I didn't bother to hide the tears welling in my eyes.

I didn't have to hide anything from Tanner, not anymore.

"I can feel her in this place now, but not in a creepy way, like she's haunting me," I said, staring at the collection of photos Dad had on the walls of our cabin. "And not because of these photos."

"Maybe it's you, Abbey. You found a place for her…in you." Tanner talked with a faraway voice and stared out our window. "Dealing with guilt and grief doesn't leave much room for anything else. I know about that dark stuff, but one day if you're real lucky, you get tired of feeling bad all the time. It's like a curtain opens and light comes in. First, it's only a sliver. Then more."

After a long moment of neither of us saying anything,

Tanner finally smiled and sat back in his wheelchair, coming from a shadowy place I knew he'd been before.

"I didn't know your mom long enough, but…" He nodded. "She'd be proud of you."

I wanted to think so. I really did, but when I thought of the reason I'd skipped town, avoiding the online bullies that threatened to anonymously ruin my life, my face turned from a fleeting smile to a grimace in a heartbeat. When I went back to Palmer with Dad tomorrow, I'd have to face it. I'd have to talk to my father about it before he got bushwhacked by a well-meaning neighbor and that made me sick.

"What's with the face?" he asked.

I shrugged. "It's the only one I've got."

"You know what I mean. Spill it. Something's bugging you."

"I wish there was an app for obliterating the crap in my life. Scan it with my cell and *bam,* it's gone." I heaved a deep sigh. "I was remembering what you showed me before I left Palmer. That FarkYourself website stuff. If Nate tells anyone he saw me at the hospital, that'll put me front and center again. And you, by association. Going back to town will suck for both of us."

I expected Tanner to commiserate with me, but when he fought a smile that turned into a big grin, I had to ask.

"Okay, not cool, Lange. What's so funny?"

"Cyber-banditos blew a virtual hole in that site. Threads that had pictures of us? Gone."

"What are you talking about?"

In geek speak, Tanner rattled off techno babble to explain that he'd launched an SQL injection attack on that site. I got totally lost, but I loved watching him get wired talking about malware script and keystroke loggers.

"I'd be much more impressed if I understood a fraction of what you just said," I told him. "I need subtitles, cyber boy."

"Maybe it's best that you don't know too much about the details." He grinned, clearly feeling pretty good about what he'd done. "SQL code can launch an attack that affects thousands of other sites, but that's not what happened. I only wanted the site administrator's attention and I got it."

"Then give me the highlights, Tanner. And dumb it down so I can appreciate your genius."

When his cheeks flushed red, shy boy had returned.

"Basically, anyone who wanted access to our cyber-bully thread, I redirected those users to a dummy site where I cached their IDs and other stuff. All they saw was a glitch in the site that asked them to log in again. That's when I replicated the FarkYourself header page. They never knew they were on a dummy site. Mine."

"And the real site administrator didn't catch you?"

"I made sure they had other diversions to worry about. I crashed their server for a while." He smiled. "And I planted a back door on their site that's embedded real deep. Even if they go looking for a virtual trail to find me, they have to go through a few foreign countries first, ones that don't play well with others."

Sometimes it scared me how Tanner's mind worked, but not today. Today I was in awe…and very grateful to call him my friend.

"If I ever need to access their system again, I can do it, but it's over, Abbey. That thread and those images are deep-sixed for good." He locked his gaze on me, but his serious expression turned into a devilish grin. "I would've loved to see Britney Hartman's face when she saw the warning on her computer."

"Britney Hartman?"

"Yeah, she started it. It was real tempting to return the favor, but that would make me a pathetic anonymous coward like she is."

"You put a warning on her computer?"

Okay, I had to admit. I was really getting into this. Britney was in Akk the Yak's social-studies class this last term with me, but I'd known her since elementary school. She hated my guts. If I had known that one confetti egg would have caused me and Tanner such pain, I never would have hit that girl on the head in Girl Scouts, at least not in public with witnesses. I'd never done anything to her, besides the egg. Girls like Britney didn't need much of a reason to carry a grudge, but to let one lousy egg turn into such a cruel prank almost made me feel sorry for her.

Maybe being anonymous on the internet made her feel safe to unleash her streak of mean. The girl had serious issues. Being an overindulged princess, she'd never heard the word *no* from her parents or from the tight circle of mindless groupies she'd cultivated over the years like hothouse flowers. No amount of Girl Scout badges would ever earn her what she really needed—a personality—and maybe a forgiving heart.

When Tanner saw my smile, he laughed and nodded.

"Yeah, that warning message was really choice stuff," he said.

With his voice low, Tanner tried to sound like a special agent for the FBI as he told me what Britney had seen on her computer after she logged on to the FarkYourself thread that she'd created.

Apparently he'd memorized every word of the fake message he posted.

"You are in violation of the United States federal cyber bullying law 13-068-A-0863."

Total drama, Tanner moved a hand in front of him as if he could read his warning across a theatre marquee.

"It is a felony to display a visual image of a minor that depicts explicit sexual material. An email is being sent to your parents and school, listing your name and address. Your next infraction may result in expulsion from school with felony charges pursued. This is the only warning you will get. You are being watched."

With the last two lines, he laughed really hard. Tears rolled down his face. He wiped his eyes with the back of his hand and when he looked at me, my mouth gaped open.

I was stunned.

"How did you know about that federal law thing?" I asked.

"There isn't a federal law, but wouldn't it be cool if there was? Maybe someday."

"You made that up?"

He only shrugged and smirked.

"But won't you get into trouble?" I asked, punching him in the shoulder. "You hacked a website, Tanner. You and whoever your cyber-bandito friends are."

"Any site that condones cyber bullying deserves to be hacked." He narrowed his eyes and got serious again.

Tanner explained that with his attack code, he got the FarkYourself administrators' user names and passwords, plus he gained access to databases used to maintain the site.

He permanently deleted our nasty images, even from the backup files.

For anyone who had linked to the site or embedded code for our doctored photos—to spread the word—that script no longer worked. It was like cutting off the head of the snake, Tanner said. From the sounds of it, he could have been more malicious—to Britney, to the others who joined in and to the website that hosted the abuse—but that would have made him no better than they were.

Even a hacker (and car thief) had scruples...*apparently.*

"Before I stole my mom's car, I noticed the site posted a message," he said. "They warned against bullying and said there'll be new rules posted online soon. They added an 800 hotline for complaints as well as an email contact. Guess they got the message. Even if they found me and wanted to press charges, I don't think they'd want the bad PR."

"I can't believe you did that."

"When I told you about those pictures, I never forgot the look on your face. I couldn't let anyone hurt you like that, Abbey."

I'd left town with my tail between my legs, but Tanner figured out a way to make a difference. He'd not only fixed the problem for the two of us, but he also got a very popular website to see the error of its ways.

"If Britney and her loser friends try anything like this again, I have access to their computers," he added. "I embedded code on their hard drives. I'll have their user names and passwords whenever they update them, too. Anything they do online, I can shadow them."

"Good looks and brains, too." I grinned. "Here I thought you were just another pretty face."

"I can live with pretty."

At that moment, all I wanted to do was kiss Tanner, but the creak of the cabin door stopped me.

"Hey, you two. Better get moving. Tanner's parents will be here soon."

My father's timing had never been great. When he barged through the door, both of us jumped, but Tanner recovered first.

"Thanks for the hospitality, Mr. Chandler. Your cabin has nice…ambience. I'll be sure to recommend it to Triple A."

"Next time, make sure you're legal, son."

"I better write that down, sir. By the time my parents let me drive again, I could forget that sage advice."

Tanner didn't crack a smile, but Dad did. After my father disappeared into his bedroom, I mouthed the words *thank you* to Tanner and he grinned back. My alone time with him had come to an end, but I'd have a whole new reason to look forward to going back to Palmer…*and home.*

Minutes later

With Dad inside the cabin with us, Tanner didn't say much. He packed his stuff and folded the linens on the couch so our living room didn't look like a motel. After he brushed his teeth, he looked ready to go. We exchanged short glances when Dad wasn't looking, but I noticed Tanner kept his eyes on the window. He felt the pressure. His parents would arrive any minute.

After I heard gravel crunching on the drive, I peeked through an opening in the drapes and glanced back at Tanner.

"Guess my parents are here," he said.

"Yep, I'll go talk to them," Dad offered. "Get your stuff, but…no rush." My father shot me a look before he headed out the door.

Before Tanner got too miserable about the ride home, I stood in front of him and cupped his face. When I felt his hands on my hips, I leaned down to kiss him. His lips tasted like minty toothpaste. Tanner pulled me to him and buried his face against me in a monster hug with his strong hands on my back. After I ran my fingers through his tousled hair, I held him in my arms, completely happy in our silence. The intimacy of holding him warmed me all over.

"There's something I've never told you," he said. His muffled voice made my stomach tickle. "Never told anyone, actually."

After all we'd talked about, I couldn't imagine what that could be, but I waited for him to come out with it.

"I've never been on a date," he said.

Holding him in my arms, I never let him see my smile.

"You consider that a defect, Lange?"

"I did, until I realized one thing."

"What's that?"

"I want my first date to be with you, Abbey."

I don't know what I expected from him, but that wasn't it. I looked down, not sure what to say. I wasn't anyone's Cracker Jack prize, but Tanner made me feel…*special*.

"Yeah, I'd like that." I grinned and ran my fingers through his hair again, messing up what I just fixed. Considering my best friend would be my first date, too, I had to admit it.

Tanner Lange would be worth waiting for.

An hour later

After Tanner and his parents left, I was alone with Dad and the silence in our cabin weighed heavy on me. Something unsettled had grabbed hold of me. Surrounded by the countless photos of my mom hanging on the walls, she smiled back and her eyes followed me through the room. With every image frozen in time when she was alive, those pictures stirred memories that I thought I'd forgotten.

Good memories.

I finally understood why Dad had been adding to his collection. Every photo kept him connected to her...*to both of us.* It'd been his way of saying, "I'll never forget you." Those photos helped me grasp my mother's final gift to me, too. She'd given me life more than once and she had found a way, through Death, to remind me that I'd been loved. What I did with her love and my second chance would be up to me.

With the sun going down on our last night at the cabin, shadows stretched across my bedroom as I heard my father packing in his room. Only days ago, I had argued with him about being forced to remember the death of my mother in a meaningless ritual by the lake. Now, with everything that had happened, her birthday had come and gone yesterday. Nate's ordeal had been a complete distraction. That couldn't be helped, but with us leaving first thing in the morning, I couldn't drive away without doing something that would be meaningful for both my father and me.

I knew I'd never need a reason to honor my mother's memory, but after I figured out what I wanted, I knew just where to do it. I sent Dad a personal invitation, one that I'd made for him myself. I cut a tree branch, sharpened one end with a knife, and speared a marshmallow with it. I wrote my father a note meant just for him…and it was about time I'd sent him that long-overdue invite.

Let's celebrate Mom's birthday at dusk. You know where.

After I grabbed my jacket, I slipped out of the house with the stuff I would need for the party of two that I'd have with my dad. I had a smile on my face as I headed up the mountain trail behind our cabin. It was time I started my own memories with my father. The upper-ridge clearing with the fire pit—where he had proposed to my mom—was the perfect place to do that. I was determined not to let Death taint how I felt about the special spot that I'd shared with my mother, and now would share with my dad, but I couldn't deny that I thought of my dark angel, too.

In truth—*a scary truth*—I missed Death.

I missed how he made me feel. He was an ancient soul, an immortal, who had risked everything to be with me. He may have come to me for his own reasons, but he also helped me deal with the death of my mother in a way that only *he* could. The time we shared on my mountain had an edge of danger to it. I had sneaked out at night and hidden my trips to the ridge from my father. I don't know why I'd done it, but something had stirred in me and I knew that I'd do it again.

I'd spent time with Death—*and liked it*. No matter how much I loved Tanner, the Angel of Death would always be the first boy I ever kissed.

Pushing through the switchbacks, I raced up the mountain one last time, knowing my father wouldn't be far behind. I shouldn't have been in a hurry. Roasting marsh-mallows with my dad shouldn't have made me anxious, but after I felt the burn in my thighs and realized I was pant-ing hard, it dawned on me why I felt nervous and why I'd wanted a head start.

I hoped Death would be waiting.

abbey   chapter 20

When I got to the clearing, breathless, I stopped near the stone fire pit and stared down at the brittle charred wood nestled in heaps of gray velvety powder. Gusts of the evening breeze swept over the stones of that old landmark and lifted the lifeless ashes into the air with ease. Mounded at the base of the evergreen trees, the lingering snow was covered with a fine layer of soot from past fires. As I stood in that spot, holding a knapsack filled with the fixings for s'mores, I fought to keep memories of my mother in my head, but I couldn't do it.

Death had taken center stage and my dark angel was impossible to forget.

I hugged the rucksack to my chest and let my gaze jump to everything that moved as my breath fogged the air. I looked for Death in the deepening shadows. Every chilly gust of mountain air that swept through the evergreens and each call of a bird grabbed my attention as I searched for him in everything I saw. When I didn't find him, I shut my eyes tight and listened to each sound that carried on the wind until the crushing weight of my expectation closed in with the darkness.

What did I expect? *What did I need from him?*

I set down my knapsack and occupied my unsettled mind by gathering wood for the fire. Like Dad had taught me, I gathered dry cedar bark that I shredded off trees and I looked for dead branches, dried brush and old pinecones to nest in the fire pit as kindling under the larger pieces of firewood. After I cupped my hand to block the wind, I started the fire with a lighter I'd brought from the cabin. Smoke wafted into my face and stung my eyes as I bent down to breathe life into the growing flames.

But every crunch of snow under my boots and each crack of a twig that echoed through the trees raced through my mind, too. Those sounds stirred memories of my dark angel from the last time I'd shared a fire with him.

I remembered his perfect face, Nate's face, only different. His pale skin radiated the flickering light from the fire. His mesmerizing blue eyes glistened as he stared at me with a preternatural stillness that now I thought I should have recognized as unnatural all along.

Whatever his real reason for coming here, Death had not forgotten me. He held my mother's soul in his care and with his need to feel human—even for a fraction of an eternity—he had come to me for answers, answers I didn't have. Threatening Nate's life, Death left me with no other choice. No matter how much I tried to justify what I'd done, I had betrayed him to save Nate. I'd made a choice. Although I would make that same decision again and again, I still didn't feel any better about what I'd done—and how things turned out for him.

But now that I stood here, and Nate's life no longer hung in the balance, I came to the clearing for a reason I was only beginning to understand.

I needed Death's forgiveness and now I'd never get it.

As far as I knew, he'd been punished for what he'd done. I didn't feel him anymore. Not like I had before. If there was a God in heaven, I wanted to believe that my mother and the other innocent souls in Death's care wouldn't have been forsaken because of his actions.

But the emptiness I felt came from my fear that he had not been spared.

That strange boy—wrapped in Nate's beautiful body and soul—had given back what he'd taken and denied his obsession with being human for me. He was gone now. I couldn't get his haunted face from my mind and as I warmed my hands by the fire, I felt the chill of tears on my face. An aching emptiness started in the pit of my stomach and left me feeling numb as I thought about the bargain I tried to make with Death.

In the end, I had counted on the compassion of Death's brand-new humanity. *Nate's humanity.* And because the Angel of Death had my mother inside him, I gambled on his love for me. *Her love,* a love I knew I could always count on. I should have been happy at how things turned out, but I wasn't, not with the flood of memories filling my mind. Old ghosts and new were with me now, bleak memories that I had a hand in creating.

Death—with his unforgettable kiss—would be one more.

But when a distant sound carried on the wind, I almost didn't hear it at first. In disbelief, I stood and searched the darkening skies as I stepped beyond the glow of the crackling fire to see.

The soft flutter of wings made me turn in a rush. The biggest raven I'd ever seen had found a perch on a branch behind me. It cocked its tufted head and stared down at me, unafraid. Its iridescent feathers caught the reflection off the fire and turned its inky-black wings a striking color of purple and blue.

I smiled at the creature and almost said something, but another distant sound stopped me cold. My heart leapt as a raspy caw echoed across the valley. One. Two. *Then more.* When I looked over my shoulder, I stood breathless.

"Oh. My. God!"

One by one, ravens filled the skies—hundreds of them. They crisscrossed the horizon, with their slick wings catching the fire of the dying light. When they found a place to land, they squawked and cackled in the trees behind me and with every flutter of a wing, I felt Death with me. Each feather-tufted head with shiny onyx eyes reminded me of him. They were his eyes and ears—*his* messengers.

I laughed as if I'd lost my mind. *Maybe I had.*

"Poof," I whispered, fighting back fresh tears as I grinned at a sky filling with ravens.

"What the hell?" My father's voice cut through my stunned silence.

If I hadn't been distracted, hearing my father would have scared me. I hadn't seen him coming up the trail, but as he stared into the darkening night sky and the trees that surrounded us, I couldn't help but laugh harder at his reaction…*and mine.*

"Isn't it amazing, Dad?"

With my head back, I spun where I stood and laughed until tears came, gazing into the heavens, black with ravens.

The elegant, graceful birds gathered in the trees and made lazy circles in the sky, with more coming in the distance.

"*Gawd!* Have you ever seen anything like this?" My skin rippled with goose bumps and my voice grew shrill with uncontrollable and boundless joy.

Beautiful!

Amazing!

The Angel of Death came to me now in the only way he could and put on a show meant only for me. He'd sent me a message—*on a dark wing*—that he would always be with me.

Death never forgets. And now, neither would I.

★ ★ ★ ★ ★

Acknowledgments

After living in Alaska for ten years, it's hard to get the haunting beauty of the land and the endearing qualities of its people out of my blood. I pray that will never happen, but writing about it helps bridge the gap in my soul.

For his technical help on climbing Mount Denali, I wish to thank Niles Woods, who has made the dangerous trek more than once. Teacher, adventurer and dear friend, I thank you from the bottom of my heart.

For sharing his personal experiences about being wheelchair-bound and breathing life into my character, Tanner Lange, I have David Clampitt to thank. I've always admired Dave's strength in dealing with the challenges he faces every day and his humor always makes me laugh. He works as an Occupational Therapist, getting others back on their feet. Dave is one of my heroes.

I'd like to also thank my wonderful editor, Mary-Theresa Hussey, who makes collaboration a joy. The emotions she can add to a story make her input invaluable to me. She really knows how to balance the business-minded editor with the passionate heart of a die-hard reader and romantic. And to the team at Harlequin Teen, thanks for everything you do. I heart you.

To my agent, Meredith Bernstein, I have nothing but gratitude for your common sense and good humor. You are my guardian angel in designer shoes.

Special thanks as always, to my crazy family and my loving husband, John (Salsa Boy). And to the latest members of my growing Texas *fam-damily*—The Supper Club (Gracie & Ignacio, Marta & Kevin, Nelson & Janice, Annie & Patrick, Gale & Mike, Jim & Jeannie, and brave soul Denise)— I want to say: laughing is a vacation where you don't come back ten pounds heavier. Thanks for the weekly vay-kay. You guys ROCK!

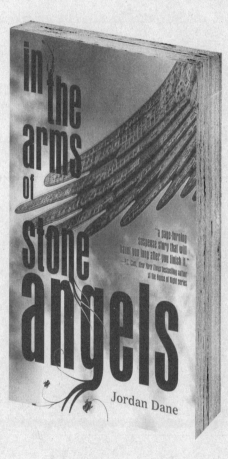

CRAVE

Book one of *The Clann* series

Vampires and powerful magic users clash in a contemporary tale of forbidden love and family secrets. Outcast Savannah doesn't know why she's so strongly attracted to Tristan, Clann golden boy and the most popular guy in school. But their irresistible connection may soon tear them apart and launch a battle that will shatter both their worlds.

Available wherever books are sold!